Come Back to Me

Melissa Foster

WORLD LITERARY PRESS

ISBN-13: 978-0989050814
ISBN-10: 0989050815

This is a work of fiction. Names, characters, places, and
incidents are the work of the author's imagination, or are
used fictitiously, and any resemblance to actual persons,
living or dead, business establishments, locales, or events
is entirely coincidental.

First Printing, Revised Edition, July 2013

Praise for COME BACK TO ME

"..a hauntingly beautiful love story against the backdrop of betrayal in a broken world."

Sue Harrison, bestselling author of MOTHER EARTH FATHER SKY

"COME BACK TO ME is passionate, romantic, and moving. A vivid story of loss and hope - a fine read for a wide audience."

Midwest Book Review

"A story of dark realities and faith in the future--validation of love and friendship--a love story with twists and turns that will keep you reading to the end."

Kaira Rouda, author of HERE, HOME, HOPE

"Foster's writing captures the complexity of life and keeps you flipping the pages until the end—surprising you all the way through."

Kathleen Shoop, bestselling author of THE LAST LETTER

Dedication

For those who put others first, and for everyone who has lost someone they've loved.

Chapter One

Suha huddled over the hand-drawn map, wishing the shadows from the candle would stop dancing across the page and thankful that the sandstorm had finally ceased. The cadence of helicopter blades grew closer. She blew out the candle and stared into the darkness of the makeshift tent, fingers clenched, eyes wide, certain that her end had come. Samira and her three children lay sleeping on blankets they'd strewn across the sand, oblivious to the sounds of their hunters. The chopper's rhythmic thumping passed overhead, then faded slowly into the distance.

Suha allowed herself to breathe once again. She unfurled her fingers from the edge of the thin blankets beneath her, her only cushion from the dense sand. One hand covered her racing heart, the other held her balance. Suddenly an explosion broke through the silence. Suha scrambled on her hands and knees toward Samira.

"Have they found us?" Samira asked Suha, pulling her daughter against her side and taking quick inventory of her two young sons, both also fast asleep.

"Shh," Suha commanded. She ran out of the tent and into the black of the desert night, pulling her frayed sweater tight across her plump body. Plumes of smoke rose in the distance. She whispered a fast prayer. Her heart pounded against her ribs as she spun around, looking for insurgents. The distant smell of sulfur assaulted her senses, a smell she'd become far too accustomed to since the beginning of the war. She hurried back into the tent and grabbed a flashlight.

"Suha! No!" Samira said in a harsh whisper.

"Shush. It's far away."

"Please!" Samira begged.

"Stay with the children." In the two months that they'd been on the run, Suha had worn the hat of both mother and father to Samira, and *jadda* to Samira's children. She'd never imagined herself as a grandmother, and bore the weight of the responsibility proudly. She would die before letting any harm come to them.

Outside the tent, Suha shivered from cold and fear as adrenaline carried her in the direction of the smoke. *A mile away*, she estimated. The tension in her shoulders eased. She listened to the darkness—her panting breath the only break in the silence. A deep, low moan came from her left. Suha froze. She raised the flashlight, illuminating a path on the sand before her and then whipped the light to the sides, behind her. The shelter was nowhere in sight, tucked perfectly behind an enormous dune. She was alone.

Praying that she'd made up the noise in her own mind, she inched toward the west, using her hands to pull herself up a small hill. At the peak, she crouched, catching her breath, straining to hear any sounds; she was met with silence. She waited until the sound of her heart beating behind her ears calmed. Satisfied that they remained undiscovered, she turned back in the direction of the shelter. The light swept over a dark lump in the sand. Suha gasped, jumping backward and expecting a siege of insurgents to appear. She flattened herself to the dune and thought of the children—better her than them. She pulled her body up, hoping her shaking legs would sustain her as she moved forward. She'd make her father proud, rest his soul. Gathering courage like a cloak, she lifted the light once again. A man lay in the sand, blood pooled around him, his arm cocked at a painful angle. The physician in her took over, propelling her to his side. *Male, early thirties. Pulse. Broken arm and leg. Contusions. Alive.* Arabic flew from her mouth, "Hello. Can you hear me? Hello." There was no response.

Suha rushed back to the shelter, her sixty-five-year-old body aching and heavy. As she flew into the tent, Samira's eyes shot open, "What is it?"

Suha bent over the blankets, rifling through them, casting away the smaller ones and collecting the longest, strongest ones. Her fingers worked furiously, tying them to two walking sticks as she spat orders, "An injured man. You must help me. Do not wake the children."

"Man?" Samira moved protectively closer to the children.

"Aagh," Suha swatted at the air. "Don't be foolish. I'm alive, aren't I? He's American, not Iraqi." She stood, dragging the crude stretcher behind her. "Come! Now!" she ordered.

3

Chapter Two

Tess sat across from the doctor's desk, her legs crossed, her heel kicking up and down. She bit her lower lip and wished he'd hurry up. The urge to pee was just nerves, she told herself. She'd just given a urine sample, after all. Her hand moved to her abdomen, and she closed her eyes. It's just stress, she thought. Tons of women miss their periods because of stress. *Five-year plan* ran through her mind like a dull ache.

"Well, Tess, it looks like you and Beau are going to have a little Johnson running around." Dr. Robert's deep voice startled her.

Tess stared at him. *Pregnant. Pregnant! Pregnant?*

"Tess? Are you alright?"

Suddenly, Tess's throat felt as if it were closing. She focused on street noises that snuck in through a crack in the window, magnified by the silence of the room. *Pregnant?*

"Tess?" Dr. Roberts said softly. "Do you want to talk about this? Should we discuss...options?" Dr. Robert's concern only heightened the ache in her belly that had been there since she'd missed her last period.

"Beau's away," Tess muttered. *Where did that come from? God, now I'm turning into one of those flighty women I can't stand.* "Um, Beau's in Iraq, on a photography assignment."

Dr. Robert nodded, "Yes, you mentioned that earlier."

"I did? Sorry. I'm fine, really." *Aren't I?* "He'll be back in six weeks, and I'll tell him then. I'm sure he'll be fine...good...happy." Tess feigned a smile and began chewing on her fingernail.

Tess stared out the window of her Bethesda, Maryland office, her mind as cloudy as a November sky. *A baby.* She lowered her face into her hands. In the four years they'd been married, she'd never once questioned his five-year plan. Five years to establish himself as a photographer and gain international exposure, *then* they would think about having a family. It all seemed reasonable, until now. Now she wanted him here, not off gallivanting through a war zone taking pictures of someone else's family. She pushed her chair back from the desk, swallowing against a wave of nausea that pushed at her sternum. Tess had always considered herself lucky to be married to a man of the arts rather than a businessman. One meticulous, Type-A businessperson in the family was enough. Now, she wasn't so sure "lucky" was the right word.

Her eyes drifted to a framed page of *NewsTime* magazine which boasted one of Beau's photographs. Layla, the little girl in the photo, was the daughter of Hakim Fulan, the owner of *Wartime* magazine. Beau had been documenting three-year-old Layla's life since birth, and the shots he'd taken had been picked up by several national magazines. It made sense for Mr. Fulan to hire Beau to document the changes in Iraqi family life since the inception of the war, and Mr. Fulan's position with Wartime magazine practically guaranteed the acceptance of Beau's photos. Yes, Tess was sure these six weeks in Iraq would finally lead to the international exposure Beau craved, and, with that accomplished, how could Beau be anything less than thrilled about the pregnancy?

Tess looked at their wedding photo, then sat down on the edge of her desk, suddenly feeling very alone.

"You miss him, don't you?"

Tess turned toward Alice's breathy voice and smiled at the woman who had been her assistant for the past six years. Fighting the urge to confide in Alice the news of her pregnancy, she answered, "I do." She'd save the news for Beau to hear first.

"He'll be okay, you know," Alice said.

Tess nodded. She was right, of course. Beau would be fine. If only she understood that his leaving wasn't her main concern. "It's still a war zone," she said.

Alice handed Tess a warm French vanilla cappuccino and set a light blue coaster on her desk. "When are you Skyping again?" she asked.

"He said it could be a day or two before he'd have access again."

"Bummer. Wanna catch dinner tonight?" Alice asked.

"What, no nameless men available?" Tess joked.

Alice guffawed, "Hey, just because I'm not into commitment doesn't mean I'm not choosy."

"Right." Tess chewed on her fingernail, eying the cappuccino that she had a feeling she shouldn't drink. "Doesn't it scare you sometimes? Taking men you don't know back to your place?"

Alice smirked, tucking a lock of straight blonde hair behind her ear. "I'm not twelve. Dinner?"

Tess shook her head. "My stomach's been a little off. Rain check?"

"Sure," Alice said and left Tess's office.

Tess closed her office door and made a beeline for Google. She pored over the pages of information relating to pregnancy. At six weeks, her baby would look more like a grub than a human. She stared at the images on the screen, each depicting a different stage of pregnancy. She didn't even want to think about the creature the baby would morph into in weeks seven, eight, and nine. At least by week ten it would look more like a recognizable...alien. *Alien.* That word kind of fit the unplanned pregnancy, like she'd been implanted by an alien that she'd somehow, miraculously, grow to love. Were they kidding? How could she grow to love this thing inside her? Most women gushed over their pregnancies. She'd heard them. "I fell in love the moment I found out I was pregnant." What was wrong with her, she wondered. Why did she feel so disconnected? She flipped forward to sixteen weeks—finally, an image that resembled the tiny person the baby would become. She touched the screen, her eyebrows furrowed. She sat like that for almost a full minute, until she let out a long sigh and simply gave up. Her heart had not fluttered one bit. *What is wrong with me?*

Tess clicked on an article called "What to Eat When You're Pregnant." *This should be easy,* she thought. The left side of her mouth lifted into a crooked smile. Tess had a healthy appetite, and she had no intention of changing, even if she did feel a bit nauseous in the mornings. "Skip sushi, fish, and soft cheese," she read. *What?* Her heartbeat quickened. There it was, staring at her in bold type: "Limit caffeine." The cappuccino Alice had brought her vied for her attention. She pushed it over to the side of the desk and turned back to the monitor.

7

The cappuccino still called out to her. Warm vanilla wafted directly from the cup to her nose.

"Ugh!" She stacked books in front of the cup. *There,* she thought, *out of sight, out of mind.*

She turned back to the article. *"The American Journal of Obstetrics and Gynecology* showed that moms-to-be who consumed 200 mg or more of caffeine a day had double the risk of miscarriage compared with those who had no caffeine." *Miscarriage? Jesus, will I have to watch every little thing that goes into my mouth?*

She clicked on another article, "Pregnancy and Exercise." At least that article offered some good news. Riding a bike was considered safe until it became uncomfortable. Tess's head fell forward with a loud sigh—weight gain, the bane of her existence. She'd never been thin, and once she'd hit twenty-nine, she swore her middle had expanded overnight. Beau called her shape womanly. Chunky was a better description, and even that was borderline. Suddenly the caffeine sounded good to her—a way out. She could drink this baby away, and Beau would never have to know. She began calculating how many cups of cappuccino would equate to two hundred milligrams of caffeine.

Iraq

"Marhaba," Suha whispered with a modicum of hope. "Welcome," she tried in English.

The man's eyes remained closed.

Suha muttered under her breath with a sense of urgency and shuffled across the tent, retrieving a small bucket of water. She placed a wet cloth upon his forehead, praying that he would soon open his eyes. She checked his pulse, barking orders and concerns to Samira in their native Arabic tongue.

Samira hung back from the injured American man as if he might suddenly wake up and pounce on her.

Suha had been at his side around the clock, tending to him, administering what little pain relief medication she could, and nursing his bloody wounds which covered the majority of his body. The makeshift cast that she'd secured to his left arm and leg were holding up well. As much as she'd wished he'd wake up, she was thankful for his slumber. It made the healing easier. She worried about infection and took every precaution to avoid such a fate. In her sixty-five years of living in Iraq, the latter of which were spent as a hospital physician, she had never dreamed that she would be caring for a wounded American while living in hiding.

The conditions of their dwelling were ghastly. Dirty sheets, the color of sand, were tied together to form walls, held up with sticks and brooms, whatever they'd been able to scrounge during their travels. The thin walls were sheltered within monstrous sand dunes and shoved into cracks and crevices for stability. The dunes provided ample camouflage from passing helicopters and other aircraft, but the damp, chalky smell and dust-filled air left a film on everything and, Suha was sure, coated her lungs. She was thankful for the people of the underground who had helped them plan and execute their escape, enlisting the help of others whom they knew were safe to help them along the way, putting their own lives at risk by bringing more food and supplies to them. She was riddled with guilt at the mere thought of another person risking his life for her, but she was too concerned for the safety of Samira and her children to forgo the risk. Staying at the safe house had been out of the question. As a physician, she was particularly at risk of death. Insurgents had already killed five doctors who had been aiding Americans, and as a hospital physician, she was bound to help the injured, regardless of their origin.

They had traveled for many days, far outside of the active war zone, mostly at night, led by members of the underground group who had been helping women escape the harsh realities that had become their lives since the beginning of the war. They took routes that were not well traveled, and disguises had become commonplace among the travelers. Suha knew safety was an illusion during the war, and in their temporary shelter, she clung to that illusion like a lifeline.

Maryland

"Hello?"

Tess hadn't even heard the door open, much less Alice walk across the room. She clicked to her home screen and began shuffling papers.

"What's up with you today?" Alice stood beside Tess, looking from the computer to Tess, and back again. "Are we going to do any work, or have you been overtaken by sadness because your dear, sweet, handsome husband has left you for a faraway land?"

Tess fumbled with the papers and stood, glancing quickly at the computer. The word *pregnancy* was nowhere on the screen. "I'm just...uh...looking for the Caton file."

Alice held up the file with a smirk.

Tess walked toward the door, hoping Alice, in her perfect taupe pencil skirt and crisp white blouse, would follow. The sound of Alice's Jimmy Choo heels on the wood floor eased Tess's panic.

She forced herself to focus on Mr. Caton. Eventually, thoughts of her pregnancy were replaced with the comfortably-familiar contemplations of her client's staffing needs, fee schedules, and prospective applicants.

Several hours later, Tess pushed back from the conference room table and stretched. She and Alice had been poring over potential clients' files for hours.

"I'm beat, can you close up?" Tess asked. She was dying to run into the bathroom again, but she'd gone so many times that she was afraid Alice might start to ask questions, and not the comforting, warm, concerned questions, but the efficient, cold type, like, *Do you have diarrhea?* or *Perhaps you need some Senekot?* Alice may not be warm, but she was sharp as a tack and tirelessly efficient.

Alice looked at her watch. "It's only six. Your stomach again?" Tess hadn't left the office before eight o'clock since Beau had left town.

Something like that. She put her hand on her stomach and nodded.

"No problem. Want me to drop by some Pepto?" she asked. Then she added, "Wait, Kevin called for you while you were in the bathroom earlier."

"I'm fine. I'll call him later," Tess said. Sweet, caring, Kevin, Beau's best friend, best man, and the lucky recipient of the daunting task of making sure that while Beau was away, he took care of anything Tess wasn't able to do, a.k.a. move boulders or perhaps scale the side of Mount Everest.

Chapter Three

Tess clicked through her emails, her right toe perched on the ground, bouncing her leg up and down in short, fast motions. It had been six days since she'd heard from Beau, and she didn't know if the burning in her chest was from worry or anger. Now she understood what her mother had felt like when she'd stayed out overnight as a teenager without calling to check in. *Sorry, Mom,* she thought, missing her for the umpteenth time since she'd passed away.

Why had they been so damned frugal? They should have just paid for international cell phone coverage. She could have gone without her cappuccinos, hell, she could have gone without groceries if she'd known it would have meant going this long without contact. She pushed away from the computer and paced the small den. She'd expected a day or two without contact, but six? Six! All in a row? Her mind fabricated scenarios ranging from Beau wandering the streets of Iraq, unable to speak the language, lost and hungry, to his being holed up somewhere with a gorgeous young woman, using her wiles to entice him into a world of lust and debauchery. Her face grew tight. She hated when her mind strayed into ridiculous territory. *Great. I'm here waiting day after day, while you're off gaining international exposure.*

Tess stared at her reflection in the window. She lifted her hands to her hips, turned sideways, cocked her head, then faced the window head on again. She wrinkled her nose at her reflection. Her pursed lips and strained forehead looked more like an angry schoolteacher's than a woman who had recently found out she was pregnant. Fatigue followed her from morning until night, but there was no other indication of a baby—no bump, no heavy breasts, just dark arcs under each tired eye. She could end this now, and he'd never know. Why should she give her body up to this baby if he didn't even care enough to call her and let her know he was okay?

"Damn it, Beau!" she spat into the empty room. "Where the fuck are you?"

Tess rode her bike through the neighborhoods, her eyes trained on the strip of pavement before her. She peddled fast, weaving in and out of joggers and past other cyclers. She rode until every movement of her legs took insurmountable energy, panting, drenched in sweat.

Her legs ached as she peddled up the monstrous hill that led to her house. A car sped over the crest of the hill, catching air and heading directly toward her. She swerved behind a parked car. "Slow down!" she yelled. She'd been yelling at airborne teens for so long that it had become second nature. She usually raced down the street behind them, hollering, and secretly praying that they wouldn't die right before her eyes. When they'd first bought the 1950s bungalow, she'd inquired at the county about putting in speed bumps and cautionary road signs, but the county had denied her requests, blaming budgeting and the poor economy.

She crested the hill and peddled into the driveway, propped her blue Schwinn up by its kickstand, and sat down on the concrete stoop. She picked a leaf from the ivy that had taken over half of the front stoop and rolled it between her fingers. Tall grass sprouted up through the patch of mulch around the weeping willow they'd fallen in love with when they'd moved in, four years earlier. Maybe Kevin could mow and weed the yard, she thought, and immediately chided herself for relying on a man. You'd think she'd never started her own consulting business or had a life of her own. She could do this. She'd mow the damn yard.

Tess closed her eyes, wishing she could fall back in time—to a time before their five-year plan had been knocked out of the water.

By Sunday night, Tess had already straightened, vacuumed, dusted, and reviewed her files for the next morning. She sat at the round kitchen table and lined up her collection of coasters, a ritual that she'd used to soothe her anxiety since she was a little girl, first organizing them from light colors to dark, and then from largest to smallest. Anxiety still gnawed at her. Her feet tapped beneath the table. Tess opened the drawer with the take-out menus, leafed through them, and threw them back in, slamming the drawer much harder than she'd meant to, flinching in reaction.

She stomped to the living room like a child having a tantrum and sat in front of the television, flipping through stations. It was no use. Questions about Beau's whereabouts riddled her mind. She went to the den and checked her computer for the fourth time in the last hour. Her fingers pecked quickly at the keys, nails chewed down to nubs. Skype worked. Email worked. She threw herself back from the desk with a loud sigh.

Tess had a love-hate relationship with Skype. She could tell when she looked in Beau's eyes if he was paying attention to her or had his mind on something else. She'd seen people walking around behind him in the small internet cafe, and pangs of jealousy had ripped through her. She wanted Beau home—with her. She wanted him to forget his five-year-plan and embrace the pregnancy.

The last time they'd Skyped, she'd almost told him about her period being late and her upcoming doctor's appointment, but she hadn't wanted to make him feel guilty for being away, just in case she was pregnant. This was his chance at international exposure and no matter how difficult it might be for her to wait for him, he'd worked hard, and he deserved the chance to gain the recognition. The desire to blurt out her secret had taken all of her concentration. By the time they'd signed off, the mantra, "Don't tell him," raced through her mind, their conversation swiftly forgotten. Had she misunderstood? Could he have told her it could be a week or two instead of a day or two? She stifled the urge to scream and checked her hair in the mirror. Mousy brown and fine as thread, she knew any amount of coiffing was useless. Tess turned her back to the mirror and leaned against the porcelain sink.

"He's in a war zone and you're the one stressing?" she said aloud. She rolled her eyes at her ridiculous insecurity.

In the bedroom, Tess pulled a journal from her underwear drawer and opened to a clean page. She wrote the date and pressed the pen against the paper, but no words came. She flipped backward through the pages, skimming through the first few days he'd been gone. Waking up alone had been a guilty pleasure of which she'd quickly grown tired. She couldn't count the number of times she'd picked up the phone to tell him about a new client, or a big contract, and then remembered that he wasn't reachable. She flipped backward through the journal and read an entry about a silly fight they'd had. *I wish Beau would just go away so I wouldn't have to look at him!*

Tess slammed the book closed, her chest burning. If only she'd told him about the baby. Maybe he'd have left Iraq immediately, photography assignment be damned. Maybe he'd have been happy to change his five-year plan.

Chapter Four

The clock in the living room chimed midnight. Tess sat nestled into the couch in the den, her laptop across her legs. She gnawed on a fingernail and made a conscious decision not to allow any more negative thoughts into her mind. He'd Skype, and she'd tell him about the baby. Why wait until he came home? Surely he'd profess his excitement and possibly come back early from Iraq. Tess convinced herself that it would be as easy as that.

The green Skype icon by her name, *ConsultGirl,* was bright, indicating that her account was online. The icon next to Beau's screen name, *BethesdaShooter,* was white, offline. Tess sighed. She closed the top of her laptop then settled into the cushions and leaned her head back, eyes closed.

Tess wiped away the crust of sleep from her eyes and eyed the clock, 2:23 A.M. The persistent knocking that had awakened her continued. Tess groaned, moving cautiously through the darkened living room. She peered through the front curtains. An unfamiliar dark car was parked in her driveway.

"Who is it?"

A deep, male voice with a familiar accent answered, "Mrs. Johnson?"

"Who's asking?" Tess's heart raced. She pulled Beau's shirt tight across her chest and crossed her arms, looking around for her cell phone.

"Ms. Johnson?"

His serious tone sent a chill down Tess's spine.

"It is I, Mr. Fulan."

Mr. Fulan? "Do you have identification?" she called through the door.

After a moment, a driver's license slapped lightly against the sidelight. *Hakim Fulan, 5200 Abercombe Street, Washington, DC.* Tess's heart sank. Another identification card appeared against the window above the last, *Amira Fulan,* his wife. Tess's throat closed, her body trembled. *Beau.* She flipped the deadbolt and threw the door open.

"I haven't heard from Beau. Is something wrong?"

Mrs. Fulan dropped her gaze, her eyes damp and red, tissues clutched in her hands. Mr. Fulan cleared his throat, "May we come in, please?"

"What is it?" Tess led them to the living room. "Is something wrong?" Goosebumps riddled Tess's arms. Tormented by the silence, Tess sank to the couch.

Mrs. Fulan sat next to her and folded her hands in her lap, her eyes conveying a silent, horrific message.

Tess shook her head. Her chest was being squeezed by a vice. She didn't want to hear what they had to say, and at the same time, she needed to know immediately. Every second became a torturous abyss, until she couldn't take it any longer. "Wha—"

"Mrs. Johnson," Mr. Fulan interrupted in a serious, yet gentle tone, "I am sorry for what I must tell you."

Tess silently pleaded for his words not to come.

Mr. Fulan stood before her, his shoulders pulled back in his perfectly-pressed suit. His musky smell filled the room. Mr. Fulan took in a long, deep breath. Mrs. Fulan reached for Tess's hand.

"Beau was traveling in one of our corporate helicopters, with our most trusted pilot," he began. His words faded into the sound of the ticking clock. Tess tried to concentrate. She couldn't breathe, the musk was suffocating her.

"Helicopter crashed...bodies burned..."

Tess's body shook. Her teeth began to chatter.

"I'm sorry," Mrs. Fulan whispered.

Tess shook her off. She lifted her swollen eyes toward Mr. Fulan. "No," she shook her head, "there's been a mistake. He wasn't on the helicopter," she cried.

"I'm sorry," he said.

Tess gritted her teeth. "You're wrong. He's supposed to Skype me. There's been some mistake." Her voice escalated, "There's been a mistake!" Tess leapt to her feet. "He said he'd come back!" She pounded his chest with her shaking fists. "No! You're wrong! Why are you doing this?"

Mr. Fulan put his arms around her and held her to his chest as she shrieked, flailing her arms, trying to beat away the news she couldn't bear to accept.

"I'm sorry," he said. "He's gone."

Iraq

The man lay before Suha on the cleanest blankets they could find, his head just inches from the dune wall. Without running water, cleaning wounds well was nearly impossible, and she worried infection was inevitable. The trek to the river and back would take nearly a day, and it was dangerous. But what could she do? She and Samira could not go back. They would not go back, not even to save the life of the American man who lay before her. She glanced behind her at the two sleeping children: Edham, who, at seven had begun sucking his thumb again. His flawless face looked so peaceful that it brought a prayer of safety to Suha's lips. His younger sister, Athra, lay curled against his back, her own little thumb tucked deep into her mouth. The sight of sweet Athra renewed Suha's strength. She knew the terror that lay behind them, and she couldn't fathom the thought of Athra being exposed to those dangers.

When she looked at Samira, she found it difficult to look away, she was so beautiful—and yet so full of anguish. Her eyes held horrors beyond her twenty-two years. Suha listened to Samira's hushed argument with her nine-year-old son. Zeid, the mirror image of his wretched father, Safaa, argued daily with his mother. He wanted to go back to their home, back to the fighting, and stand up for his country. He was as fierce as he was intelligent and belligerent. Suha shook her head. That boy would be the death of them all, as uncontrollable and angry as he was. Suha knew what she had to do, and she was petrified; not of telling the child what to do, but of what the child might choose to do once outside the confines of their tent. Zeid held all of their lives in his hands, and if he chose to go off on his own, they'd surely be killed—or worse.

Suha spoke in a harsh tone to Zeid, hoping his respect for his elders would take over his misguided youth. "Stop arguing with your mother, the woman who bore you, fed you, changed your rancid diapers." She told him that he was despicable, the way he talked back to his mother. A mother, she said, was the soul of the Earth, to be respected and praised. Suha unloaded her misdirected anger at their situation on the boy, and couldn't help but set his loyalties

20

straight. "Iraqi men are mistaken in their abhorrent treatment of women! If not for women, the men would not exist!" she spat.

Zeid's jaw dropped open. He'd never heard a woman speak in such a way about men. If his father were there, he advised Suha, he'd put her in her place.

Suha approached the slender boy, his eyes as large as hard-boiled eggs, his short dark hair rising in unwieldy sprouts from weeks without a proper cut. She loomed her ample body above him, knowing it would cause him discomfort, and she told him, in an even, stern voice, "Your father was not a man at all. He was a pathetic coward of a man who abused women to make his small manhood appear larger."

"Suha!" Samira was quick to her feet, placing her body between Suha and Zeid. "Do not say such dreadful things about his father." Though her words were strong, her voice betrayed her, trailing off at the end, sounding weak and unsure.

"You speak those words out of habit," Suha implored. "That man beat you. He used you like a dirty rag and left you to bleed to death."

Samira took Zeid by the arm and dragged him to the far corner of their shelter, away from the ugly words Suha spoke.

"You will not go back—ever. You have seen the abuse by your papa. Think of your sister. It is your job to protect her," Samira ordered.

Zeid stared at her with hardened eyes. His father had spoken of his role as the protector, but he'd also seen the treacherous treatment of his mother and other women at the hand of his father. It had plucked at the recesses of his mind when he was younger, but he'd learned at a very young age that standing between his father and his mother would only lead to a heavy hand used on his own body. The need to make his father proud had become stronger than his need to protect his mother. In the end, he'd relented, and the elitist attitude of his father had become his own.

Suha watched a saddened look wash over Samira. She knew Samira recognized the cold look in Zeid's eyes. Samira had seen it many times before, from an older set of eyes. Suha wondered if Samira felt the need to break Zeid of his father's beliefs, and if she understood that now, with the absence of his father, was her chance to erase those beliefs and patterns from her son's young mind.

Zeid stared through her, his jaw taut and angry.

Guilt coursed through Suha. The boy needed a stronger hand if he was ever going to break out of his father's mindset. The shame of wanting to break a young child of paternal ways coalesced with the belief of how right she was to do so, and she shook her head, as if to shake the conflicting thoughts away.

Chapter Five

Tess curled into a ball on the living room couch. She covered her head with a pillow, trying to escape the incessant pounding of flesh on wood. She must be dreaming. She'd wake up any second and see. The past twenty-four hours couldn't have been real.

There was a hard rap on the living room window, followed by Alice's voice, muffled by the window between them. "Tess! Open the door!"

Tess moaned and pulled the pillow tighter against her head.

"Tess?" Alice's anger lessened, replaced with concern. "Are you okay?" She banged on the glass until Tess lowered the pillow and glared at her. Alice lifted her palms toward the air.

Tess sat up, her hair a tangled mess, her clothes disheveled. She dragged herself to the front door and unlocked the bolt, shuffled back to the couch, and collapsed into it.

Alice was in the front door and on Tess's heels in seconds. "Tess? What the hell's wrong? Are you sick?" She looked Tess up and down. "I've been calling you all day. When you didn't come to work, I got worried," she sat next to Tess on the couch. "What is it? The flu?"

Tess shook her head, turning away from Alice's frustration. Thoughts of Beau brought fresh tears.

Alice tucked her silky blonde hair behind her ear, "Tess?"

Tess turned toward Alice and tried to speak, "They…" The words stuck in her throat like peanut butter. She handed Alice Mr. Fulan's crumpled business card, which she'd held in her hand since he'd left the night before, his home phone number scribbled across the top.

"What's thi—" it took a moment for Alice to understand. "Oh, my God, Tess, what's happened?"

Tess tried to explain. She opened her mouth to speak, her voice absorbed by her sobs.

"I'm so sorry," Alice awkwardly pulled Tess into an embrace, patting her back as if she'd just gotten a good grade on a paper. She pushed back quickly, "Why didn't you call me? What happened?"

Tess didn't answer.

"What can I do?" Organization, that's what Alice was good at.

Tess shrugged.

"Did you call his parents?" Alice asked, the gears of her mind in motion.

Tess shook her head, "Couldn't."

Alice was on her feet in seconds heading toward the front door, "Be right back." She whipped out her cell phone and called Mr. Fulan, walking outside so Tess wouldn't have to endure the hurt all over again. She returned to Tess's side ten minutes later and whispered. "I'm so sorry."

Tess stared straight ahead, her eyes vacant, her body numb.

For two days, Alice milled around the house, cooking food Tess would not eat, trying to engage Tess in conversation, and working very diligently to lift Tess's spirits. Alice was not known for her warmth, and Tess was grateful for Alice's lack of skill in that area. She didn't have the energy to be coddled—her being there was more than Tess could handle. She lay in silence for two days, finally asking Alice to leave, "I just need some space."

Kevin had stopped by a few times. He cut the grass and tried to comfort Tess, his own private pain hovering like a dark cloud.

Iraq

The sun shone brightly in the clear sky, filling the tent with a heat so dry that as quickly as sweat poured off Suha, it immediately dried up. Suha focused on the task at hand, rousing the injured man.

She wiped his brow with a damp rag and spoke softly, "Wake up, *Jameel*." Suha was surprised when the word rolled off her lips. The Arabic word, *Jameel*, translated to *beautiful male* in English. She sat next to the man that she'd dragged to safety, the man she'd monitored throughout the long nights, dressing his wounds, and had come to care for. His dark hair, the color of stones in a riverbed, not quite brown and not quite black, had grown in the passing weeks, sticking out in odd places. It was much less coarse than the hair of local men. Suha tried to attribute his peaceful look to his medications, but something told her that the man who lay before her was not a mean-spirited man. She was not afraid of this man. Suha thought of her kind father, grateful that he'd insisted on schooling her in English. *A woman in the medical field*

25

would need such knowledge, he'd told her. She'd spent years studying her father's library of English dictionaries and learning to translate medical books. The memory warmed her. She wished she could see her father once again, thank him, hear his voice. The American's eyes fluttered.

Hope soared through Suha. She asked him to open his eyes, told him that he was safe.

He moaned.

Samira rushed to Suha's side.

Suha reached for the American's hand, urging him to open his eyes. He moaned again. She wiped his face with a cloth, hoping to revive him.

Sounds washed over Beau. Pain coursed through every inch of his flesh. He tried to open his eyes. His eyelids were too heavy. He wiggled his toes, sending searing pains through his calves and thighs. He listened, trying to figure out where he was, trying to remember how he had gotten there. His mind was too foggy, he could not focus. He felt a hand on his wrist and heard the softly-spoken words that accompanied the tender touch. *Damn,* how he wished he could understand what was being said. He tried to speak, but his voice failed him.

Suha spoke excitedly, her heart racing. "Jameel, please. Open your eyes," she pleaded.

His eyelids fluttered. Beau's mind drifted in and out of fogginess. He'd heard a woman's voice, but it was not Tess. *Tess.* The thought of her made his heart beat faster. He felt a warm hand caress his own. He tried to lift his index finger.

Samira felt the slight pressure of the movement. "Suha!" she called and held his hand as if it were a delicate piece of art.

He moved his index finger slowly around her palm. The message he drew was lost on Samira. He could hear the Arabic words flow from her mouth, and his heart sank. He wasn't home.

"Yes, Jameel," Suha said. "That's it, my son. Move your fingers. I knew you were in there." Tears brimmed in her eyes.

Zeid approached his mother from behind. His high-pitched voice carried anger, though his Arabic words were cautious, "Why are you helping this ugly soldier? Father would be angry."

Suha glared at him, and he shrank away. She turned back to Beau. His left eye, the side that had taken the brunt of his fall, was still swollen shut, the muscles pulsated beneath the swollen flesh. "Jameel, wake up," she said.

Beau tried to open his eyes, but his left eye hurt too badly. To his surprise, his right eye opened, just a slit. He could not make out the blurred images before him. He closed his eye again and felt Suha's warm, capable hand on his head, lifting the back of his neck off of the blankets.

"You must drink," she said. She injected water into his mouth using a syringe without the needle. Pain followed the water down his throat. He was eager to drink. He tightened his fingers around Samira's small hand.

"More, Suha," Samira urged.

Suha quickly reloaded the syringe and dripped more water into his mouth. She repeated the effort five times, until he loosened his grip and the weight of his head became apparent in Suha's hand. "Good," she praised him.

The taste of metal lingered on his tongue. He opened his eye again. The face of the older woman slowly became clearer, as if he were looking through aged, thick glass. The woman whose voice had pulled him from the trenches of the blackened void in which his mind swam, the voice he'd held onto to keep himself from the grip of death, the woman who'd saved him, looked back at him. Her dark eyes held too many feelings to decipher: fear, hope, fatigue?

She smiled, exposing large, yellow teeth, bringing happiness to her otherwise wrinkled and strained features. Her thick black eyebrows rose with her smile, and the darkened hair above her lip, that on any other women would look manly and harsh, looked appropriate on her, softened her in some way.

Beau tried to smile, his lips lifted on the right side, still too swollen on the left to move.

Suha spoke to Samira in rushed Arabic. Samira hurried out of the shelter with Zeid in tow, careful not to wake Athra and Edham, asleep on blankets on the other side of the small tent. Suha pushed Beau's hair from his forehead, gently wiping the thick beads of sweat that had repeatedly formed.

"You are alive," she said in English with both confidence and surprise.

Beau's words pushed from his mouth, a long, low, convoluted breath, "'Hank you." Tears welled under his closed left lid and pooled in his right eye. He wanted desperately to touch his chest pocket. He needed the security of seeing Tess's face, the photo he carried. His left arm wore a heavy splint and makeshift cast, his right too pain-stricken to move, he repetitively shifted his gaze between Suha and his chest.

Suha watched his eye with pain in her heart. She knew what he wanted. She had found a photo and a pocket watch, both battered but intact. It was as if his body and clothing had been ravaged, but the photo and watch had been somehow protected. Suha had wrapped the photo of the beautiful girl with wet hair and soulful eyes, and the watch, with the touching inscription that she was glad to have been able to understand, in a piece of cloth, and tucked it underneath the edge of his blankets. Suha

28

believed the power of those items would bring him strength. She withdrew the wrapped items.

"This is what you wish? No?"

The tears on his cheeks were her answer. "Tess," he breathed.

Maryland

Tess shuffled through her days like a zombie on an automated track: moving from the couch, to the den to check Skype (just in case Beau found his way to a computer), to the kitchen, bathroom, and then back again. In the kitchen, she went through the motions of preparing food, because she knew she should, and would later toss it aside, untouched save for a nibble or two.

Without Alice and Kevin to contend with, long afternoons pressed into evenings unnoticed except for the two lights that were switched on and Tess's changing out of her sweat pants and into a pair of pajama pants. She'd taken to wearing Beau's shirts, relishing the smell of him that lingered on his clothing. Tonight Beau's blue turtleneck was the shirt of choice. It hung loosely around her body, which had become slighter with each passing day. She stared blankly at the blinking lights on her answering machine, lacking both the energy and the desire to listen to the messages. She heard a key in her front door and stared in its direction with wonder. Suddenly her eyes flew open wide and she ran to the door. *Beau!* She knew Mr. Fulan had been wrong! She flung the door open with a broad, hopeful smile.

"Hey there!" Kevin mistook her enthusiasm.

Tess's heart sank. The first thing Tess noticed was the *You hunt your way, I'll hunt mine* t-shirt he wore beneath his open sweatshirt. Beau had had that shirt specially made, with a picture of a bow and arrow, Kevin's hunting weapon of choice, next to *You hunt your way,* and a picture of a camera next to *I'll hunt mine.* Tess felt sick to her stomach. "Kevin," she said, just above a whisper.

"Thanks for the warm welcome," he said following her. The pungent odor of rotting food filled his nostrils. The house was a wreck, littered with dirty dishes, uneaten food, and half-empty glasses on the coffee table, *without* coasters. Tess was not a complete neat freak, but coasters and dirty dishes were her pet peeves.

Tess burrowed into the couch.

"How're you doing, Tess?" Kevin went to the kitchen.

Tess didn't respond.

Kevin set down the grocery bag that he'd been carrying and methodically began cleaning the dishes. He called out to Tess, "I've been trying to call you, but you never answer the phone."

"How'd you get a key?" Tess asked without turning around.

"The key? Beau gave it to me before he left, you know, in case you needed anything while he was gone."

Tess nodded, touched by the thoughtfulness of her husband.

Kevin strode from room to room, picking up dishes piled with stale food and wiping away weeks' worth of dust. When he reached the den, he stopped in his tracks. Stacks of unopened mail covered the desk. A mound of covers and bed pillows was piled on the couch next to Tess's laptop, which displayed the light blue Skype welcome page. Kevin took a deep breath and returned to Tess's side.

She stared at the television, her body slumped to one side.

"Tess, I know it's hard. He was my best friend, too," Kevin began, "but you can't stop living your life. Beau wouldn't want you to do that."

"How can you tell me what Beau would have wanted?" She turned toward him, her voice rising, "Beau wouldn't have wanted you to give up on him. He's coming back. He wasn't on that helicopter." She turned back toward the television with a loud, "Sheesh!"

Kevin shook his head and gently placed his hand on her back, "Tess, I couldn't believe it either, at first, but you know what they said."

Tess's chest tightened. She closed her eyes, listening with weary resignation as Kevin reminded her about the helicopter crash, the bodies instantly cremated. They'd found Beau's duffle bag, remnants of his photography equipment. The sickening smell of musk returned to the room. Her throat constricted. Tears burned her eyes. "He's not gone, Kevin. He's coming back."

Kevin shook his head. "Oh, Tess," he said and pulled her into his chest, one hand on the back of her head. He held her there until tears sprang from her eyes, and she sobbed like a hurt child. "It's gonna be okay, Tess," he reassured her. "It's gonna be okay."

Tess caught her breath and pulled back from him. "It's not okay, Kevin." Her body trembled. Her voice filled with venom. "He's out there somewhere," she stood. "They didn't find him because he wasn't on the helicopter."

"They found his stuff, Tess," he tried.

"Who cares?" she yelled. "So what! They found his duffle? Big deal. He could have left it there by accident, or...or...maybe the pilot was taking it somewhere for him!" Even as she screamed, she knew Beau would never leave his equipment. Tess crossed her arms over her trembling body and stared at Kevin, daring him to disbelieve.

Kevin wanted to argue the point, to make her see that Beau was really gone, but Beau had once likened arguing with Tess to arguing with a bull while you were wearing red—she wouldn't back down.

Tess paced the living room while Kevin went to straighten up the den. He folded the blankets that were heaped together and peeked back at Tess. He quickly clicked on the Skype Communication History and a new window opened. One line was duplicated all the way down the page and for several additional pages: *Call to: BethesdaShooter, no answer*. Kevin checked the dates and times of the communication attempts. Although it had been four weeks since Beau's disappearance, Tess's calls to Beau hadn't diminished in frequency. Tess was far worse off than he'd thought.

"Tess?" Kevin stood beside the answering machine.

She turned from her perch on the couch.

"You have twenty-two new messages. Don't you think we should check those?" he asked.

Tess shrugged.

"Want me to take it into another room and check them, just in case there's something important?"

Tess shrugged.

"Have you talked to Alice lately?" he asked.

Tess shook her head.

Kevin carried the answering machine into the den and shut the door, bracing himself for what was likely to be a barrage of sympathy calls. Besides several calls from Beau's parents and Alice, they were mostly sympathy calls from friends and Beau's clients, interspersed with a handful of solicitations. Mr. Fulan had called several times.

Kevin returned to an empty living room. He found Tess upstairs, curled up on her bed.

"Tess?"

She didn't respond.

He sat next to her on the bed.

Tess closed her eyes and let her body relax.
"Do you need to talk to somebody?"
Tess shook her head.
"Okay, but if you change your mind, I'm here."
She fell asleep almost instantly.

While Tess slept, Kevin returned the phone calls. He was glad to have a moment to himself. He hadn't realized how difficult it would be to appear strong for Tess. He clenched his eyes against the tears that had been waiting to fall and took a deep breath. He'd purposely saved the call to Alice for last. He had known Alice for as many years as he'd known Tess, surely she'd know what to do to pull Tess out of her depression. As he dialed her number, he thought of her lean physique, her blond hair that he'd so often wanted to touch. If it weren't for her holier-than-thou persona, he might have even tried. His purposeful glances had always gone unnoticed, and flirting? He wasn't sure Alice was even capable of such a thing. In fact, he wondered if she were asexual. Alice may have all the warmth of a cold fish, but Tess needed help, and who knew Tess better than Alice?

"No coasters?" Tess was worse off than Alice had feared. The Skype records were a bit obsessive, but she'd seen Tess's relentless ability to track down anyone and anything first hand, working side-by-side. She could not be dissuaded by a stern secretary or evasive assistant, and never walked away from a potential new client. She always reached her prey. This time her prey was Beau. Tess may be in denial, but wouldn't most wives be if their husband's body was never found? Alice was sure Tess could work through those feelings with some help. The messy house was out of the ordinary, and she didn't blame Tess for not answering the phone or opening her mail. After all, her entire life had just been turned upside down. It was the lack of coasters that sent red warnings flashing before Alice. At first, she'd thought Tess's compulsive need for coasters was driven by her love of collecting them. She'd since learned that she'd had it backwards; Tess's collection was driven by her obsession, a compulsive need to have coasters used at all times. Alice was sure it was a control issue, but who was she to judge? Tess's coaster rule had become second nature for Alice. She'd bring a client coffee in one hand, and a coaster would surely be in the other. She kept a stack of them in each room of their office, and had even gotten used to using them in her own home. The lack of coasters, to Alice, indicated that this was far more than simply denial. She needed to assess Tess with her own two eyes.

To anyone else, Kevin's soft blond hair and hazel eyes coupled with his sweet demeanor might qualify him as handsome—a good catch even—but to Alice, he was just Kevin. Although, she had to admit, it had been ages since she'd felt a spark of anything other than disdain for any man. Men had one purpose in her life, and beyond that, they were simply bodies that took up air and space.

"Hey, Kev," she smiled and walked past him, surveying Tess's house. "Wow, the place looks great. I assume this is thanks to you," she said.

Kevin felt better the moment she walked in the door. Not having to shoulder the burden alone was reassuring. "I straightened up." He pointed upstairs. "She's sleeping."

Alice nodded and checked her watch, 8:17 P.M. "Well, it's not exactly bedtime. Let's wake her up and get her back on track."

"Do you think we should? She's not exactly doing well."

"I'd imagine she's not," Alice said, matter-of-factly. "And how are you doing? He was your best friend," she said kindly.

"Good. I'm good," he walked to the bottom of the stairs. "I miss him. I mean, every time I read my email, I look for one from him, but I think that will fade once they have the funeral. Closure, you know?"

Alice nodded. "That's exactly what I think is going on with Tess. Imagine suddenly losing the one person you've woken up to for years, the person you confided in. I can't imagine," she said, hoping she was convincing. The truth was Alice couldn't imagine wanting to spend all that much time with anyone.

Kevin swallowed the lump in his throat. "Yeah, you're probably right." He followed Alice upstairs. Tess looked like a teenager, curled around Beau's pillow and wearing his shirt.

Alice walked over to the bed and crouched down. "Tess, honey, wake up."

Tess curled more tightly around the pillow.

Alice shook Tess's shoulder, "Tess? Come on, time to get up."

Tess's eyes slowly opened. *Alice?* She turned her head and saw Kevin standing at the foot of her bed. She sat up, wanting nothing more than to lie back down and go to sleep.

"You okay?" Kevin asked. "I asked Alice to come over, in case you wanted to talk."

Tess nodded.

"Tess, you need to get up," Alice said, as a mother might instruct a child. "It's only eight, not bedtime. C'mon." She tried to lift Tess to her feet, but Tess's body went limp.

"I don't want to get up," Tess said quietly.

"You have to. C'mon, you have to get back to your life now. We'll help you. Let's go," Alice's voice left no room for negotiation.

Kevin held Tess under one arm and Alice held the other. Together, they lifted her to her feet.

"I can stand," Tess shrugged them off. "I just don't *want* to."

"We know," Alice said, "but you have to. Now c'mon, let's get you showered and back in the real world." She guided Tess toward the bathroom, and looked over her shoulder at Kevin, nodding toward the bed.

Kevin took the hint and made the bed.

Alice came out of the bathroom giving more orders. "Good job, Kevin. Can you go downstairs and order some food? I don't think she's eaten in forever. I'll get her dressed and be right down."

Kevin left the bedroom, again thankful that Alice was taking control. Chores he could handle, but women, well, they had a full range of unpredictable emotions with which he would rather not tangle.

Tess poked at the sesame chicken and rice. She was cleaner than she'd been in weeks, and so, felt more awake. The house was clean, and for that Tess was thankful. It had become overwhelmingly dirty and in such disarray that she couldn't fathom the idea of mustering the energy to set it right.

"Thanks, you guys," she said.

"That's what we're here for," Alice said easily.

"Are you okay, Tess?" Kevin had asked her that a hundred times, but he didn't know what else to ask. That's what he wanted to know. Was she okay? Would she be able to break out of this lost place she'd found?

Tess nodded, "Yeah, I'm okay."

"Of course she's okay!" Alice said, as if by not paying attention to Tess's pain it would not exist. "She just needs to find herself again, to get moving." Alice put down her fork and looked at Tess; her cheeks had become hollow, her skin deathly pale. "Right, Tess?" she asked hopefully.

Tess nodded and forced down a few more bites. She leaned her chin in her palm and asked, "How do I do this?"

"Eat?" Alice joked.

Kevin gave her a disapproving look. She shrugged.

"No. This...life?" Tears slipped down her cheeks. "How do I do it without him?"

Kevin reached out and touched her arm.

"We'll figure it out," Alice said with surety, although she had no idea how to go about helping Tess, or if she should be the one to do it—but she'd sure as hell try. Whenever Alice had been in crisis, her mother would tell her to push through it (whatever *it* was) and make it happen, and that's just how she'd help Tess. She'd push Tess through this awful situation.

After dinner, Alice washed the dishes while Kevin brought stacks of mail into the kitchen. Alice was secretly pleased when she noticed Tess inspecting the tabletops for water rings.

"Tess, I'm really sorry about Beau," Alice watched Tess move from inspecting the coffee table to inspecting the kitchen counter.

"Oh, he'll be okay," Tess said as she settled onto a wooden chair.

Alice shot a look of concern to Kevin.

Tess caught the glance and cocked her head. The right side of her face showed a hint of a smile. "You know Beau, Kevin. He'll be fine. He always is."

Alice knelt before Tess. "Tess, Beau's gone. You know that, right?"

Tess made a little laughing sound under her breath. "I *know* that."

They sorted through the mail in silence. The drawn tightness that had pulled Tess's features down had

37

softened. Tess found two successive unpaid bills and hoped the electricity wouldn't be turned off. Thankfully, her mortgage was taken directly from their checking account. She wished Beau were there. He always had the patience to deal with the bills. Tess hated the time it took to get online and make sure the payments were being made to the right companies. Too many times she'd paid her Sunoco bill to Sprint, and her Direct TV bill to Dr. Roberts. She took a stack of bills into the den.

Tess pulled her laptop onto her lap and realized that she'd been spending every evening in that exact position since Mr. Fulan had come to her house. *Mr. Fulan.* Just thinking about him brought the urge to hold her breath against his scent and made her stomach hurt. How could they tell her that Beau was dead if they didn't even find his body? The Skype website greeted her, bright and welcoming. She clicked on BethesdaShooter, biting her lower lip and allowing hope to swell in her racing heart. The connection failed, and her shoulders dropped. "Oh, Beau," she said quietly. "When are you coming back?" She rested her hand on her belly.

"Tess?" Kevin said from the doorway. He spotted the light blue screen and went to sit next to her.

Tess shrugged. "I thought he might be on."

"Tess, Beau is dead. He can't be—"

Tess interrupted, "Stop saying that! You don't *know.* They never found him. Maybe he's not..." She could not bring herself to say the word. How could she tell Kevin that she would know if Beau were gone? She'd feel it, like a dark abyss in her soul. She didn't feel that emptiness. Beau's presence still remained in her heart.

Iraq

The memory of twelve-year-old Samira, torn apart and bleeding between her legs on the night of her wedding, came rushing back to Suha. Her face reddened. She turned toward the injured man, her back to the children, and willed the images to leave her mind. Samira's husband, the louse, had violated Samira roughly and left her in her marital bed to roam the streets with his particularly offensive friends, other adulterous men, looking for loose women to fill their insatiable sexual appetites.

Suha had spent her younger years in fear of Iraqi men that were outside of her community, as her father, a well-respected physician, had warned her of the demeaning, discriminatory lifestyle some led and the all-too-often harsh treatments some women, Iraqi and otherwise, endured at their hands. He did not agree with the humiliating lifestyle enforced upon those ill-fated women. Suha knew this was a gross generalization, but she'd seen it far too many times to chance her own future.

Years of witnessing this disrespect and disregard had led Suha to realize that the kindness and generosity her father displayed toward women was rare. She thought her mother, Farrah, had been a very lucky woman indeed. She had been a joyful person. Suha had fond memories of her mother's contagious smile, the way she'd touch her father's shoulder, and the way he would look at her with adoring eyes. She remembered her mother's long hair, let loose in the evening and combed all the way to the tips, which fell just below her waist. She used to long to be just like her and was disappointed in herself when she had become coarse, guarded. Her mother did not show that tension in the easy, loving way she spoke to Suha, and Suha felt the difference.

When she'd lost her mother to pneumonia at the tender age of seven, she'd had no time to mourn her loss. Her father had been devastated, taking to his room for the first month after her death. Suha had cared for him as best she knew how, and eventually he found his feet again. As the years progressed, she and her father became very close, sharing their time and discussing her father's patients well into the evenings. Even as a young girl, Suha had understood the importance of her father's profession and had longed to follow in his footsteps. She'd pored over his medical textbooks, asking in-depth questions that had caused her father to sometimes raise his eyebrows, but he took the time to answer, and his answers carried not just explanations, but lessons, as well.

Suha contributed the fact that she was never pushed to marry to not only her father's respect for her desire to be something more than a house maiden, but also to their long conversations and the camaraderie that they shared. She could never replace her mother, but she knew her father saw her mother somewhere inside her, and she also knew that he would never want that likeness far away. She had readily stepped into her mother's shoes, cooking their meals, cleaning the house, and shopping for necessities. She did all that a daughter could do in such a situation. Her father was a man of loyalty. He'd missed her mother terribly, and as far as she'd known, he'd never longed for another. There was no need to marry Suha off, no need for extra money. The inheritance his father, and his father before him, had left him had been ample for the simple lifestyle they had chosen. As Suha grew to a young woman, her father had asked her often if she wished to be married. Suha had never longed for a different life. With her education ensured and supported by her father, and his ability and desire to protect her, as fathers (and brothers) should, she'd been happy. Eventually, her father had stopped inquiring.

She'd enjoyed many years by her father's side, studying, listening to the cases he shared with her, and, she realized now, learning how to be a good person. Suha's world came shattering down around her when she lost her father in the third year of the war. He'd been eighty-six years old and taking the short walk from the hospital to their home, as he had done for all of the years Suha could remember. He'd taken that short journey so often that he'd worn a literal path in the ground. He'd insisted on walking, even after the war began and the streets had become unsafe. He'd insisted as vehemently as Suha had insisted on continuing to work in the hospital during the war, even with the unsafe conditions.

They'd met for a brief lunch of goat stew and rice, which Suha had prepared the evening before for supper and which she had carried with her to the hospital earlier that morning. This had been their practice, meeting each day around two o'clock in the afternoon for the largest meal of the day. On that unusually warm, gray afternoon, her father shuffled down the path toward his home, too slowly for a group of angry, impatient insurgents who had been terrorizing families in the neighborhood with their guns and loud voices, scavenging and eying the women as if they were just awaiting the right moment to attack. Suha knew of women who had been raped and killed—women without husbands, fathers, or brothers to protect them. A neighbor had seen trouble brewing—loud, irate threats toward the old man. He'd run to the hospital to fetch Suha. Her father had made it to within thirty feet of their front door before the heartless insurgents destroyed Suha's life—without an ounce of remorse. At the moment of his death, she'd been running down the path toward her home as fast as she'd been able, panting, her heavy bosoms swaying painfully against her ribcage. She'd prayed aloud for his safety as she ran. Her dark abayah stuck to her large body from the unrelenting heat of the sun. Her house had come into view. She'd thought he'd made it. As the door had come into view, her eyes drifted toward the ground, and she'd collapsed to her knees at the sight of her father's bullet-ridden body. She sobbed, rocking back and forth, and screamed into the road, *Baba!*

Baba! Blood pooled around him, and his face—the face of the only man she'd ever worshiped, the face of her protector, the face which, forever more, she would recall as blood streaked and lifeless—lay still, distorted and filthy, against the cold, hard earth.

Chapter Six

The evening loomed like a forbidding forest. Tess had known the time would come when she'd have to go back to work. Her bills would not pay themselves. She stared into her closet at her business suits, their creases fresh. The feel of them used to give her an energized high. Now, just the thought of taking charge, being responsible, pained her. How would she ever be ready to face the world by tomorrow? Tomorrow! She threw herself down on her bed and let out a frustrated sigh. Tears came easily. "Oh, Beau," she said softly. She contemplated the bottle of Xanax that had helped her through the difficult nights, then kicked them off of the nightstand with her toes. She wasn't going to become *that* woman. She dropped her hand to her abdomen. Tears spilled down her cheeks as she rolled over and punched the pillow. The thought of pitiful looks and people using words that had taken on new meanings, words like *sorry, passed,* and *accident,* made her as angry as it made her sad.

Tess remembered Beau's promise, made the days before he left for Iraq. "I'll come back. I promise," he'd said with feeling.

"I know you will," she'd answered, without as much confidence as she'd hoped.

Beau had gently pushed her back from his chest so he could look into her tear-filled blue eyes. "Baby," he said, "what have I told you since we decided that I should take this opportunity?"

Tess looked down at the floor and said in almost a whisper, "You'll come back to me."

He tilted her chin up so she couldn't help but look into his eyes. "And I will. I promise you that."

"But you can't make that promise," she said quietly. "There's still a war going on, Beau."

"Don't doubt me, Tessie. I love you, and I promise, come hell or high water, if I have to walk and swim back from Iraq, I will come home."

Tess took Beau's hand and outlined in his palm, lightly, with her index finger, the letter *I*, the shape of a heart, and the letter *u*. He smiled and kissed her cheek. They had done this silent ritual for many years, in the darkness of theaters, reaching under the table when dining with others, in the darkness of night just before they fell asleep.

She sat up and wiped her tears. "Goddamn it!" she yelled, and wrapped her arms around herself. "How am I supposed to do this, Beau?" she asked the empty room. Silence pressed in around her until she felt claustrophobic and hauled herself off the bed. She opened the top drawer of Beau's bureau, reaching past his nicely-folded boxers and rolled socks, and withdrawing his unwashed blue cotton t-shirt that she'd stashed. She pressed it against her nose and breathed in the familiar smell of Beau's scent. A smile spread across her lips, and she exhaled, as if she'd taken a deep drag of a spectacular drug. *I can do this*, she told herself. *I have to do this.*

Alice rushed around the small office. Tess would be there any minute, her first day back since Beau had died. Alice wanted everything to be perfect. She hoped Tess would slip right back into her old routine without stress or what she feared most, having to watch her friend fall apart before her eyes. She knew Beau's memorial was a source of contention for Tess, she'd spoken to Beau's parents, Carol and Robert. They wanted to hold a service for Beau, and Tess wanted no part of it. She wasn't sure how, or if, she'd be able to help with that situation. At this point, she just hoped the day went smoothly, without any tearful breakdowns. Alice was good at pushing through, but she wasn't very good at hand holding. Her mother had never coddled her, though she knew her mother's love was as deep and pure as love could be. One didn't have to coddle, she reasoned. One only needed to express love for another, be there for them, be strong for them—and Alice could do that for Tess.

She smoothed her blue pencil skirt and glanced in the mirror on the wall. She stroked her hair and smiled. She loved her hair. It was her strongest feature. Sure, she had a slim, toned body, but that was easy to come by with hard work and a little discipline. Good hair, on the other hand, that was something that you could only be born with. It fell just below her shoulders, straight and full. Her natural color, somewhere between Asian pear and just-ripe banana, was cool and soft. She had worn it in the same style since she was seven: center parted, blunt across the back. If something worked, why change it? She ran the edge of her finger under one eye, then the other, though her eyeliner never needed repair.

Satisfied with her appearance, she pulled the new coasters she'd purchased from her Coach purse (one of her guilty pleasures) and laid it on Tess's desk. She set a tall Styrofoam cup of Tess's favorite drink, French vanilla cappuccino from 7-11, on the coaster. It never failed to boggle her mind that her friend's favorite beverage could be purchased for a dollar seventy-seven from a convenience store.

Tess stood in the hallway, staring at the office door, wishing she could just hide forever. Reality, however, pressed on, even if you were scared, alone, and spending every second of the day waiting to hear your husband's voice. *He's coming back to me. He promised*, Tess told herself. She knew she had to put on a brave face for Alice, and she was determined not to have to deal with the looks that Alice and Kevin hadn't realized she'd seen, the eye rolls and pity-filled glances. She took a deep breath and pulled her shoulders back. Beau would expect to find her whole, with her business still intact. For him, for when he returned, she would be strong. The feigned eagerness felt like an ill-fit jacket—too loose and too tight for comfort. *He's coming back.*

Tess breezed into the office. "Hey, Al, how's it going?"

Alice answered tentatively, taken aback by Tess's quick turnaround. She looked healthier than when Alice had last seen her, fuller in the face, the drawn, gaunt look she'd held was gone. "Fine."

"I can't wait to get back to work," Tess said. She flung herself into her chair and thanked Alice for the cappuccino. She moved the cup to the side of the desk and picked up the coaster, turning the warmed ceramic in her hands, running her fingers over the taupe, green, and peach flowers.

"This is gorgeous! Where did you find it?" she gushed.

"You know that little women's market, on Wisconsin Avenue?"

Tess nodded. "By that handmade rug store."

"Yup. I found it last week and knew you'd love it." Alice smiled. She was relieved to hear the happiness in Tess's voice.

"It's beautiful. Thank you." Tess put the coaster in her top right desk drawer and sipped her drink.

Alice watched with disbelief. "Aren't you going to use it?" she asked.

Tess scrunched her face and shrugged her left shoulder, "Nah, but I do love it."

Alice was uncertain if she should be concerned about Tess's newfound freedom from coasters or if she should be happy about it.

"What's happening around here?" Tess skimmed through the stack of messages on her desk.

"Beau's parents called." Alice watched Tess's face tense and knew it was not the time to bring that up. "They, uh, were just making sure we didn't need anything here in the office."

Tess's shoulders relaxed, "What else?"

"I hadn't wanted to worry you, but we're getting close to having issues with payroll. Everyone understands, but payroll is payroll."

Tess's face grew serious again. "Right. Payroll." She dropped her gaze, thinking, then popped up from her chair. "Well, we'll have to push some new clients through. What's happening with Mr. Mason?"

"He's ready. He was waiting for you to come back." She sifted through the folders until she found the one marked *Mason Press*. "Mid-level manager, fifty-five, maybe sixty-K."

"Did he agree to the twenty percent?" Tess asked.

"Yup. He's all set. Just needs you to go down and finalize."

"Great, set it up. How about that Tole guy? The one that was referred but didn't return my calls? Any word from him?" Tess asked.

Alice shook her head.

The corner of Tess's lips turned up, and in a conniving voice, she said, "Oh, he's ours. Don't you worry."

Alice laughed. "Oh, I'm not. I figured you'd pull him in." She left Tess's office and came back with a stack of five blue folders. "I've been going through our mid-level management résumés. I think these are good matches." She handed them to Tess.

"I'll look through them now. Can you get me Tole's number? And set up a meeting with Mason for Wednesday, three o'clock."

Alice felt a surge of adrenaline. Tess was back!

On her way back from sealing the deal with Mr. Mason, Tess was on fire, enthused to be accomplishing her goals instead of pining away at her computer. She could do this—the pregnancy, waiting for Beau to return. *Yes*, she thought, *I can do this*. No longer would she try to convince Alice and Kevin of Beau's being alive. It was a futile effort. She'd noticed how Alice had watched her every move the last few days, and how she'd scoffed when Tess had made reference to Beau's return. They were too closed-minded to understand that had Beau been dead, Tess would have known—and the one thing she knew for certain was that he was not dead. He couldn't be. He was just…detained, and that thought gave her the strength to get up each day and reclaim her life.

Tess turned onto Wisconsin Avenue and headed toward Bethesda. She was on top of her game, and if Mr. Tole wouldn't return her calls, she'd knock on his door.

The fine leather furnishings and expensive hardwood that adorned the accounting office of Tole and Whitcomb would be intimidating to most, but to Tess, a woman who had built a company from the ground up with nothing more than sheer will and an idea, the pricey façade was merely an ego boost for the people within. Tess didn't care much for over-inflated egos, but her business needed the income. The six weeks she'd taken off had stretched their bank account about as far as it could go. Sure, the insurance companies were sending her letters and calling her, trying to get her to file the necessary paperwork in order for her to claim the life insurance that Beau had so thoughtfully left behind, but Tess would not take a penny of it. Doing so would validate Beau's death.

Tess held her head high and approached the middle-aged secretary who glanced up from behind rectangular red glasses.

"Tess Johnson for Mr. Tole, please," she said.

The secretary scanned her day planner and then looked at Tess disapprovingly. "What time is your appointment, Ms. Johnson?"

"I don't have one," Tess said. The attitude and smug sneer of the secretary did not dissuade Tess. She handed the woman a business card, *Top Staffing Consultants, Tess Johnson, President*. Instantly, the woman's sneer morphed into something vaguely reminiscent of a pleasant smile.

"Just a moment." She stood, settling an efficient telephone headset upon her perfectly cropped, coiffed, and recently-dyed honey-blonde hair. She towered above Tess's five-foot-seven-inch frame and sauntered as if she were on a runway, straight backed and smooth gaited, into the next room.

Tess peeked over the top of the reception desk and quickly eyed the calendar. Mr. Tole had no appointments until 3:30 P.M. She glanced at the clock behind the desk, *1:42*. Tess smirked.

A moment later the receptionist returned, sat her capable self down behind the desk, removed the headset, and donned a fake smile. "Mr. Tole will be right with you. You can wait on the sofa, if you'd like."

Tess thanked her and remained standing. She'd learned early on that sitting gave the client an advantage, and she'd wanted the upper hand in this initial meeting. She'd arrived on his turf. She'd have to establish her ground quickly. She took a deep, empowering breath, the scent of leather reminding her of her deceased father. She bristled. Not now.

A man about Tess's age neared the doorway. He stopped to speak to a younger man, who, unlike him, was dressed in a suit. Tess assumed he was a client. It wasn't uncommon for clients to show up for appointments in any office in jeans and a t-shirt. She turned away and glanced at the paintings on the wall.

"Ms. Johnson?"

Tess turned around and was met with the jean-clad man. "Yes?"

He reached his right hand out to her and smiled, "Louie Tole. It's a pleasure to meet you."

Tess shook his hand and couldn't help but look over his clothing.

"I know," he laughed. "My mother tells me to dress like a grownup all the time."

Tess blushed. "I'm sorry. I didn't mean—"

"It's okay. I'm used to it." His smile was warm and welcoming, his disheveled brown curls brought a softness to his rugged face. "C'mon back to my office. Let's chat."

Tess hurried next to him. *Chat? What man used the word chat?*

The large, mahogany desk was in complete disarray, cluttered with files and loose papers. Tess eyed the empty Styrofoam cups piled on the Indian print chair in front of the desk.

"Let me get those," he swept the mess off the chair and into a small metal trash can.

"Thank you for seeing me without notice, Mr. Tole." Tess settled into the surprisingly comfortable chair.

"Louie, please," he said and leaned back in his chair, hands clasped behind his head. "What can I do you for?" he asked. His glance at her crossed legs did not go unnoticed.

Tess questioned her choice of the black, above-the-knee skirt she wore. It had given her confidence when she'd put it on that morning. Now, however, she wondered if that skirt should be kept just for Beau. She smoothed it down toward her knee, and Louie smiled.

"You were referred to me by Katelyn Rafael of Layona Farms?"

"Katie," he nodded, "of course. She's always sending pretty ladies my way."

"She didn't refer me for…that," Tess said, irritated.

He laughed again and brought his seat back to its upright position, lowering his hands to his lap. "I know. I'm sorry. It was meant to be a joke. Katie's an old friend of mine. I know who you are."

"You do?" Tess asked, a little miffed by his innuendo.

"Of course. You've called me on eight occasions, the last one being yesterday at four."

Tess looked at him inquisitively.

"I'm not very good at returning calls," he admitted. "It's not that they're not important." He held Tess's gaze as he spoke of his inability, or lack of desire, really, to return phone calls, and his rampant ability to take on far too many things at once.

Tess warmed to his confession. She told him, with a little laugh, that he was not at all like her, that she was just the opposite—she leaned toward the compulsive side; every phone call returned, every milestone met, every client followed-up with. Then she quickly added, "I don't mean that how it sounds, like I'm better than other people. In fact, I think it's a detriment, being so compulsive about things." What was she doing? Where was her upper hand? For once, Tess had no ulterior motive during her client meeting. They fell into a conversation about missed opportunities for him and instances when she'd driven her clients crazy with constant follow-ups. Worrying about sealing the deal had fallen by the wayside. Tess liked Louie's off-beat personality. At 3:30, when the completely capable receptionist buzzed Louie's phone, Tess had not only *not* sealed the deal, but she'd accepted his invitation to dinner—to further discuss how they might work together.

The phone rang as Tess was heading out the door to meet Louie for dinner. "Hello?"

"Mrs. Johnson, I'm glad I caught you."

Mr. Levy's voice made Tess's heart race. *Damn.* She'd been avoiding the overzealous insurance agent. "I'm just on my way out the door," Tess said, hurriedly.

Mr. Levy rattled on, "Can we schedule a time to talk? I've been leaving messages for weeks. We have insurance that needs to be tended to. The funeral—"

Tess interrupted him, "Sorry, I have to go." She hung up the phone without an ounce of guilt. "Where the hell are my keys?" she strode toward the table by the front door, snagging the keys with her shaking hands. Pushing the sadness away and replacing it with a feeling of hope had become almost a physical task as much as a mental one. The mantra she'd adapted, *He's coming back, he promised*, helped her through the excruciating emptiness that she knew would easily disable her if she let it.

Tess entered the quaint Thai restaurant five minutes later than she'd hoped, the smell of fish, lemongrass, and garlic hovered in the air. The lights were dim, creating an aura of relaxation and romance. Romance! Suddenly Tess worried that she'd given Louie the wrong impression. They had decided to meet to discuss work, hadn't they? She was sure they had. So why were her nerves all tingly? *You're pregnant and married, remember?* The restaurant was busy, and for that she was thankful, though she was sure she'd overdressed in her black slacks, pale yellow blouse, and black blazer. She quickly decided it was a good thing to be overdressed. She looked professional, and that was just what she needed to portray.

Tess mentally transformed from nervous woman to business professional, standing up straighter, and tightening a curt smile across her lips. She was led to a darkened corner by a beautiful Asian woman as thin as the day was long. Louie stood when she arrived, welcoming her with a smile. Dressed in the same jeans and t-shirt he'd worn earlier to the office, he made no apologies for his appearance and didn't comment on Tess's either. Tess wasn't sure if she found his nonchalance rude or appealing.

Conversation came easily. Louie told Tess about a client that he had met with in the afternoon, a gentleman who owned five retail chain stores and had recently "lost" his accounting records. Tess could not imagine having the patience to deal with that type of situation. She'd have confronted the man about poor business practices or tax evasion. Louie explained that he'd told the client to find them before April, or he'd have to back out of being his accountant. He was ethical, Tess concluded, and she found that to be admirable.

"So tell me about the phone calls," she said. "What can you possibly gain by not returning phone calls? How do you stay in business, much less grow a business?"

Louie smiled and flagged the waitress over. He ordered another glass of wine for himself and another seltzer water for Tess.

"I do return my clients' calls," he said and took a bite of his Shrimp Pad Thai.

"So it's just non-clients that you ignore?" Tess asked.

"No, I don't *ignore* anyone. Usually, my secretary, Kay, returns calls that are from non-clients, and if they appear to be potential clients or need my attention, *then* I return them."

"So..." Tess was a little annoyed about his lack of explanation about her phone calls.

"So I wasn't ignoring your calls. I know you're a headhunter, and I haven't really decided if I want to use one or not."

"I thought you had used Klineman Staffing, and before that, PermaStaff."

"You do your research," he smiled. "Impressive."

Tess prided herself on knowing how to win a client over, memorizing their hiring practices better than they know them themselves, which was easy because it was rarely the principles doing the actual hiring. Be persistent, professional, and offer them a fair market value for services rendered. Last, but not least, always present candidates that are thoroughly screened and tested, their backgrounds investigated, and only represent the people that she, herself, would hire in her own office.

"Let's see how good I am at this game," Louie said conspiratorially. "You've been in business for ten years. Your first office was a small townhouse in Rockville. You moved to Bethesda seven years ago and have been renting the same office space ever since. You've negotiated a smaller increase in rent the last two years than other renters. Your right hand is the lovely Alice Workman, and your primary means of support is mid to upper level management—although as far as I can see, you work with just about any type of business, with the exception of law firms, and—"

Slack jawed, Tess blinked rapidly. "How do you--"

Louie smiled broadly. "You see, two can play at these games." He took a sip of his wine, and his eyes danced above the rim of his glass, then suddenly became serious.

"Well, you nailed it—dead on," Tess nodded, perhaps she'd met her professional match. Her mind reeled through a way to one-up him, but while her mind was running, he kicked her legs out from under her.

"And…you recently lost your husband," he said in a serious, quiet tone.

Tess's smile faded. She rolled her lips into her mouth. *He's coming back. He's coming back to me.* She steeled herself against the pressing heartbreak and straightened her back against her chair. "I haven't lost him," she said confidently.

Louie cocked his head and furrowed his brow. "Oh, I'm sorry. I thought…the crash…"

Tess shook her head. "They—" she waved her hands as if displaying an item, "his family, my friends—they all believe he's gone, but I don't think so. They simply haven't found him yet." Her voice told Louie to back off, and he did.

He nodded. "Alright then."

An uncomfortable silence passed between them.

"Let's talk about hiring practices. What can you offer that no one else can?" Louie taunted.

Madonna interrupted Tess's thoughts, more specifically, Madonna's "Vogue." *Odd choice for a man's ring tone.*

"Excuse me," Louie turned away from Tess, whispering into the phone. "Is she coherent?" Louie ran his hand through his hair and said with a sigh, "Okay, I'll be there soon." Louie turned toward Tess, a concerned look in his eyes. "I'm sorry. I have to go." Without further explanation, he excused himself from the table, paying the bill on the way out the door.

Tess slipped into her car and replayed the evening in her mind. She wondered who had called Louie. *A wife? Babysitter?* He hadn't mentioned a wife or a child, but then again, Tess had never asked. She had been too caught up in enjoying the diversion from her grief. What was she doing? How could she have pushed Beau aside in her mind like that? Guilt wooed her. She wanted to feel stricken—lost even—by Beau's absence, as she had in the weeks prior. She knew she should feel those emotions, and yet, somehow, each day, she was becoming stronger. Her faith that Beau was not gone forever extinguished her fear that he might have been. It was almost as if he were on a business trip, and she knew he'd be coming home— only she didn't know when.

Iraq

Beau stared at the photo of Tess, remembering fondly the afternoon it had been taken. They'd been dating for about a month, and Beau was head over heels in love with Tess. They were fishing on Kevin's father's boat, joking about one of them falling in the water. Tess was deathly afraid of any body of water larger than a swimming pool, and she wasn't too keen on those, either. She'd clung tightly to Beau's arm. Suddenly, the wind kicked up and the small boat rocked from side to side. Beau had to pry himself away to help bring down the sail, and somehow, at the very moment that Beau had turned his back, the boat had tipped. Tess had gone flailing into the water, shrieking and petrified. Kevin and Beau had pulled her out seconds later.

He ran his hand over the picture. Tess hated everything about that photo, from her soaking wet hair to the frightening memory it held. Beau's love for the photo was equal to her hatred, for the simple fact that five minutes after it was taken, Tess had held onto Beau like a lifeline, soaking wet and shivering. Through chattering teeth, she'd told Beau what he'd been waiting to hear— that she loved him.

He was not ashamed of his tears as they streamed down his cheeks. He could not have stopped them if he had tried. Flashes of memory flooded his mind, the sounds of explosions echoed in his ears. He lay on the strangely-printed blankets, wondering how and why he had survived the helicopter crash. Whatever the reasons, his life had been handed back to him, and for that he was grateful. His mind ran in circles. He had to come up with a plan. He had to get back to Tess.

Suha wiped his tears, speaking in her broken but understandable English. "She is yours, yes?"

Beau nodded slightly. His cheeks hurt, but he could no better hide his pushing smile than walk away from his makeshift bed. "Tess," he whispered.

"Tess. She is beautiful, yes? Your wife?" Suha asked.

Beau nodded.

"She will be worried. You will, *come back to me*," Suha said, and placed the shiny, dented, pocket watch in his right hand, curling his fingers around it with a gentle squeeze.

Beau closed his eyes, relishing in the feel of his watch, their watch. *Yes, I will*, he thought. *I will come back to you.*

"Sleep," Suha said, and for the first time in many weeks, Beau closed his eyes without anxiety.

Chapter Seven

Tess lay on the table in her obstetrician's office, her belly covered with warm, gooey gel. She stared at the black screen of the ultrasound monitor, tapping her fingers on the paper sheet below her.

"Excited?" Dr. Roberts asked.

My husband's missing, I had dinner with another man, and I'm lying here naked under a paper gown. Would you be excited? Tess shrugged.

The ultrasound wand pressed against her abdomen, sending a cool shiver up her arms. The outline of a bubble came to life on the monitor as Dr. Roberts expertly aimed the wand to the right, down, then to the left, ever so gently. A tiny shape appeared. Tess's heart jumped, "Is that her?"

"Well, I don't know if it's her or him. It's a little early for that, but yes, that's your baby," he smiled.

Tess lifted her head, "That's my baby? That tiny thing? Is she okay?" Her baby had become real.

"So?" Alice said from her usual morning perch in Tess's office. They'd sat across the desk from one another for eight years, and never once had Tess dodged Alice's questions as she had that morning. Alice had received the finalized paperwork from Mr. Mason and had been trying to gather details of Tess's meeting with Mr. Tole.

Tess sipped her water, wishing it were cappuccino, and lifted her eyebrows. "The deal's not sealed just yet," she said, avoiding Alice's glare.

"Okay, I got that much. So where do we stand? Did you discuss business at *all* last night?" Alice became annoyed with the silence, "Tess? Hello? What is it?"

"I don't know, okay?" Tess said, frustrated. "I *think* we're going to seal the deal. I mean, we always seal the deal. So yes, we *will* seal this deal." Her words were confident but her mind was not. "There's something…I don't know…weird about this guy."

"Weird?"

"Yeah, but in a not-so-weird kind of way." Tess knew that she was avoiding Alice's eyes, and she didn't know what was going on in her own head. She'd had a client meeting—she'd had a million of them. Why was she so hung up over this one?

"Okay, Tess, spill. I want it all, every last detail," Alice said curiously.

Tess looked up and smiled. "There are no details to spill. We had dinner. We talked about work…sort of…and about life. He's just," she looked out the large picture window that overlooked the busy streets of Bethesda and let her mind wander to the prior evening. What was it about the evening that had her so dumbstruck? She couldn't define the fine line that she teetered upon, wavering between comfort and discomfort. Alice's voice brought her back to the present.

"Just what, Tess?"

Tess shook her head and shrugged. "He's the kind of guy who runs a business in jeans, Alice. Jeans! It's just...I don't know." She scooped up a pile of files from her desk and rose from her chair. "Let's get started setting up interviews for Mason Press. Who do you have in mind?" she hurried out of her office with Alice close by her heels and spread out the files on the conference room table. They were discussing potential candidates when the phone rang. Alice answered it on the second ring.

"Sure, she's right here," she put the caller on hold and handed the phone to Tess. "It's Beau's mom," she said. Tess gave her an annoyed look, waving her hands as if to say she was not there. Alice busied herself with the files, pretending not to see.

"Hi, Carol," Tess feigned a smile. Tess closed her eyes and listened to Beau's mother's plea for a memorial service.

"We can't move on with our lives until we have closure," Carol said.

There it was—the words that pulled Tess's heart right from her chest and infuriated her all at once. Heat raced through Tess's veins. "He is not dead," she said into the phone.

Alice's head shot up. She glared at Tess with disbelieving eyes.

Tess held the phone a few inches from her ear, and Alice could hear Carol's tearful pleas on the other end, trying desperately to talk some sense into Tess. Tess's cheeks burned, her eyes filled with tears. "Carol," she said in a detached, professional voice, "I have to go now." Tess hung up the phone and stormed out of the office. Alice was on her feet in seconds, following Tess into the ladies' room. Tess locked herself in a stall and sobbed.

Alice pressed her hand against the stall door. "Tess?" she said softly.

Tess sniffled, blew her nose.

"Do you want to talk?" Alice asked.

Tess steeled herself for what she knew would come next. She'd tell Alice that Beau was still alive, and Alice would tell her that she needed to deal with the reality that Beau was dead. She'd heard it so many times already from Alice, from Carol, from Kevin. If she heard it one more time she thought she might throw up. She knew what she believed, but she also knew that no one else held that same belief. No, she decided. She would not go through that again. If Carol and Robert needed a damned memorial, then so be it. She didn't need to be part of it. She'd be damned if she was going to have that useless discussion with anyone else—ever again. She lowered her hand to her abdomen and thought, I can do this. *For you. For us.*

She wiped her eyes, held her head high, and pulled her shoulders back before exiting the stall. *Alice.* Alice knew how to push her, make her do things that she didn't want to do. Alice's full lips turned down at the ends, her eyebrows drew together and lifted ever so slightly. The emotion Alice gave her was real, and Tess couldn't, no matter how much she steeled herself, turn her back on that. Against her will, tears tumbled down her cheeks and she fell, sobbing, into Alice's open arms.

Back at her apartment, Alice set her purse on the impeccably-clean black countertop and settled into the white Scandinavian recliner. She still got a rush of excitement from the crispness of the black and white furniture, highlighted by smooth wooden braces that arched and essed. Scandinavian designs made her feel successful and comfortable. In her condo, she was in control, and she liked it that way. Everything had its place, and it was rarely set awry. A few male visitors had left their shoes in all the wrong places, carelessly tossed their shirts onto the floor—something she despised—and had, in general, made her wish they would leave shortly after they had arrived. Alice felt complete just the way she was. She didn't understand the gushing need that so many women had for men in their lives. Even Tess's preoccupation with Beau had been almost too much for Alice to endure.

She enjoyed the amenities she owned, which did not come cheap. She'd been knee deep in debt when she'd taken the job with Tess, and it hadn't taken long for her to understand the earning ability that Tess possessed.

Alice quickly discovered which tasks she could take over, enabling Tess to build the business, and rendering the need to hire two more recruiters. Alice's salary had soared, as did Tess's, and Tess was generous with the profits, a little too generous, if you asked Alice. She tossed an extra thousand dollars to the recruiters whenever they had produced more than ten thousand dollars of income during any one-month period. Alice never complained, though. Tess had always been fair with Alice, allowing her to naturally increase her responsibility without question, and with the added responsibility, she increased Alice's salary exponentially, while still providing lofty bonuses. Alice had quickly climbed out of debt and into a place of comfort, maybe even a little elitist. She reached for her black, designer telephone.

"Hey, Alice, what's up?" Kevin was in good spirits.

"A lot, let me tell you," Alice sighed. "Can you meet me somewhere?"

The last time Alice had asked Kevin to meet her was when Alice wanted to complain about Beau sweeping Tess away on an unplanned vacation in the middle of their busiest season. She'd wanted Kevin to step in and talk sense into Beau, delay their trip.

He hesitated, then agreed. "When?"

"Tonight." It wasn't a question.

Alice assumed Kevin didn't have plans. Her assumption was correct, of course, and she didn't care if it undermined his masculinity—nor was she perturbed at his annoyed tone of voice when he answered, "Yeah, sure. Bailey's Pub, eight o'clock?"

He could not say no to Alice when it might concern Tess.

Alice strolled into the pub ten minutes early. Though she stared straight ahead, the hostess seemingly her only focus, she was not oblivious to the lascivious, hopeful stares emanating from the men at the bar. As disinterested as she appeared on the outside, inside she was scoping, planning. It wasn't their lifted eyebrows or the way they tried too hard to look cool that roused her or enticed her curiosity. Conquering men, being in control of which one, how long, and what she'd let them do, had become a finely-tuned art. Men had such weak minds. It almost disgusted her how easily they could be had. She stood tall and proud, and followed the waitress to a nearby table where she would wait for Kevin and let the horny hoverers stew. She ordered a drink, knowing that if she didn't, eventually one of the bar oglers would order one for her, and she'd just as soon skip that playful game tonight. She had Tess on her mind and wasn't in the mood for fake flirting. Cat and mouse games bored her. She'd make her choice, introduce herself with the sole purpose of getting her chosen stud into bed, use him, and cast him off, as she'd done hundreds of times before.

Kevin breezed into the pub, stopped at the bar, then sat across the small round table from Alice. "I ordered you a piña colada from the bar," he smiled. "You look great." Alice's cocoa brown silk sleeveless shirt set off her eyes perfectly.

"Down boy," she laughed.

"No worries there," Kevin smirked.

His *not interested look* came across loud and clear. "Anyway," she sighed, "How are you?"

"Great."

Alice caught the hesitation in his response. "Not great, huh?" she asked

Kevin shook his head. His hair had grown since Alice had last seen him, falling below his eyes and hiding them perfectly.

"Beau?" she asked gently.

He nodded, clasped his hands together, rested his chin on them, and looked up at Alice through his wavy bangs. He breathed in through his nose.

"It's been harder than I thought it would be."

While Alice had felt Beau's loss as a devastating loss for her friend, she now realized that she hadn't felt it personally. For the first time, she questioned her own lack of emotion. She fiddled with a napkin. A strand of insufficiency wheedled its way through her thoughts.

"It must be hard to lose your best friend," she said.

Kevin pinched the bridge of his nose between his thumb and forefinger and closed his eyes. When he reopened them, his mood had changed dramatically.

"Yeah, well, what are you going to do, right?" he announced with feigned bravado. He looked around the pub and noticed the glances toward Alice from a neighboring table of men. He chuckled inwardly. "So, what's up?"

Alice took the hint and refrained from inquiring any further about the emptiness Beau had left in Kevin's life. The change of subjects suited her just fine.

"Tess," she said, and half-smiled, "I'm worried about her."

"I haven't seen her in a while," he confessed. "It just got to be too hard."

"Because seeing her reminded you of Beau?" Alice asked.

He shook his head. "Because Tess wouldn't let him go."

"That's kind of why I'm here," she confessed. "I think she's really in denial."

"Denial?" he laughed. "She's in no-way-in-hell-is-my-husband-dead land, not denial. She'll have no part of any conversation about Beau being gone." He gulped down his beer and waved to the waitress, pointing to his empty bottle. "I tried. I spent time with her, even cut her grass a couple of times, but it was just...too hard. She really believes that he's alive."

Alice wasn't surprised by his statements. Her own observations had her concerned. "Do you think she really believes it, or she just doesn't want to talk about it?"

Kevin leaned back in his chair shaking his head. His voice grew louder, "Nope. She believes it. She still checks Skype every night—or at least she was still doing it a few weeks ago."

"Really?" That surprised Alice.

"Yup, and when I tried to talk to her about that, she laughed at me, like I was the crazy one."

Alice immediately stood up for Tess, "I don't think she's crazy, Kevin. Maybe she's depressed, or in denial, but not crazy."

"That's just it, Alice. She's going through her days like there's nothing wrong, but she won't even let us have a memorial service for him. That's why I stopped going over. I need that. I need closure. He was my best friend for God's sake." He stared at her.

She looked down. Normal people knew how to comfort others. All she could do was push through the discomfort. "I know," she said awkwardly. "There's got to be something we can do. We can't just turn our backs on her. This is seriously wrong. I mean, Beau's gone. He's not coming back, and she's causing conflicts with his parents, and now you." Alice shook her head.

"I talked to Carol and Robert. They called me this morning. They're going to hold a memorial anyway, and if Tess doesn't want to be part of it, then so be it."

Conflicting emotions beleaguered Alice—guilt for knowing about the memorial and feeling as though it was the right thing to do, and heartbreak for recognizing that it went against Tess's wishes.

"Can you talk any sense into her?" Kevin asked.

"I have to admit, I kind of tippy toe around the topic myself. I didn't realize that she really thought he was alive. I figured she was just having, you know, a hard time with it."

A few drinks and two hours later, they laughed about Kevin and Beau's hunting trips—Kevin with his bow and arrow (he had yet to actually kill any animals), and Beau with his camera, hunting his prey.

"There's this one raccoon by my grandfather's hunting cabin. It gets into the trash every time we're there. I swear I've been trying to kill the damn thing for five years, and Beau's been trying to capture it on film." He laughed at the memory. Kevin told Alice that Beau had always seemed to him like an old married man, even when he was single. Marrying Tess had brought a certain contentedness to Beau that Kevin had secretly envied. He'd had a hard time committing to the movies, much less a lifetime.

Kevin swigged his fourth beer. What was that sexy scent she was wearing? "So, Al, what's really up with you?" His inhibitions were nowhere to be found.

Alice sucked down the last of her third (or was it her fourth?) drink and waved to the waitress for another. "Whaddaya mean?" she asked. If she wasn't mistaken, her words sounded almost flirtatious. Her body was numb, and it felt damned good to let go for a while.

66

"C'mon. You know what I mean." Kevin laughed, "Men, guys, doing the nasty." *There was that scent again.* He tucked his heightened sexual impulses away.

Alice feigned insult, pulling back from the table, her eyes wide.

"I've known you for what…forever? And I've never seen you with a dude." Kevin's head rocked to the beat of the bad rap song playing loudly in the background.

"Date? I date." She leaned over the table. "I date guys, I mean."

"Well, I didn't think you dated chicks!"

They fell into fits of drunken laughter.

"Maybe I do! How would you know?" she quipped.

"That'd be cool, too. Maybe I could watch," he roared.

Alice grinned.

Tess hesitated by the bed, thinking of Beau. She'd been such a mess earlier, with Alice, she'd felt as though she were on an emotional roller coaster. Even the bike ride she'd taken to clear her mind hadn't helped. She touched Beau's side of the bed, lingering in thought, then made her way to the bathroom where she pulled off her bike shorts and stepped into the shower. Lather slid down her chest. She washed her stomach, the heel of her hand feeling a tiny bulge. She looked down and froze. There it was. She tried to wrap her mind around the idea that there was a little person inside of her. A fact she'd successfully ignored. *What did it feel like to be inside a person's body?* she wondered. Even with the baby inside of her, she felt hollow, alone. If Beau had been there he'd hold her, tell her he loved her. If Beau were there, she wouldn't be wondering how she was going to raise a baby alone.

Iraq

Samira and Zeid made their way to the river and trudged back toward their shelter across the dark, arid desert. Zeid tried his mother's patience during the long, hot trek.

"But, Mother," he said in his high pitched, pre-adolescent voice. He spoke only Arabic, though now that they were living with Suha, Samira had hopes that he might learn English. "I want to fight. I am a man," he pleaded.

Samira, scared for their safety, shushed him and ignored his relentless plea to return to the city. Her heart swelled with pride that her son would want to protect their people, though the attitude he showed toward Suha was deplorable. She was shamed by his words, though he'd acquired them by no fault of his own—a remnant from his bully of a father.

Zeid had given up his arguments or was simply too exhausted to put forth the effort. He walked a few feet in front of Samira as they neared their temporary shelter. He carried two containers of water, and when Samira looked at him, his feet dragging, his shoulders hung low, she felt the weight of sadness upon her. She'd taken him out of one hell and led him into another. Although she did not mind the temporary shelter, she worried how living in constant fear would impact Zeid and the other children. Zeid was a child, and yet he'd been thrown into the role of a young man.

She sent Zeid inside the tent. Samira needed a moment to refocus her mind before seeing the handsome man inside. Over the past few weeks, she'd stolen many glances at the injured foreigner. *What was his life? Did he beat his wife?* Oh, how she wished she knew! She was embarrassed by her schoolgirl infatuation, but could not deny the excitement of her rapid heartbeat as she stole those peeks, or her adulation of the man who lay helpless in a bed that she had hastily thrown together.

The day after they'd found him in the sand, she'd gone out and scoured the area, looking for clues of his life. All she had found was a broken camera, which now lay hidden amongst her things. It was not her intent to keep the jewel hidden, but she had been unwilling to relinquish it. Having that small token of the intriguing stranger brought her happiness, and she hadn't had much joy in her short life.

Samira's life had been one of sadness and great pain. She had never forgiven her parents for giving her to Safaa, her husband, when she had been just a girl. Safaa was twenty years her senior and well versed in the ways of men and women. Samira had pleaded with her parents not to be made a bride at twelve years old. She promised to help her mother, to cook, clean, sew, to do whatever was necessary, although she had already been doing those daily chores for years. *It was not the way anymore*, she had told them. *Girls no longer married so young!* Her father would not hear her. He demanded her marriage, ignored her pleas without so much as an explanation. He'd turned his back on her for money, and to Samira, for what seemed like a pittance when compared to what she'd be losing. Prior to the war, Iraqi brides bid a much higher dowry, and Samira was no different than those brides, though much younger than most.

A smooth-skinned girl, blessed with dark tendrils that fell to her waist, small, fine features, and a willingness to work hard in the home, Samira was a relative gold mine for her family. Her father had demanded twice the typical dowry of 350 U.S. dollars. Safaa, a wise business man, negotiated for Samira, and in the end paid her father the equivalent of roughly 425 U.S. dollars. He was proud of the negotiation. Samira was sickened by it.

With one older brother and no sisters, Samira had learned her place in a home early on. Her marriage was no different. Her wedding night brought pain, shame, and the understanding that complaining would only lead to bruises and harsh words. Samira accepted her place in her husband's world as more of a concubine, nanny, and housekeeper than a wife, with grace and outward patience. Inside, however, she harbored disgust and resentment. Shame for what she had become, and anger toward not just her husband, but also herself, gnawed away at her. When her husband was killed by an improvised explosive device, she'd been secretly, shamefully, thankful. She played the role of grieving wife flawlessly. She did feel grief, but only for the protection that a husband had provided, not for the loss of her husband.

After Safaa's death, Samira had tried to get a job, initially being one in the home of a kind gentleman whose wife had taken ill, but Suha worried about what it might look like to others, and she'd left that job after only two days. Most of the men who interviewed her leered lasciviously, and she had grown increasingly frightened. One of the men came to her home after dark, her children each tucked safely in their beds. Samira had tried to keep him from entering their modest home, but she was no match for the large man. He forced himself upon her, leaving her unconscious and battered. When she awoke the next morning, thankfully before Zeid, Edham, and Athra woke up, she summoned Suha immediately.

Suha had delivered her three children. She trusted her. She'd seen to similar wounds on Samira on her wedding night, and had secretly advised her of the power of silence—advice Samira had been grateful to receive and had smartly abided by. Suha had also delivered Samira's fourth child, whom she could not bring herself to name.

She had been just six months pregnant when a blow to her side, artfully bestowed by Safaa, had caused him to leave her body, a slippery, lifeless weight. Samira prayed for her husband's death from that day forward, and once her prayers were answered, she realized that his death just brought the need for new prayers, prayers of savior from the hell that Iraq had become for her. Suha answered those prayers. After nursing Samira back to health from the violent rape, she took the steps she had been planning since her own father's death. Suha arranged for them to defect.

The process had been long and difficult, and the planning had taken much longer than Samira had thought she could bear—but she did—and she would endure this last leg of their journey, as well—even if that meant living in the desert for another year or more. Samira had the patience of a python mapping out its hit on unsuspecting prey. She would never go back to her homeland, and that resolution brought her great pride.

Maryland

Tess washed her salad bowl, having finally begun eating again. She lifted a dish towel out of the kitchen drawer, exposing her collection of coasters, lonely and forgotten in the bottom of the drawer. A sharp pang raced through her chest. The colors and flawless edges called out to her. She swiftly slammed the drawer shut, turning her back against the sink. *Damned coasters.* How dare they show up now when she'd been so strong? She threw the dish towel onto the counter and walked into the den where her laptop sat cradled among a nest of blankets, her nightly perch. Tess sat upon the blanket, placing the laptop gently on her knees, her delicate fingers hovered over the keyboard. She closed her eyes and raised her chin toward the ceiling. *Please. Please*, she begged. She logged onto Skype and was about to type in Beau's screen name when her cell phone rang. It was a sign, she thought. She pushed the laptop to the side and ran to the ringing phone.

Before looking at the caller ID, she pushed the green button.

"Hello?" she said, hopeful and breathless.

"Tess, hey. Did I catch you at a bad time?"

Her hope deflated, "Uh, no." *I thought you were my husband.*

Louie didn't pick up on her disappointment. "Good. Sorry I didn't call you earlier. It wasn't that I wasn't going to call you this time, I promise. I was stuck with that client I told you about, you know, the guy who lost his ledgers. Anyway, I wanted to talk to you about your company."

Tess was still a little miffed about his quick retreat, and apparently he wasn't going to offer her any explanation. Two could play at this game. She didn't respond when Louie paused.

"I know I said that I'd call today, and I'm really sorry," he said sincerely.

Busy with your wife? "That's okay," Tess managed.

"Is now good or would you rather I called you in the office tomorrow? Or do you want to meet for lunch, maybe?"

Tess smiled despite herself. His enthusiasm was hard to ignore. "Now's fine." Tess slipped into her professional persona. She inched to the edge of the couch, her legs crossed, notepad and pen in hand. "What would you like to discuss?" She was well practiced in answering the basic questions that most clients asked: how she recruited her applicants, what her criteria was, testing used, etc. Almost every client she'd ever worked with wanted to know how she started her business at such a young age. Her pulse never failed to respond to the excitement that she still felt when talking about her company.

She answered Louie's questions without pause. They commiserated about the difficulties of being one's own boss, the pressures of growing and maintaining a business, the weight of having employees, and how managing often equated to babysitting. Tess had become sidetracked, her annoyance had vanished.

An hour later, Tess was lying on her back on the living room couch, phone pressed tight against her ear.

"I can't think of any," Tess said honestly.

"No hobbies? You're kidding me, right? Everyone has hobbies."

Tess laughed, "I guess not everyone."

"Knitting?"

"Maybe when I'm one hundred," Tess laughed.

"Skiing, running, gardening?" Louie prodded. "Don't tell me you're one of those work-only people."

"No, I'm not a work-only person," she wondered if perhaps she was a work-only person after all. She rolled the thought over in her mind and finally said, "I bike ride."

"Really? You ride? That's marvelous. I'm so relieved," he teased.

"Great revelation, huh? I guess I am sort of boring."

"Riding is a great hobby. I've been riding forever. Where do you ride?"

"Around the neighborhoods," she answered, realizing how ludicrously small her world was.

"Well, then. How about a ride through Rock Creek Park some time?" he asked.

Tess frowned. The memory of riding with Beau was too strong when she rode through Rock Creek Park, which is precisely why she'd begun riding around the neighborhood streets instead. "I...I'm not very fast," she lied, "and I don't do hills very well."

"Neither do I." Tess could hear his smile through the telephone line.

"I don't ever ride with a partner," she tried.

"I'm not a partner. I'm a potential client," he answered.

Tess blushed.

"It's a ride, Tess. If you can't make it, no sweat."

How had she been so dumb? Of course he wasn't flirting. Who would flirt with her anyway?

Louie sensed her hesitation, "It's okay, another time."

"No," she said before she could stop herself, "I'll ride with you."

Chapter Eight

Tess stared at her answering machine, teeth clenched, breathing hard and fast through her nose.

"We've scheduled the memorial service. I'm sorry, Tess, but it's been over three months, and you won't even take our calls. It's not fair to Beau," her mother-in-law sounded apologetic.

She wanted to scream—no, she wanted to hurl the answering machine across the room. Why had she insisted on the goddamned answering machine when Beau had been so adamantly against it? He hated what he called *extras* in the house, and she hated relinquishing control— always afraid the automated voice mail would swallow her messages, and she'd never get them back. *Stupid machine!* It stared back at her accusingly. She unplugged it from the wall and shoved it roughly into the bottom of the television console, mumbling under her breath, "You can have your damn memorial! I won't go!" She swiped at her tears as if they were the enemy and threw herself onto the couch, taking several long, deep breaths. *This is not about you. This is about them,* she told herself. She nodded, confirming her thoughts, and feeling good about her decision. Carol and Robert had turned their back on Beau. Kevin, too, as far as Tess was concerned. *Kevin.* He was Beau's best friend! How could he do this to him? The hell with him, too, she decided, and she stood, calmly, as if she'd put away her anger, put Carol, Robert, and Kevin away, too, stowed them away with the answering machine.

Iraq

Suha's days were consumed with taking care of Beau, Samira, and the children. She was thankful for the neediness of them all, which left her no time to worry about their tenuous situation. Beau had progressed to standing on his own, albeit awkwardly with one leg splinted. She'd been diligently working with him to strengthen his healthy arm and leg again, knowing all too well what a few weeks of bed rest could do to a person's spirit, much less the atrophy it could cause. She was determined to help Beau to become strong again, and felt a little guilty for her tactics. Suha hadn't believed that a man should be made to feel weak. She knew his confidence would come from his ability to provide for others, and to do so, he had to get well again, become the strong man she was sure he had once been. Beau had responded with the strongest of intentions, reluctantly giving in to his body's own weakness. He'd fought through the initial pain, allowing his right side to become strong and stable once again.

When Beau had healed enough to carry on conversations without fading in and out of sleep, his lacerations healing into red, puffy scars, Suha had learned his proper name, though *Jameel* still sailed swiftly from her lips. She'd felt bonded to Beau in a way that she could only imagine to be maternal. As Beau's body became stronger, his need to speak followed. He spoke of his love for his wife and his physical need to be with her, the pain inside his heart, which was caused by the span of earth and sea between them. The longing in his eyes had drawn Suha in. She wanted desperately to reunite the two lovers. She ached for the kind man's yearning.

Suha scrunched her face as she worked to remove Beau's makeshift cast from his left arm without accidentally cutting his skin. Working with a knife, she cut through the fabric and wood that had held his arm firmly in place. She'd already removed the stabilizer that she'd been using intermittently from his injured leg. The memory of setting the bones brought chills to Suha as she worked to free his limb.

Beau stared, slack-jawed and wide-eyed, at his pasty, thin leg. His left leg had looked ill compared to his right, healthier leg.

Suha tore the stabilizing pieces of the sling away from his arm, sensing Samira's eyes behind her, watching Beau. Samira had become like a teenager worshiping an idol. She was oblivious to Suha's knowledge of her crush. From Suha's place, she wasn't sure how anyone could miss the longing looks she'd cast in the man's direction. Beau, however, had seemed unaware. *Men*, Suha thought with a smirk.

Edham watched with curiosity as Suha worked to release Beau's arm. "Will he be able to walk? Will he do helicopter again? Will he leave?"

Suha tried to be patient with his peppering of questions. She understood that he was just an inquisitive child, but found herself rolling her eyes and hoping he would relent.

Since the third day he'd been able, Beau had played games with Edham. They'd used rocks as marbles. He'd drawn English letters in the sand, and watched Edham morph them into animals, houses, and others pictures—his small slender fingers working the sand carefully into thin lines and little hills, his lower lip hidden under his small straight teeth. Edham's eagerness to please Beau was in direct opposition to Zeid's anger toward him. Beau tried to teach the children simple English words, like "game", "dog", "play", and "house". Edham worked hard to learn the unfamiliar words and their meanings, carefully sounding out each syllable with pride, while Zeid cast harsh looks in Beau's direction. His mouth never once uttered a single English word.

Samira had watched from the background this man who was trying to teach her children. His attempts were gentle, first writing the word, then speaking it, slowly, and then asking the children to repeat it. She found herself embarrassed by Zeid's non-compliance and sheer defiance. She tried to reprimand him, though she also tried, she had to admit, not to come across as a mean parent in the eyes of the stranger. She was not successful in the first effort, and hoped she was able to succeed in the second. If she'd come across as stern, Beau had not let on so. *Beau*. What a name that was! She had yet to dare call him by his name. When in private, though, she whispered the smooth word, caressing it. She felt a blush when he cast a look in her direction, wrong as she knew it was. The tumbling in her stomach was new to her, exciting and welcome, yet threatening at the same time. What if this man meant harm? What if once he gained his strength, he was just like the others, just like Safaa? She told herself this was a possibility, but her heart refused to believe it could happen.

Samira quietly cared for Beau, helping Suha in every way she requested. She offered him water and food, unsolicited. She often helped him to his feet with soft, gentle hands, or brought his blankets up to cover his chest when she thought he was sleeping. Beau felt strangely like one of her children. Her eyes held compassion, and just beneath, he saw fear.

Athra sat on Samira's lap, watching with her big brown eyes, her thumb planted firmly in her mouth. Beau winked at her. From behind her thumb, she smiled. Her fine dark hair curled up at the ends, just the slightest bit, like the edge of a page folded over to mark a reader's place. Something in him began to stir—a feeling that he'd not encountered before. He found himself questioning his five-year plan, and wondering if he'd been missing the point these last few years. Beau had become very fond of all three of the children, even Zeid, as tortured and angry as he was. He'd learned from Suha that the children's father had been killed in an accident of the war, and she'd provided a glance of the type of man that he had been. She didn't have to elaborate. Beau read the story of Safaa in her eyes. He was not a man who agreed with generalizations, and was sure that all Iraqi men were not created equal, just as all American men did not treat their wives in the same fashion. Some people were good, some were bad. Samira had been married to a bad man. He had watched her with her children, the loving way she spoke to them, the tender touch on their shoulder or head as she passed by them in their small living quarters. He damned Safaa in his mind for hurting such a gentle and, seemingly, naïve creature.

The more Beau learned about Safaa, the more he cared for the children and Samira. When Suha spoke of Zeid, her words carried a certain sting, almost a hint of disgust, though not quite. Beau had been watching the angry boy, who was on the cusp of pre-pubescence. He saw in him a young boy caught between two worlds; one in which he had been schooled and of which he understood the confines, and one that seemed only a thought, a world that he could neither visualize nor understand. Beau believed confusion lay at the heart of Zeid's anger. He felt sure that Zeid was dealing with his troubled, fear-ridden life in the best way he knew, even if it was painful for the rest of them. He'd seen grown men deal with less stressful events in a more aggressive way. Perhaps he was jaded, seeing Zeid's attitude as acceptable, given his circumstances. Beau saw beyond Zeid's angry front. Hope? Fear? He could not say. He made a pact with himself to show Zeid that all Americans were not hateful, and that men did not have to belittle women to be confident and strong. He tried to imagine what Zeid was feeling, but could not fathom the thought of losing a parent and leaving his home, all in one fell swoop. His empathy for Zeid fueled his desire to help him, and sparked a deeper empathy for Samira, for what she'd been forced to endure.

"Ah, now that feels better," he said, as the last of the cast was removed.

"No *alaam*?" Suha said, then corrected herself, "No pain?"

"No alaam," Beau responded, and smiled at her effort. Suha's English was becoming more fluid. She was patient with Beau's efforts to speak Arabic, which he found to be a very difficult language to grasp, or perhaps he had difficulty because his mind was already overwhelmed with the task of healing.

Suha moved Beau's arm in a careful fashion. He grimaced, but felt no greater ache than the sadness he felt from being away from Tess. Suha and Beau would spend the next few weeks rehabbing his injured arm and leg, reconditioning the muscles, and rebuilding his overall strength. At first they exercised his limbs with small, careful movements, short weight-bearing exercises which included things like bicep curls with a can filled with sand, and tying the same can around his ankle with a sheet, then lifting it slowly off the floor. As he grew stronger, Beau took short daily walks, increasing his distance over time, and pushing through the pain. He kept the pocket watch and photo of Tess in his pants pocket, which Samira had mended as best she was able. The familiar lump against his thigh drove him to push himself harder.

Beau set off on his rehabilitative walk with Edham at his side. Those walks were cathartic for Beau. He spoke of his desire to get back to Tess and his worry of the emotional pain she'd likely been through. He was glad that Edham could not understand him or respond to his rhetorical questions. It helped to cleanse his thoughts, to release stress. He wondered what Tess had been told and longed to know if any others had survived the crash. When he'd asked Suha about the accident, she was hesitant to give details, telling him only that he must have been thrown from the helicopter long before it crashed because the explosion was miles away. He couldn't think of the accident, or Tess, for too long—the burden of the sadness would grow too heavy, weighing down his thoughts and hindering his recuperation.

Edham looked up at him now, as they walked away from their humble dwelling across the naked desert. The dunes masked what lay a mile or so beyond—dark sand eking out from a glorious, flowing river. He smiled, his smooth skin glistening with sweat. "You leave?" he asked in English.

Beau stopped in his tracks, looked down at the boy, and cocked his head to the side in question. He was sure he had heard him incorrectly.

Edham looked embarrassed, fearing he'd said the wrong words. "You leave?" he asked tentatively.

Beau put his hand on the boy's slim shoulder. He'd been listening and learning all along, he realized, to more than what Beau had been teaching him. He'd been listening to Beau and Suha's conversations about how he might get home, and when their next move, as a group, would begin. Beau was happily surprised, and instantly worried. How much of what he and Suha had discussed had he understood? He wracked his mind, running through the words he had tried to teach Edham and the others, and could not recall teaching them the word "leave".

"Leave?" he repeated. His goal had been to return to Tess all along, and suddenly that word, *leave,* brought conflicting emotions. How would he leave? Where would he go? There was a war going on out there, and he had no idea where or how badly it had turned in his absence. He shrugged in Edham's direction, noncommittally, and turned to follow the path they'd worn in the sand.

Edham shrugged, too, wondering if perhaps he'd used the wrong words after all. He reached up and took hold of Beau's hand.

Maryland

Louie quickened his pace, kicking up billows of dust from the dirt path adjacent to Rock Creek. He caught up with Tess. They were heading south—a quick trip to the National Zoo. Tess breathed deeply, taking in the smell of the fallen leaves. She could do this, a bike ride with a friend. This wasn't so bad. Wearing her bicycle helmet made her head look out of proportion to her newly-slim shoulders and sleek arms. She'd shed weight like a molting bird, and worried that soon she wouldn't be able to hide her burgeoning bump. Louie raised his arms off of the handlebars and held them out to his sides, cackling like a teenager.

Tess laughed. "You're a fool!"

They'd gone riding together a handful of times, and life had slowly rejuvenated within Tess. They'd taken their first ride along that very path a few weeks earlier, an awkward, silent ride that began with a "hello" and ended with "see ya," without as many words in between. By their third ride together, they'd found their groove. Tess now had a reason to look forward to Sundays, and, without realizing it, she'd stopped sitting in front of her computer on Sunday evenings waiting for Beau to Skype.

Louie lowered his arms just in time to swerve around a branch that had fallen across the path. Tess roared with laughter as his balance faltered and his wheels wobbled to the right. Louie floundered for balance.

"It was all in the plan, my friend," he joked.

The bike path intersected another and Tess turned quickly, leaving Louie to stop and turn around in order to follow her. Tess wasn't thinking of Louie at that moment. She pedaled faster as the dirt path turned to pavement, pushing herself to gain speed up the small incline that led to the cemetery. Her heart thumped against her chest, not from the effort she exerted, but from the thoughts that reeled through her mind like a tornado. She rode around the outer path, staring into the sea of headstones, oblivious to the flush that covered her cheeks. A green canopy came into view, interrupting the cemetery like a sore thumb. She slowed her bike, coming to a stop behind a large oak tree.

Tess leaned her bike against the tree and then pushed herself against the rough bark, peering like a child around the girth of its trunk. Mourners stood in a small group, huddled close together, leaning on one another for support. Tess recognized Carol and Robert, standing before the newly-planted headstone. The lack of a casket glared like a missing tooth. At six feet three inches tall, Kevin was usually difficult to miss, though on this day his stooped shoulders made him more difficult to distinguish.

Tess heard the rattling of Louie's bike being positioned next to hers, Louie's footsteps behind her. Her body tensed. She remained focused on the group in front of her. She shifted her stance to the right to get a better look at the woman who stood next to Kevin. Her blonde hair was pulled back into a tight bun at the base of her neck, her clothing looser than normal, but there was something in the woman's stance that was undeniable. *Alice?* Tess's hand covered her mouth. *How could she?*

"Tess?" Louie whispered, putting his hand across her lower back.

Tess shrugged him off, turned away, tears stinging her eyes.

"Do you want to go?" he asked kindly.

Tess shook her head, her shoulders curled inward.

Louie watched her from behind, feeling inadequate. Quiet sounds of hidden sobs filled the air around them. Louie waited patiently.

"Tess?" he moved toward her.

"I'm okay," she said. "It's—"

"Beau?" he said thoughtfully.

She nodded and turned toward him, wiping her eyes with the back of her hand. "I'm sorry," she said.

"Don't be," he said. He knew why she hadn't attended the memorial, at least he thought he did. Tess hadn't told him much, but she'd alluded to the fact that she didn't think Beau was really dead. Louie knew all too well that there wasn't much anyone could do to help her accept the truth. He stood before her, awkward in his unsure stance, his curls poking out randomly from the properly-fit bike helmet, his shirt wet with sweat, and his heart heavy.

Tess watched his chest rise and fall with each breath. She focused on the movement of his clinging t-shirt. It was easier than focusing on the ceremony that had progressed to hugs and milling attendees one hundred feet before her. Without moving her eyes from the sweat stain between his pectoral muscles, she said, trancelike, "We'd better go." She made no move to leave.

Louie recognized the stillness in her. He swallowed his own memories, took her gently by the elbow, and led her to her bike. She grabbed the handlebars with both hands and pushed the bike back down the path toward Rock Creek Park.

"Are you okay?" Louie followed Tess down the path. When she didn't answer, he said, "Why don't we turn back and head towards home?"

Tess shook her head. When they reached the bottom of the hill, she climbed onto her bike, straightened her t-shirt, and said, "Let's keep going."

The ride to the zoo was swift and uneventful. The fresh air whipped against Tess's skin. She breathed it in, shedding her sadness with each exhalation, pulling herself together, reminding herself that Beau wasn't really gone. She tucked her thoughts of Beau away in some imaginary treasure chest within her mind, knowing she could retrieve them with a thought. She was not going to torture Louie, who at this point felt like her only friend, with her angst of her in-laws, Kevin, and Alice. *Alice!* The thought of her at the memorial made Tess's stomach burn. She took several deep breaths and thanked God that Louie was now riding ahead of her, unable to see her face.

They hopped off their bikes and chained them to an empty bike rack at the end of the parking lot. The National Zoo had been one of Tess's favorite places when she was a child. She'd been there only a handful of times in her life, each one better than the last. As she and Louie walked up the path toward the giraffes and elephants, the scent of manure recalled a childhood memory. She and her mother had been waiting long hours for the elephant's feeding time. Her mother had pleaded with her to see other animals until the scheduled event, but she'd have no part of leaving. She had been a pixie of a girl, with paper-thin arms and legs, pale skin, and a mind as stubborn as a full-grown bull. She longed to hear her mother's voice just one more time.

"What are you thinking about?" Louie asked. "You were smiling, just then."

Tess shook her head.

"If this is too difficult, we can go," he offered.

"I'm fine." Tess looked up at the sky, as if watching a scene unfold in the clouds. She waved her hand through the air. "They have a need for closure," she explained. "It's okay. It's what they need. I was just surprised to see Alice, that's all."

Louie understood the feelings of betrayal. He also understood Alice's need to say goodbye.

The crisp afternoon turned into a brisk evening. Louie and Tess stood in her front yard, the leaves of the weeping willow whispering in the breeze.

"How about that gorilla?" Louie laughed.

Tess rolled her eyes. "He was nasty."

"No, just horny."

"Whatever." She swatted his arm. "You men are all alike," she laughed.

"Aren't you going to ask me about getting my business?" Louie asked in a serious tone.

"No," Tess said.

"Why not?" he asked.

Tess shrugged. She'd picked up a number of new clients in the past few weeks and knew that when Louie was ready, he'd work with her. Until then, she needed his friendship more than his money.

"Do you want to talk about today?" He kicked the ground, contemplating the afternoon. His own painful memories rushed forward.

"Not really," she said with an edge.

Relieved, he said, "Okay. I just thought—"

"I know," she said with a sigh. "Everyone thinks I need to talk about it, talk about Beau. But you know what? I don't. I'm okay with him being away. I know he'll come back. I know he's not gone." She stood and paced.

"Tess, it's okay to grieve. You don't have to be strong."

"I'm not being strong," she said heatedly. "He's not gone!" her words were accusatory. "Why does everyone feel the need to make me talk about him?" Her body began to tremble.

Louie turned her shoulders gently toward him. "No one can make you do anything. I just thought you might want someone to listen." He brushed a few strands of hair from her forehead.

She shrugged him off.

"You don't have to get mad," he said. "I'm trying to be a friend, that's all."

"Well, maybe I don't need that kind of friend," she dug in her purse for her keys.

"I'm sorry, okay? I didn't mean to upset you." He tipped her quivering chin upward. "I'm sorry."

Tess trembled like a frightened bird. She'd been strong for so long that she'd forgotten what it was like to be taken care of. Loneliness seeped from her pores. Louie put his arms around her, his breath on her cheeks. Heat spread up her chest. His eyes washed over her, comforting, wanting. She pressed her body against his, her mind cautioning her every move. He lowered his lips to hers. Salty tears slipped between them, the smell of sweat, the feel of his tense muscles, drew her in. Guilt engulfed her, pulling her back from him, fighting her desire. The minty taste of him lingered on her tongue. Tess unlocked the front door and stepped inside. Without uttering a word, she closed it behind her.

"Vogue" rang out from across the threshold, a barrier between them.

Chapter Nine

The man came in the night, as silent as the moon swept across the evening sky. He gave Suha directions for their departure and assured her that he'd be traveling with them. They were to leave the next evening.

He'd charted a course outside the red zone that would take them to the next underground safe zone, where, he assured Suha, they'd be taken care of along with other families that were being housed there. Soldiers who were party to the underground process would transport them to a location where they'd receive new identities and visas and be taken out of the country. The man, who called himself Abdul Hadi, or Servant of the Guide, was swathed in fabric, his long, unkempt beard, more gray than black, poked out from the scarf he'd wrapped around his head. His face was weathered, his hands thick and dry.

Abdul Hadi's loose brown pants and soiled button-down shirt looked as though he'd been sleeping in them for weeks. His heavy boots must have been hell to wear, trekking through the desert sand. Beau watched the man like a hawk, trying to translate his conversation with Suha, but falling too far behind to follow.

The man's eyes shifted to Beau several times as he spoke. Beau could tell from Suha's expression that the man was not happy with his presence. Abdul Hadi hunched as he spoke, the fabric of his wrap moving with each forceful expression. Beau tensed, fearing the worst. This went on until the sun began to rise, and eventually, Suha rose too, standing before Beau with a bowed head.

"Jameel," she said, "Abdul Hadi, he worries. You put us in danger."

Beau clenched his teeth. She was right. With Beau, they were harboring an American. Without him, they were merely traveling Iraqis, not easily explained, but easier than explaining their allegiance to him. He looked down, unsure of what to do or say.

Suha turned back to Abdul Hadi, speaking rapidly in her native tongue. She stood with her back to Beau, a protective shield between him and the stranger.

Abdul Hadi ran his eyes up and down Beau's body.

Beau pulled his shoulders back, raised his chin, and looked the man in the eye.

The man spoke in slow, clipped English, "You come with us. You become one of us."

Beau nodded, unsure of what he meant.

Suha placed her hand on his arm with a nod. The hint of a smile crossed her lips.

Suha packed supplies while Samira and the children slept, unaware of their pending upheaval. Beau did as the man directed, tying bundles of blankets and bed linens around utensils. They were to leave nothing behind. The man shed his outer wrap and handed it roughly to Beau.

"You wear this," Suha explained.

Suha nodded toward the man's bag, indicating the change of clothes Beau would be wearing, a concession that the man had not planned.

The children awoke, frightened, at first, of the strange man who had come in the night. Zeid watched the Iraqi man with interest, as if deciding if he were friend or foe. He whispered sharp comments in Abdul Hadi's direction. Samira snapped at him, lowering her eyes and apologizing to Abdul Hadi, who disregarded her concern.

Beau took offense to his disrespect of Samira, but said nothing, afraid of the trouble his reaction might bring. Instead, he stayed near Samira and the children.

They waited until the sun made its arc over the desert and descended toward the dark sand. Athra made nary a sound all afternoon, nestled into her mother's side, thumb planted in her mouth like a never-ending lollipop.

Edham listened carefully to all that was said. The skin between his thick eyebrows tense, his dark eyes watchful of the man's every move. When Beau passed by him, Edham reached up, his fingers trailing along Beau's arm, as if he were making sure Beau were really there.

Beau smiled, tussled his hair.

Abdul Hadi spoke in harsh tones.

The hair on the back of Beau's neck stood on end. He pulled Suha aside, "Is there a problem?"

Suha pulled him further away, whispering, "As part of the underground movement to save women from honor killings, they must remain emotionally unattached. Doing so allows greater strength and concentration." She took Beau further from the children and Samira, to the opening of the tent, and leaned close to his ear. "Some women would not make it out of Iraq safely," she explained, a risk she was willing to take.

Beau glanced at Samira and the children. His eyes locked with Suha's, as they stood on the edge of an unspoken understanding. He knew he would do whatever it took to keep Suha and Samira safe. They'd saved him, and he'd do the same in return.

Maryland

Resentment raced through Tess like a river. She sat behind her desk tapping her foot against the floor, a scowl fixed across her face. She waited for Alice to arrive. She'd spent the night tossing and turning, beating herself up over kissing Louie, and finally decided that it was Alice she was angry at, not herself.

Alice breezed through the door with a smile. "What on earth are you doing here so early?" she asked and put a steaming cup of coffee on Tess's desk.

Tess pretended to be engrossed in a file, her silent fury unnoticed.

"New client?" Alice asked.

Tess stomped into the conference room, feeling completely inadequate at handling her inner tumult. Alice followed.

"Something I can do?"

Tess turned to face her, calm and stoic, "Yes. Stay away from me," *before I fire you.* She turned and walked away.

"What? Tess?" Alice rushed after Tess, "What's going on?"

"How could you?" Tess choked out.

"Oh, this is about the memorial?" Alice set the files she'd been carrying down on the table and put her hand on her hip. "Just because you can't say goodbye doesn't mean that we shouldn't." She sighed, "What am I supposed to do, pretend Beau's coming back?" She knew it was a mistake the second the words flew from her lips.

Tess stormed out of the room.

Alice followed. "Wait. I didn't mean it like that. Tess, please!"

"He's my husband!" Tess said between clenched teeth.

"Yeah, and he's Robert and Carol's son, and Kevin's best friend," she stared into Tess's eyes, unwilling to relent. "Tess, he's gone. It's been months. He's not coming back."

"Don't say—"

"What, Tess, don't say the truth? You know he's not coming back. I know you love him, we all know you love him. We know how much you hurt—"

"I can't listen to this," Tess covered her face and threw herself onto the couch in her office. "Please, just go away."

Alice sat next to her, her back straight. "No, I won't go away. This isn't going to go away. You have to deal with it."

Tears streamed down Tess's cheeks.

"I know it's hard. I know it hurts. Beau loved you more than life itself, you know that."

"Leave me alone," Tess spat, her face red, eyes swollen. "Please," she pleaded.

Alice shook her head. "No, Tess. No one else will stand up to you. You have to move on. You have to live your life." Tess looked at Alice with such sadness that Alice almost backed down.

"What do you want from me, Alice? I'm working, I'm even biking again. Why isn't that enough for you?"

"It's not enough for you, Tess. This isn't about me," Alice said gently.

Tess stared at the floor.

Alice rested her hand on Tess's arm. "It sucks, Tess. I know it does."

Tess shook her off and rose to her feet. "You don't know, Alice," she spat. "You've never loved anyone.

You've never breathed the same breath of a man, day after day, thinking the same thoughts, wanting the same things, wanting to touch him, to hold him, to—"

"You're right. I haven't. But I have a friend who is grieving. I have two."

Tess squinted at her, the realization of Alice's friendship with Kevin coming clear.

"And the hurt that I see in them, that's real. I may not feel the same hurt, or have felt the same love, but I'm not a cold fish, Tess. I know it hurts."

Tess took a deep breath and let it out slowly.

Alice went to the credenza and pulled out their secret stash—the celebratory bottle, saved for their largest sales. Today it would serve as a sanity saver. She poured a vodka tonic with a dash of lime for Tess, and one for herself, then sat down next to her on the couch.

Tess pushed the drink away.

"Come on, Tess. It'll ease the pain."

Tess shook her head. "I'm pregnant." *Where the hell did that come from?* She stared at the drink, longing for the liquid relief. Silence stretched between them as a weight Tess hadn't realized she'd been carrying lifted from her shoulders. "What am I going to do?"

Alice forced her slack jaw closed. "You're what?" Before Tess could reiterate, she said, "I don't know, but we'll figure it out."

Two hours later Alice was tipsy, Tess, relieved. Each lay at one end of the couch, shoes kicked off.

"What do you see in him?" Tess asked.

"Kevin? I don't know if I see anything in him. I mean, it's not like we're dating or anything. God, that would be weird."

"But you hooked up with him?" Tess asked.

Alice laughed, rolling onto her side and almost falling off of the couch, "In his dreams! We had drinks a few times. He wants to see me and a few chicks going at it," she smirked.

"What? Is there something I should know?" Tess laughed.

"No!"

"C'mon, you can tell me," Tess egged her on.

Alice pulled herself up to sitting position, swayed, then held onto the side of the couch for stability. "Don't you think he's hot?"

"Kevin?" Tess laughed. "Cute maybe, hot? I don't know. He's not my type."

Alice ran her finger up Tess's foot, tickling her, "Oh yeah, those short ones, those are your type!" she roared with laughter.

Tess froze.

Alice stifled her laugh, "What? You have to admit, Beau's pretty shor—" Her jaw dropped open. "No!"

Tess sat up.

"Oh, my God! What'd you do?"

Tess turned away, her cheeks burning.

"Whose baby is this? Oh, my God," worry filled her eyes.

"Beau's! Jesus, Alice."

Alice waved the thought away, "Sorry." She pointed to the bottle that lay on the floor, "It's that's fault. I didn't think…"

Tess stood and tripped, landing on her butt. They both burst into hysterics.

The front door of the office creaked open. Louie's voice sailed through Tess's open door, "Hello?"

"Oh, shit!" Tess scrambled to get off the floor.

Alice scooped up the bottle and the glasses. She hung onto Tess's arm and whispered, "Quiet, he'll hear us." They laughed.

"Too late." Louie stood in the doorway wearing jeans and a gray long-sleeved shirt that read, "Just do it" across the chest.

Alice hurried past him. "How *à propos*," she giggled.

"What was that about?" he asked Tess.

Tess held on to the end of her desk and lowered herself into a leather chair, waving the comment away with her hand.

"Did I interrupt something? A celebration?" he looked at his watch. "Well, it is eleven-forty," he joked. "Happy hour?"

Tess flushed. "We don't usually do this. It was a rough morning."

"I can come back," Louie offered.

"Why are you here?" she asked, brazenly.

Louie sat down across from Tess. He rubbed his hands nervously down his thighs. "I just thought, after last night, we should talk."

Butterflies swept through Tess's stomach. She swatted the air again, "Oh, that. That was nothing."

"Nothing?" Louie asked.

"Yeah, I'm sorry. It shouldn't have happened. Just forget it." She leaned back in her chair.

Louie looked confused, "Oh, okay." He hesitated then rose. "I guess I'll be going, then."

Tess pretended to be busy with the files on her desk.

"Okay, then," he turned and walked out the door.

When the front door closed, Tess dropped her head onto her desk with a thud. *What the hell am I doing?*

The front door echoed against the headache that Tess had earned. She dropped her purse and flopped onto the couch. The *ding* of a Skype notification rang out from the den. Tess was on her feet in seconds, plucking away at the keyboard. A solicitous message from SkypeMarketing appeared. Tess closed her eyes and let out a long sigh. She made her way back to the couch, closing the door to the den behind her.

Iraq

The red night sky brought a chill to the desert. A sandstorm had come without warning, delaying the anxious group's departure for another twenty-four hours. They unpacked enough supplies to prepare canned beans for dinner and unrolled their bedrolls. Abdul Hadi ate in silence, watchful of Beau and ignoring the women and children.

Beau did not sleep during the night. Unease kept him alert and fearful. He watched the hulk of Abdul Hadi's body as it moved up and down with each slumbering breath and wondered what the journey might bring.

Athra made a soft, cooing sound in the dark.

Beau worried how the children would fare on the trek across the desert. He reached for the photo of Tess, bringing it close to his face. He was unable to make out her fine features in the dark.

"I'm coming," he whispered.

In the darkness, Samira listened.

Morning brought anxiety. The children's discomfort came in drones of whines. Edham followed his mother asking question after question. Beau took Edham aside and together they walked a short distance. Beau's leg ached. Edham chattered beside him. Ten minutes later, Edham's questions had run out, and though Beau could not understand the Arabic he spoke, he'd smiled and rested his hand on the boy's shoulder, calming him. They returned to the tent where Zeid stewed. The cold stare Zeid aimed at Abdul Hadi would unnerve even the toughest adult. Abdul Hadi began glaring back.

Beau tried to distract Zeid, enticing him with rocks and drawing games. Zeid would have no part of it. He remained disgruntled, angry toward the stranger who was there to help him.

Edham separated the marbles of many colors from the majority of the pile, the solid-colored marbles.

Beau whispered to Edham, "There are certain marbles that don't belong to any group. They're not noticeably big or small, not solid colors, not easily categorized, but don't cast them aside. Those marbles are the most special ones." He knew Edham did not understand, so instead he picked up the marbles that had been cast aside and held them close to his chest. "Special," he said and smiled. He continued, more for his own benefit than for Edham's, "They're just finding their way in a big marble world, trying to blend in. It takes a special person to take those marbles as his own. It takes courage and strength to be the one to protect those marbles."

Edham reached for the marbles.

Zeid guffawed.

Abdul Hadi sneered at the boy and turned his back.

Suha yanked Zeid's arm and chided him in her native tongue.

Beau had learned enough of the language to understand the mild threat she'd made, "Quiet down before your mother pays the price for your behavior."

Zeid stewed in silence, eyeing Abdul Hadi with a vengeance and looking at Suha as if she were the devil.

Samira looked like a troubled teen caught between a peer and a parent, afraid to move in either direction. Beau stood next to her and motioned for her to follow him. She walked shyly behind him. Once outside the tent, she inhaled deeply.

"This is difficult," she said with tentative precision.

Beau nodded.

They sat in silence just outside their makeshift home. Samira stared at the ground, her shoulders carrying years of fear and pain. Her hands lay in her lap, one upon the other.

"Scared?" he knew she understood the words he spoke, fear had been one of the easiest words to communicate. Suha had schooled Samira well. She understood enough of the English language to make sense of their brief conversations.

Samira looked up, her dark eyes held the answer to his question.

Beau leaned his head back against the hard dune.

Suddenly Abdul Hadi's voice boomed through the silence. He exited the tent in a rush of insistence. Suha followed. Samira was on her feet and hurrying inside before Beau registered Zeid's wail.

Inside the dwelling, Zeid sobbed, angrily pushing his mother's arms away and throwing looks of spears toward Abdul Hadi. Suha mumbled under her breath. Beau instinctively grabbed Zeid's flailing arm and pulled it away from its target—Samira's body.

"What are you doing?" he commanded. "You don't hit your mother."

"Zeid!" Samira snapped, then continued in her language.

Zeid tugged against Beau's steadfast grip. "What's going on?" he asked Suha.

"Zeid called Abdul Hadi a traitor."

Abdul Hadi breathed heavily in the entryway, breathing in short, fast breaths, clouded by anger.

Beau released Zeid's hand, standing between him and his mother. "Suha, tell Zeid to calm down."

Suha sighed, as if she had no inclination to do so.

"Suha! You cannot let him do this."

"The child is angry. He is his father," she said with disgust.

Beau stared her down. "He's scared. He does what he knows."

"He knows hatred," Abdul Hadi said.

"Then teach him otherwise," Beau's voice was firm. He turned to Zeid, and spoke with jilted foreign words, "Hate will kill. Let it go."

Zeid spat in his direction. Edham gasped, huddling fearfully next to Athra on their bedroll.

"There is no hope for this one," Suha said.

Beau shook his head. "There's always hope." He walked out of the fury-filled dwelling and into the heat of sun, which instantly dried the sweat from his forehead. He had become used to the treacherous heat of the desert— the feeling that a hairdryer was on his skin, full blast, at all times, the way the dry, hot air saturated his mouth when he spoke. Abdul Hadi's hand on his shoulder startled him.

"You are right," Abdul Hadi said. "There is always hope." He handed him a bottle of water. "The boy's hate, that's what makes this war."

Beau had been sent to document the changes in the Iraqi families since the inception of the war. He wondered, now, if perhaps most of those changes were invisible to the eye of the camera. He bowed his head and found himself wanting to apologize for all that the Americans had done, the hurt they'd caused, no matter what the catalyst had been. Instead, he simply nodded.

"You cannot control where you are born, or whom you are born to," Abdul Hadi continued, "Iraq or America." He spoke carefully, with practiced English, taking Beau by surprise. "We spend our lives making up for something, no? Something we did, maybe? Something our parents did?" he shrugged.

Chapter Ten

"I think she's made progress," Alice said across the bar of the crowded restaurant.

"I feel so guilty. It's been weeks since I've seen her." Kevin eyed a tall brunette across the bar. He and Alice had been meeting regularly since shortly after Beau had died, filling the gap that Beau and Tess had left in each other's lives.

Alice eyed the brunette. "Please, Kevin, have some taste," she said with disdain.

"What? She's totally hot."

"If you like the kind that tries too hard," Alice said.

"I happen to admire a woman who does anything hard," he laughed.

Alice rolled her eyes.

"So what's the plan for Halloween?" he lifted an eyebrow.

"No plans. I guess Tess will give out candy in her neighborhood, like usual." Alice had forgotten that

Halloween was only days away. She tried to remember what her costume had been the previous year. *Darth Vader*, she remembered with a smile. "What are you doing?"

"Party," he said, still eyeing the brunette, who smiled back at him.

"Focus, Kevin," Alice drew his face back toward hers with one finger. "Where? Whose party?"

"Neighbor's. You don't know him. He manages a bookstore in D.C. Not your type."

"Like I care," Alice quipped.

"Come with me?" he asked. "Maybe we can get Tess out of the house a bit? Dress her up, you know? You two can be Cuddy and Thirteen. I'll be Dr. House."

"Right, a hot bisexual and a woman you could never conquer? That should be fun."

"Seriously," he said, "it'll be fun. Besides, Tess needs to get out."

Alice scanned the men at the bar, caught the attention of a dark-skinned burly man who looked like he smelled of a construction site. *Bingo!*

"Louie's on line three again," Alice's voice sprang from the speakerphone.

"Tell him I'm busy," Tess said.

"I've told him that the last million times. You can't avoid him forever," she said.

"Watch me," Tess said. She clicked off the speakerphone and returned to her files. It had been over two weeks since she'd kissed Louie, and one day less since she'd told him it was a mistake. Then why was she still thinking about it? Why could she still taste him on her lips when the lights were out? Why did she wait by the phone last Sunday for his call, and then ignore it when it finally came? What was she doing?

Alice stood in her doorway, her white, pristine slacks crossed at the ankle, her perfectly-pressed silk blouse open almost to her navel, lying flawless across her svelte figure, and the question Tess had just asked herself rolling off her lips.

"God, Alice, leave it alone."

"Tess, he's a good guy. He could mean business for you." She moved to the chair across from Tess. "Besides, in your...condition—"

"He could mean trouble for me," she retorted.

"Trouble? Because you guys ride bikes together?" Alice smirked. "I don't think so. I was thinking security."

Tess sighed, "You wouldn't understand. Never mind." She sank back into the plush leather chair and tossed her pen onto the desk. "Tell me about your latest conquest. Give me something else to think about."

Alice rubbed the bruise she'd hidden under the sleeve of her blouse. "Nothing special." Her eyes lit up, "What aren't you telling me?"

"Nothing!" Tess lied.

"O-kay," Alice said. "Well, there's a Halloween party Kevin's going to. He wants us to come—some bigwig in D.C. Whaddaya say? Wanna go with me?"

"No thanks," Tess said.

Alice had expected as much. "Come on, I wanna go, but I can't go alone. Besides, you can't wallow alone in that house forever."

Tess lifted her eyebrows as if to say, Drop it.

"Please?" Alice begged. "I won't bug you about Louie anymore. Promise."

"Promise?" Tess asked. She put her hand on her belly. "I don't know. It seems wrong."

Alice rolled her eyes. "Even pregnant women go to parties, Tess—and yes, I promise."

"And we'll be home by ten-thirty?" Tess added.

"Midnight."

"Eleven."

"Okay, okay, eleven-thirty," Alice stood. "By the way, you're Cuddy, from that show, 'House'." She walked out of the room before Tess could protest.

It was easy for Tess to convince herself that she was going to a business meeting rather than a party dressed as Cuddy in a tight, cleavage-bearing business suit. Her hair had grown to her shoulders and she was wearing it parted in the middle. The button on her skirt pulled against her burgeoning baby bump. She buttoned the jacket, covering the straining fabric. *Oh yeah,* she thought. *I could rock this look for about an hour. I'd be home by ten, easy.*

She found the location of the party easily, she simply followed every other person dressed in costume. It seemed the entire northwest section of D.C. was headed to the party. *Who is this guy, anyway,* she wondered. The house was immaculate, a three-level townhome, easily worth over a million. The scent of marijuana drifted out from underneath a closed door. *Great, pregnant woman arrested for smoking pot.* Tess hurried toward the back, marveling at the elegance: mahogany floors, wrought-iron banisters, stone columns. She moved around Raggedy Ann and Andy and was about to tap the Tin Man on the shoulder to move around him when a very handsome Dr. House appeared before her.

"Cuddy!" Kevin took Tess into his arms. "I've been looking for you!" His breath reeked of alcohol.

"Where's Alice?" she asked, pulling the top of her jacket across her newly rounded bosom.

"Thirteen? I dunno," he slurred.

"Great," Tess mumbled, wishing she'd stayed home.

Princess Leia tugged Dr. House away, leaving Tess looking more like an out-of-place businesswoman than a television star.

"Cuddy, come on!" Kevin called over the princess's shoulder.

The clanking of glasses, laughter, and bits of random conversation filled the air. Tess squeezed through the crowd, heading toward the kitchen. She turned from the hall into the living room, stopping dead in her tracks. His thick dark hair was the first thing to catch her attention, followed by his height. He stood with Kevin, watching him, as he always had. *Of course*, Tess thought. *This was all planned.* She swallowed hard, nervously twisting her wedding band on her finger. She tried to walk toward him, but her legs failed to move. Her voice stuck in her throat. He turned in the other direction, his camouflage shirt stretched tight against his back. Why wasn't he looking for her? How did he get last year's Halloween costume without her seeing him in the attic? *Kevin, the key.* The din of the party fell away, leaving her in a trancelike state.

"I thought you weren't going to come!" Alice sidled up to Tess.

Tess stared straight ahead, unable to believe that he was finally back.

"I brought a friend," Alice continued, and pointed to a matador in full regalia. "Tess?" Alice followed Tess's gaze. "Kevin looks great, doesn't he?"

"Beau," was all Tess could manage.

Confused, Alice looked around. After a second, she realized Tess's mistake.

"Tess, that's not Beau," she put her hand on Tess's shoulder.

Tess shrugged her off and moved toward him. She reached for his arm, grazing the side of his sleeve as he turned toward her. He smiled, a broad, surprised showing of perfect white teeth. The blood drained from Tess's face. She stumbled backward, turned, and ran down the stairs and out of the house. Louie was close behind.

Chapter Eleven

Beau took one last look at the pocket watch and looped it around the belt hoop of Abdul Hadi's pants that he now wore, dropping the watch itself into the pocket. Abdul Hadi had instructed him to leave his American clothing behind. Beau's longer hair and scruffy face provided a modicum of disguise. He glanced back at where the hidden dwelling had been—the sand freshly turned, marking the outline of where sticks had been pounded into the ground, the center flattened, a footprint of where their camp had been. The surrounding dunes lurked behind them with ledges chopped into their darkened walls, an evil villain with a secret. He couldn't fathom that he'd remained in the tiny enclosure for so many weeks. In the past, he'd have been looking for the best angle, the right lighting, now he yearned only to get home safely, to hold Tess in his arms, and to feel her gentle touch on his face.

They made their way in the dark, Suha and Abdul Hadi leading the group, Zeid silently plodding behind them. Edham kept pace next to Beau. He tugged on Beau's sleeve and nodded toward his mother, who struggled to keep up with Athra in her arms.

Beau reached for Athra. Samira held tight. Athra leaned toward Beau, taking the decision out of her mother's hands. Athra laid her head on Beau's shoulder and closed her eyes. Time disappeared for Beau. He no longer thought in terms of days, but rather in events: when he healed enough to travel, when they reach the next camp. He noticed Samira's shawl had pulled loose from her face, leaving the lower half of her face exposed to the sun. Her lips had already begun to chap, the skin stretched tight. Beau gently pulled the shawl up.

She glanced at him shyly, a smile in her eyes.

Zeid moved between Beau and his mother.

Abdul Hadi had the strength of a camel, carrying their supply of water and much of the rolled bedding. It looked as though he were hiding a small person within the confines of the bundle. He walked with ease across the dense sand, as if he were used to carrying such weight.

When the children could move no longer, they moved in the direction of the river and made camp. Samira and Suha bathed the children as best they could, filled water bottles, and helped Beau and Abdul Hadi prepare a tent made from the same dust-battered sheets they'd used before. Dirt caked the sheets, strengthening them like strong starch as they stretched the sheet between four tee-peed sticks on either end.

Suha pushed medication into Beau's hand, curling his fingers around the small pills.

"I'm fine," he lied.

Suha shook her head. "Jameel, take them," she said in a maternal fashion and handed him a bottle of water. Her body hunched forward, her eyes heavy.

Beau recognized the fatigue she worked so hard to disguise. His own pain had become almost unbearable. He swallowed the pills and remained outside the tent to suffer in silence. The light of dawn threatened, pinks and grays clawing their fingers across the horizon. He stretched his limbs on the hard sand, rubbing the ache from his leg and hip.

Samira appeared next to Beau, squatting on her heels.

"Sleep," Beau whispered.

Samira shook her head. She pointed to his leg. "I help," she said, uncomfortably. "I help Safaa," she explained, "when he fell, in army. His leg—" she grit her teeth and scrunched her face, as if in pain. "I make better," she moved her fingers in a deliberate motion.

Beau looked toward the tent, afraid Abdul Hadi might get the wrong impression.

"I help," she said again and began kneading the area just above his knee.

Beau put his head back in relief, sighing in spite of his worries.

"You hurt, yes?" Samira asked.

Beau nodded, glancing inside the tent, every muscle taut.

Her hands worked on his pain, massaging their way up the side of his leg in a methodical, practiced fashion. She looked at his leg as if it were inanimate and kneaded with determination, not seduction. Beau could not ignore the heated sensation that grew within him. He laid his hand on hers, stopping her movement.

She stared into his eyes.

He placed her small hand on her own leg.

"No help?" she asked.

Beau laughed. "It helps, yes. Sleep," he said and closed his eyes, pretending to sleep.

Samira returned to the tent, her head bent in disgrace.

Beau opened his eyes. He hadn't meant to make her feel ashamed. He reached out and touched her back. "You did nothing wrong. Thank you. It helped."

Samira ducked inside the small tent.

Beau removed the photo from his pocket and stared into Tess's eyes. As the sun peeked above the horizon, he fell asleep, the photograph clenched in the palm of his hand.

Chapter Twelve

The cold air whipped against Tess's cheeks as she ran awkwardly down the unfamiliar street, the cacophony of the costumed revelers falling away behind her.

"Tess! Wait!" Louie called.

His footsteps were fast approaching. Tess crossed her hands over her stomach and pushed herself to run faster, catching her heel in the crack of a sidewalk and stumbling forward.

Louie grabbed her arm before she fell to the ground. "Tess," he pleaded, "I didn't know you would be here."

"Why are you dressed like that?" Tears ran down her cheeks.

Louie looked down at his clothes. "My costume? My friend's in the army. I borrowed it."

"You knew!" she yelled. "Did Kevin put you up to this? Alice? Did they give you Beau's costume from last year?"

Only then making the connection, Louie said, "Oh, my God, I'm sorry. I didn't th—. It was all I had. I was invited at the last minute, and I had no costume. It's a friend's."

Tess ripped her arm from his grip and huffed away toward a park at the end of the road.

"Tess, wait," he pleaded. "I promise. I didn't even know you'd be here."

"Whatever," she said. "It doesn't matter."

"Why are you even mad at me? You don't return my calls, you haven't spoken to me since we kissed—"

The night was busy with trick-or-treaters, and though Tess knew they were too busy with their costumes and candy to think about the lady running through the park, she slowed her pace and walked hurriedly toward a bench where she plunked herself down and swiped at beads of sweat along her brow.

Louie caught up to her and knelt down before her. He put his hands on her knees, the look in his eyes a mix of confusion and concern.

She pushed at his hands, the weight of his touch frustrating her.

"Are you okay?" he asked.

She let go of his hands and wiped her eyes, though the flow of tears did not cease. "No," she shook her head.

He sat next to her on the bench. "What can I do?"

She turned away. "Nothing. It's just," she turned toward him again and motioned toward his clothing, "I thought, when I saw you, I thought you were him." She closed her eyes. When she opened them again, she feigned a smile. "I thought you were Beau. I thought—" suddenly she was sobbing again.

Louie brushed her hair from her face, sending a shiver down Tess's spine. He put his arm around her back, pulling her into an embrace.

"Tess!" Alice's voice rang through the air, the quick tap of heels on concrete followed.

Tess pulled back from Louie and stood, smoothing down her skirt. She wiped her eyes as Alice appeared.

"Thank God!" Alice said. She shot Louie a look of contempt. "What's wrong? What did you do to her?"

Louie stood, hands splayed in front of his chest. "I didn't do a thing," he said.

"Right. That's why she avoids your calls and flees the party the second she sees you!"

Tess wiped her eyes again. "Al, it's not like that," she said.

"Right, Tess. I know you. What'd he do to you?" She turned toward Louie, "So help me, if you hurt her—"

"Settle down, Tomb Raider. I didn't do anything more than wear military clothing. She's having a hard time right now, remember?" His eyes flashed a plea for leniency.

Tess settled herself back down on the bench, her head once again in her hands. "He's right, Alice. It's not him. It's me."

"I'll leave you girls alone," Louie said, then hesitated in front of Tess. "If you need me, you know how to reach me."

Alice watched Louie walk briskly away from them before turning back to Tess.

"What the hell?" Alice asked. "What's going on that you're not telling me, Tess?"

"I thought he was Beau. The clothes, his hair, I don't know. I thought," she looked up at Alice, her eyes streaked red, "I thought you and Kevin set this up. When I saw him? I thought..."

Alice leaned back against the bench. "Oh, my God, Tess. I'm sorry. I thought you'd made great strides. I thought you accepted that Beau was dea—not coming back." Her voice was more frustrated than soothing.

Ugh! Tess stood and began walking toward her car. Alice followed, apologizing, asking Tess if she understood that Beau wasn't coming back, and peppering her with questions about Louie. Tess didn't say a word until she reached her car and unlocked the door. "I don't know, okay, Alice? I don't know what the hell is going on anymore."

Alice climbed into the passenger seat, uninvited. Tess glared.

"I'm coming with you."

"Where?" Tess snapped.

"Wherever you're going. You're not fit to be alone."

"I'm going home." Tess stared at the road as she started the car.

"I'm worried about you, Tess. You're living in some alternate world, someplace that doesn't exist, someplace where Beau's death didn't really happen."

Tess let her forehead fall to the steering wheel and rest there. She held the wheel with both hands and gently banged her head against it.

"I get it, okay? I know he's gone, but I can't help it. I feel like he's not really...dead." The word was like a knife in her heart. She gasped a breath. "I feel like I'd know if he was, so I'm stuck. I'm fucking stuck! I can't move forward, because what if I do, and he suddenly shows up? And I can't stand still, because life doesn't stand fucking still." She stared at the road before her, as if the answer would appear in the asphalt.

Iraq

The sun beat down on Beau. He was lying on a beach next to Tess; her presence as real as the sun that warmed his face. A cloud crawled in front of the sun, stealing the warmth it spread. He lay listening to her faint breaths. She ran her finger along his arm.

Beau turned to face her and opened his eyes. Reality, shadowed by disappointment set in. *Damn*, he thought.

Samira touched his arm again.

"I cover you," she said, pointing to the sun.

Beau groaned as he stood. Every muscle in his body ached. Sand had settled in his nostrils and ears. His eyebrows were thick with the tiny, rough crystals. He wiped them away with his dry fingers—coarse sand had become caked beneath his fingernails in thick dark lines.

"Hurt?" she asked in a shy voice.

"No," Beau lied. "I'm okay." *A dream. Goddamn it.*

Suha and Abdul Hadi studied the map while the children rolled the bedding. Beau limped toward the adults, noticing, for the first time, the stale smell of baked canvas.

"Medicine?" Suha asked.

Beau nodded. He kneeled by Abdul Hadi, ignoring the searing pain in his leg.

"We are very exposed," Abdul Hadi explained. "We must move."

Suha advised the children of their responsibilities: they must remain compliant if they were to live, they must respect their mother, and, of course, Abdul Hadi, their savior. The children did not speak for the first few hours of the grueling walk through the arid desert, flat to the horizon. Fear and fatigue had a way of stealing one's voice.

Suha spoke in hushed tones, walking so close to Beau that their shoulders almost touched. He limped with pain, she with age. "Bringing shame to one's family," she said.

"Who does these honor killings?" Beau asked, trying to hide his disgust.

"Family members. If a woman dishonors her family, another family member must take her life. I worried, of these killings. I worried for Samira," she glanced toward

Samira, who walked with her head down. "She did nothing to dishonor Safaa, Safaa say different. He accuse her of dishonor."

"Dishonor, like infidelity?" Beau asked.

"Yes, if he believe, can bring on honor killing," her voice carried contempt.

"If she flirted, she could be killed?" He asked.

Suha nodded. "Women, children, raped, killed. There is no reason. War is not good."

"But you were a doctor. Weren't you protected?" Beau couldn't wrap his mind around what he was hearing. This wasn't the dark ages. The thought made him sick to his stomach. "Did you dishonor your family?"

Suha shook her head. "Never. After war began, women fell back in rights. Maybe ten percent of women left the home, always with the knowledge they may not return. Insurgents." She lifted her eyebrow. "Many doctors are killed. Kidnapped, held for money, killed."

Zeid said something in Arabic.

Suha turned scornful eyes toward him, retorting in Arabic.

Samira's eyes grew wide. She opened her mouth to speak, catching a harsh glare from Suha.

Zeid slowed his pace, sinking back from Suha's sight.

"Hateful boy," Suha muttered beneath her breath.

Abdul Hadi walked with purpose, his eyes on the horizon, where the beige of the land blended into the washed-out blue of the sky, blurred from the heat. "Be thankful for the milder weather of October," he said to Beau. "This heat," he waved his hand toward the sun, "it's ninety, maybe, no longer one hundred and twenties. Hot, yes. Livable, certainly."

Beau was relieved when Abdul Hadi stopped to make camp in the early afternoon. His limbs burned with such intensity that he wasn't sure he would have been able to walk much further. Sweat poured from his skin.

Abdul Hadi studied a hand-drawn map and crouched next to Beau, his dark skin glistening in the sun. He pointed a thick, dirty finger toward a brown square.

"That is where we meet," he said.

"We're right out in the open. Are we safe?" Beau asked.

Abdul Hadi smiled, "What is 'safe'?"

Beau stared at him, incredulously.

Abdul Hadi explained that just over the edge of the horizon was the camp that would protect them. They would have medical supplies—he motioned to Beau's leg—food, water, and protection. The problem, he feared, would lie beyond the safety of the camp, after they were given new identities and would be traveling to Germany. "That transport, that is the worry." Abdul Hadi glanced at the others.

The children. "Does my presence create more danger?" Beau asked.

Abdul Hadi stared into his eyes with a serious look. "Life presents danger."

The tiny hand on Beau's back could only be Edham's. Beau reached behind him and took the little hand in his own, pulling the boy forward. Edham's eyes were wide, his face a slate of innocent excitement. He thrust his other hand toward Beau and opened his palm. Four small rocks rolled to the center of his palm.

Beau smiled, "Marbles?"

Edham smiled eagerly. A game of marbles ensued, complete with giggles, and watched by Athra, Samira, and Suha. Zeid sat off to the side, his head hung low, his shoulders drooped.

Abdul Hadi motioned for Zeid to join the game.

Zeid shook his head.

Abdul Hadi sat next to him on the sand, unwrapping the cotton fabric that protected his head and face from the sun, the black and white diamonds expertly intermingled. He relished the sensation of his head being freed from its binding. He pulled the fabric through his fingers and spoke in a soft voice, the Arabic words smooth and iridescent. "Your father would be proud, yes? You have trekked the desert like a man."

Zeid's eyes remained downcast.

Abdul Hadi folded the fabric and set it between him and the boy. "Your mother," he lifted his dark beard in Samira's direction, "she is a strong woman. She looks at you with pride. You are the man now."

Zeid tilted his ear in his direction, listening.

"Yes," he nodded, "you took your father's place." He picked up a handful of sand, letting it sift slowly through his fingers, as if he were mulling over his thoughts.

Zeid played with his toes, walking his fingers back and forth across them.

"You have a choice, Zeid."

Zeid's hand stilled.

"Your mother, she lives in fear. She has not known a life without fear. She will have a chance to know that life. You will have a chance to know that life."

"I'm not afraid," Zeid protested.

"No, I can see you're not," Abdul Hadi replied. "You can help her feel safe, too. You can lend your strength to her."

Zeid turned his body toward Abdul Hadi and sat up straighter.

"Yes, you can protect her instead of fighting her. That is your job," he emphasized 'job'. "Your mother, she is smart, she is strong, but she needs protection. She has babies to care for." He motioned toward Edham and Athra. "You owe your life to your mother—and to Suha."

"But—"

Abdul Hadi spoke over him. "You would have been killed, had she not saved you and your brother, your sister. That takes intelligence, strength. She is a smart woman."

"She—"

Abdul Hadi deepened his voice. "She risked her own life for yours." He filled Zeid's head with the values of his mother and Suha. He took great care not to disparage Zeid's father. When his lesson was complete, and Zeid had the look of a drunken soldier, he moved away.

Maryland

"She's fine," Alice listened to Tess's footsteps in the upstairs hallway while she sat on the couch, talking to Kevin on her cell phone. "She's just hurting, confused, but she'll pull through." At least Alice hoped she would. "Hey, I didn't know you knew Louie Tole."

"I didn't, until last night, I mean. I met him at the party."

"He's our client, sort of," she said.

"Hey, that movie's out, the one with Will Ferrell? I'm meeting a few friends there tonight, wanna go? Bring Tess?" he asked.

Alice weighed the idea. She'd seen more of Kevin in the past few weeks than she had in the four years since they'd met, and she didn't necessarily mind it.

"Never mind," Kevin said.

"I didn't say no."

"You didn't say yes, either," Kevin replied. "It's cool. We'll be at the Cinema and Draft House if you change your mind."

Tess appeared on the stairs, and Alice rushed off the phone.

"Was that Kevin, making sure the crazy woman is okay?" Tess asked.

Alice went to the kitchen and set a kettle of water on the stove. "It was Kevin, but he was asking about a movie later, not the psycho bitch."

"Ha ha," Tess said. "Thanks for staying up half the night with me."

"No biggee." Alice had listened to Tess's fears about letting Beau go and hoped her responses had been appropriate. She never really trusted herself in intimate situations—not that she let herself get tangled up in them often. The last time that a woman had confided in Alice, it had been her mother. *I knew, but I was never strong enough to help you.* Alice bristled at the memory.

Tess stood before Beau's closet, running her hands along his shirts, bringing the sleeves up to her nose, inhaling what scent remained of him. Airing out her fears about letting Beau go had brought with it an unexpected respite. Tess had yet to admit to Alice that she'd kissed Louie. *Baby steps*, she thought, *baby steps.* Maybe Alice had been right. Maybe she needed to let go, for the baby's sake. Loneliness spread like a disease through her body, until it encompassed her.

One by one, Tess slipped his shirts from their hangers, folded them, and set them in careful piles on the bed. She'd decided to pack them up and put them in the basement, where they wouldn't be a constant reminder, a constant hope, of what was surely not going to come.

Tess sat amongst the piles of clothes. In her lap lay the leather box his pocket watch had come in. She'd found it tucked behind a cashmere sweater in the back of the closet. Tess felt as if she were watching someone else's hands go through the motions of storing away pieces of their life. She laid her hand on her belly. "This is Daddy's stuff," she said. A tear slipped down her cheek. "He'll always be with us, but his things need to leave for a while. We'll be okay."

She remembered the party she'd thrown for Beau the night before he'd left, when she'd given him the pocket watch. She'd watched Beau and Kevin from across the room, a pang of jealousy ripping through her chest. *Great, she'd thought, now I'm acting like one of those insecure wives that need all the attention on her.* Beau was leaving, and if he wanted to spend time with his friends, he had a right to. She'd be just fine.

She'd escaped to the dining room, hovering over the hors d'oeuvres she could barely stomach looking at. The weight of a familiar hand on her shoulder brought a smile to her lips. She closed her eyes and, without turning around, put her hand on top of his.

"Dance with me," he whispered.

Their bodies moved as one to the edge of the make-shift dance floor where they swayed to their own beat, slowly, lovingly.

"Marry me?" Beau said softly into her ear.

"My husband might not like that," she joked.

"Would you marry me again, Tess?" Beau asked seriously.

"I'd marry you every day until the day I die," she answered.

Tess had led him to a quiet corner by the window. She reached up to the top of Beau's bookshelves, littered with his photography books, Stephen King novels, and war stories.

She pressed something cold into Beau's palm. "You promised me. Now you have to keep the promise."

Beau opened his thick palm to find a gold pocket watch. Inscribed on the back were four simple words in a fine cursive script, *Come back to me.* He pulled Tess close and whispered, "Always."

"Right," she said sarcastically. *Four and a half months. Goddamn it.* Tess pushed herself off the bed and packed Beau's belongings in three large suitcases. With his belongings packed neatly away and the closet bare, she lowered herself to the floor and stared into the cold, empty space. "Oh, Beau," she whispered.

Tess took a long, deep breath as she stood over the phone. She dialed Carol's number from memory.

"Carol? Hi. I'm sorry."

Chapter Thirteen

The children climbed on hands and knees to scale the enormous dune. Suha panted, her breathing labored. Beau helped her up the hill, one hand supporting her elbow. They trudged up the hill until finally the camp came into view, stuck in the middle of the desert like a giraffe in an ant farm.

Edham gasped with delight. Samira's eyes welled with tears, and Suha gave Beau a look as though she might drop to her knees and pray. Abdul Hadi held his palms out, silencing the group. He eyed the camp. Four small buildings, two army vehicles, and a line strung with clothing. If it weren't for his knowledge of who was housed there, he'd have thought it to be abandoned. Abdul Hadi watched for many minutes, then lowered his hands. They moved tentatively toward the camp.

As they neared the first of the buildings, two men came into view, ushering three women into a building. Sand and dust plumed around their feet.

Samira gasped, grabbing the boys' arms.

Abdul Hadi halted the group.

The men approached, guns drawn, speaking in fast and adamant Arabic.

Abdul Hadi raised his arms in surrender, Samira and Suha huddled the children behind them, Suha, calm, in control, Samira shaking with fear, her eyes shifting from the men to Beau and back again. Beau stood sentinel in front of the women and children, nerves afire.

The words Beau could translate were "order" and "war". Abdul Hadi motioned toward the women, his eyes lowered, his hand extended as if he were offering the women to them. Beau took a protective step backward, closer to Suha and Samira. One man laughed, the other moved toward Beau, gun ready. He looked Beau up and down, walking first to his left, then to his right. He lowered his gun to his side and smiled.

Beau's heart pounded against his ribs. For the first time in months, he realized that the fear that had filled every pore on his body had not been fear at all, only a sample of fear to come. He shifted his eyes to Abdul Hadi.

The gunman laughed, mocking him.

Beau lifted his arm, the muscles in his neck bulging with rage. Abdul Hadi rushed to his side.

"Easy," he said, lowering Beau's arm. "Their job is to keep us safe. You are a stranger. Let it be."

Beau lowered his arm but not his defenses.

The other gunman lowered his gun, eying the women as if they were cargo. He spoke directly to Suha, who kept her eyes trained on the ground, one arm around Edham, the other across Samira's back. She pleaded with him. The man spoke again, then Suha lifted her eyes, a look of relief momentarily flashed across her face. She turned to Samira and spoke quickly in Arabic. Samira hissed a question in reply, pulling Zeid and Athra closer to her chest. Suha nodded and reached for Samira's hand.

The exchange took only seconds, but to Beau, it felt like an eternity he could not circumvent.

"We are safe here," Suha advised Beau. "They are soldiers, yes, but soldiers of the underground."

"How do you know?" Beau made no effort to hide his skepticism.

"I know," Suha responded.

The men tossed their guns across their backs on the dark, tattered tethers that held them. They took the bulging packs from the women and led them around an ominous wall of sandbags—a blatant reminder of the ever-present danger—to the safety of the inner camp. To their right, a child's shirt and a single pair of pants hung still from a thick piece of rope strung between two buildings. The taller of the two dwellings was a hodge-podge of cheap, mismatched wood and tin. Bent and mangled wire lined the tin roofline.

Beau's eyes shot from side to side, an uneasy feeling trailed along his nerves. He kept pace next to Samira, watching the strangers with distrust.

They were led inside the building where three women and several children sat on the blankets on the dirt floor. The women did not smile when they glanced up. Their faces were gaunt, their eyes haunted, shadowed, and sunken. They turned back toward each other and began speaking in hushed tones.

The air inside the building was cooler than the direct heat of the sun. Without a breeze, however, the heat still slowly tugged at their energy.

Athra wiggled to be set free from Samira's arms. Another young girl of about five years old approached Samira, her eyes wide and hopeful.

In Arabic, she said, "I had a little sister once. I play with her?"

Samira looked to Suha, who nodded.

She set Athra on the ground. The girl took her hand and led her to one of the blankets. Athra looked over her shoulder at her mother and smiled.

Beau wondered how many shared moments Athra had experienced with other little girls in her three short, tumultuous years of life.

"You will remain here." The soldier spoke in practiced English. He repeated the same sentence in Arabic, in a tone that was more authoritative than welcoming. The two soldiers left the building.

Beau unclenched his fists. "What's going on?" he asked Abdul Hadi.

"They will help us."

Beau had his doubts.

Samira and Suha joined the group of women in the center of the room. They introduced themselves and the children in whispers. Zeid and Athra remained by their mother's side. Zeid's eyes darted around the group, as if he were determining the threat in the room.

"This is their job. They are not here to make us feel good, just to keep safety," Abdul Hadi said. "We will remain here until they come to get us."

"Who's 'they'?" Beau didn't like the ominous aura of the camp. The other women did not appear to be relishing their safety.

"The underground."

"But we're in the middle of the desert. We stand out like a sore thumb. We can be attacked at any moment."

"We're in a safe zone. Trust in the system. We know what we do." Abdul Hadi turned his back, done with this line of questioning. He left no room for discussion.

The night grew cold, and the two soldiers appeared with cans of beans and vegetables, two thick loaves of bread, and enormous plastic jugs of water. At the sight of the men, the children who had been there when the group had arrived quickly stacked blankets in a line on the floor along the back wall of the building, preparing bedrolls. Next they doled out chipped and stained plastic plates, while the women prepared the cold food. Edham and Zeid watched, only joining the others in their duties when a boy of Zeid's age invited them.

The men spoke only to Abdul Hadi. Beau remained watchful, absorbing what he could of the conversation, every nerve alert to protect the women and children. When the men left, Abdul Hadi motioned for Beau to follow him away from the group.

"We leave tomorrow evening," he said.

A new sense of unease bore into Beau's gut. "That fast? How long have these people been here?" he motioned toward the other women and children.

"Two months. They stay."

"Why?"

"They want refuge but refuse to leave the country."

Beau grasped for understanding. "Stay? They can leave with us," he said. He looked at the others. "We can't leave them behind," he implored.

Abdul Hadi shut him down. "They are not our business. Loyalty is strong, even when death is imminent."

Suha waited until Beau and Abdul Hadi stopped speaking, then handed a plate to each of them. She laid her hand on Beau's forearm and squeezed, a newfound habit she'd used when she wanted his attention.

"Do you hurt?" she asked.

Beau shook his head.

"You must rest. You have been through much," she said.

Abdul Hadi interrupted, explaining the plan to Suha.

"We will take a vehicle to the airstrip," he explained. "There are risks. We'll need to insure the children mind

126

our positions." He shifted his gaze to Samira. "She is not strong."

"I'll take care of them," Beau said.

Abdul Hadi nodded. "Insurgents can attack without warning." He went on to explain that there had been one event where one of the soldiers helping the women out of the country had turned on them. They'd had to change every safe route they'd used. The threat remained with every rescue. Beau's nationality might present a problem, he'd explained. He would dress in typical Iraqi garb, the untamed nature of his hair and his sun-tanned skin would help, but it was not a solid disguise. He would not use the bucket of water to scrub the dirt from his face that evening. The filth would add to his disguise.

Beau did not worry for his own life. He worried for the life of Suha, Samira, and the children of whom he had become so fond. No longer were the stakes simply making it back to Tess. Suha, Samira, Zeid, Edham, and Athra were part of him now. He would protect their lives without fear. The weight of that knowledge stirred torment within him that felt a lot like anger.

"If it is not to be, Jameel, then it was not meant to be," Suha said to Beau.

Later that night, Beau lay awake, listening to the tender sounds of slumber filling the small building: Athra suckling her thumb, Abdul Hadi's light snores flitting across the room from where he slept. Edham had pushed his blanket against Beau's, his body curled against Beau's side during his first hours of sleep, like an extra appendage. Beau worried about the trip. He did not know what to expect, but he knew that Americans were blowing up insurgents' vehicles, and insurgents were blowing up just about everything that passed by. In his right hand he gripped the pocket watch, in his left, an empty, clenched fist. Beau wasn't a religious man, but that evening he prayed they'd make it to Germany safely, with the group intact, and without issue over his being an American. He prayed to be reunited with Tess. He didn't let his mind wander to what she was doing, for he didn't want to admit that she very likely believed him dead. Time had become an unknown entity to him. He hadn't a clue what month it was, but he felt the slow passage of time deep within his heart, an inconsolable ache. *How long have I been gone?* he wondered. *Three months? Four?* It felt like forever. He opened his fist, releasing the watch, letting it fall beside him on the thickly-ribbed blanket. He ran his hand over the familiar fabric. Tess had a pullover hoodie made of the same rough material. She'd called it her hippie jacket. With his index finger, Beau outlined the letter 'I', the shape of a heart, and the letter 'u' in his palm, hoping Tess might somehow feel it on her own skin. He closed his eyes against his fear.

Maryland

When the phone rang, Tess was sitting on the floor before the empty closet, her journal in her lap. She'd drafted a letter to Beau—one that she knew he'd never see—and she'd tucked it into the journal. She stood, not as if in a dream, as one might expect, but rather like nothing out of the ordinary had just taken place, as if clearing out the remains of her dead husband was something she did every week.

"Hello?" the normalcy in her voice startled her— *Shouldn't I feel overwhelmed or different? What the hell is wrong with me?*

"I'm sorry. I couldn't not call. I had to make sure you were okay," Louie spoke quickly.

Tess smiled. "It's okay. I'm sorry. I've been a bit of a mess lately." She glanced in the mirror, and for the first time since Beau left, realized how thin her limbs had become. She turned sideways, touched the area above her hip bones that used to carry a few extra pounds. She frowned at the mound she'd been ignoring, centered between two sharp hip bones. All those years of wondering how she might lose the love handles she'd acquired, and now that she had, she preferred herself a bit more plump. She took note of the feeling, and assured herself that she'd be more conscious of eating.

"Just wanted to see if you needed anything."

Tess startled, then quickly turned her back on the mirror. She pursed her lips and took a deep breath. "I need a bike ride," she said, surprising herself.

"Really?"

"Absolutely."

Tess couldn't remember the last time she'd felt so invigorated. They'd biked for two hours along the C&O Canal and now sat on an outcropping of rocks, fifteen feet above the Potomac River. The water produced small whitecaps where it swirled into the rocks. The gentle sounds of the ripple and flow of the water sifted through the air. Tess stared into the blue afternoon, more relaxed than she'd been in weeks.

Louie sat a few feet from her, one leg bent, his elbow leaning across his knee, fiddling with a twig.

"Wanna talk about it?" he asked.

"About what?"

"The kiss?" he said.

Tess blushed. She turned away, then back toward him. No words came to her, no excuses, no apology. She shrugged.

He laughed. "Okay, then." Louie lay back on the rock and stared up at the sky. Tess did the same.

"You know, this friendship is a bit unfair," she said. "You know a lot about me, personal stuff, I mean, and I only know that you're an accountant who doesn't return phone calls. Seems kinda one-sided, don't you think?"

He turned to face her, then looked back up at the sky. "Not much to tell."

"There has to be something. Ever married? Skeletons in your closet?"

He laughed, "No, and maybe."

"Aw, come on!" she teased. "Tell me something juicy, something I can hold against you."

He was quiet for a minute, contemplating. "I sleep with the same blanket I've had since I was seven."

"That's a start—weird, but a start."

"My grandmother made it. It's brown and tan and has my initials in the center. It fits a twin sized bed, but I still use it on my king."

"Like I said, weird, but okay. Give me more."

"I've got nothing," he reiterated.

She sat up and stared at him. "Nothing? No one has nothing. Come on!"

He shook his head, "Sorry."

They rode back into Bethesda and stopped at Rock Bottom Restaurant and Brewery for dinner. Tess had just finished her last bite of salmon when Louie excused himself to say hello to a friend who was sitting at the bar. She watched him from behind, his jeans and t-shirt wrinkled from their ride, his hair awry from the wind. Suddenly, she realized that she'd seen Louie before she'd ever met him.

He came back and settled into his seat. Tess wore an ear-to-ear grin.

"Do you frequent bars?" she asked playfully.

"Uh, no. Why do you ask?"

"Rock Bottom, maybe?"

"I don't know, a few times. Why?" he shifted uncomfortably in his chair.

"You were Nineties-Guy," she laughed, taking a sip of her wine.

"Okay," he moved his plate to the side and leaned forward. "Am I supposed to know what that means?" he raised his eyebrow. "Ninety-inches? Was I into a ninety-year-old chick? Ninety—"

"Nineties guy," she laughed. "Beau and I used to watch people and—" she turned away, suddenly embarrassed. What she'd done with Beau may have been way out of the norm for other people. "Nothing, never mind."

"No way! C'mon, now you have to tell me," his energy was contagious.

Tess threw caution to the wind, recognizing that speaking Beau's name hadn't sent her crying, running from the room—it actually felt good. "Nineties guy, you know, old jeans, t-shirt, long hair, like in the nineties? We used to make up stories about people while we were waiting for our table, or in lines, you know," she waved her hand through the air. "It's silly. Never mind."

"Wait, wait, wait! You mean like, What's her story?"

Tess looked at him cockeyed.

"You know, when guys make up stories about the girls standing at the bar? She's looking for a father figure. She'll take your wallet. She's got a penis," he laughed.

Tess covered her face, laughing. "Okay, make fun of me."

"I'm not," he sat back and roared with laughter. "We're pigs. We really do that, or at least we did when I was twenty."

She told him of his made up history and enjoyed his pleasure at her choice of professions for him. Tess couldn't help but ask him again about his past. He gave no hints of anything more than college and work. "Long-term relationships?" she asked.

"Overrated," he said.

They biked back to Tess's house, the brisk night awakening their senses. Tess pulled her sweater around her shoulders after parking her bike on the side of the house and invited Louie in for a drink.

"I don't think so," he said. "I know how you work. First, you invite me in for a drink, then you're all paws, clawing at my clothes and taking advantage of me."

She laughed, unlocked the door.

"Seriously, I have to go. I have a long ride home and an early meeting tomorrow," he said.

"Okay, Mr. I-don't-return-calls, blow me off then," she teased.

He leaned in to kiss her cheek and she quickly turned, taking his face in her hands and kissing him on the lips.

"See?" he said softly as they pulled apart. "I knew you'd take advantage of me."

"Did you say Kevin asked you to go to the movies?" Tess and Alice had been reviewing files in the conference room all morning. Monday was typically a busy day for them, and this one had started out with a storm. One of the managers Tess had placed had been accused of embezzling from the company's charitable fund, and it was up to them to find a replacement—fast.

"How about this one, Joe Soloman? Six years investment banking, three years management," Alice offered.

"Skirt the question much?"

"Focus, Tess, our butts are on the line here."

Tess rolled her eyes. "Sure, set it up, then tell me about you and the Kevster."

"Nothing to tell," Alice said, furiously searching through files.

"Okay," Tess said, making a big show of waving her hands and sighing loudly. "You can keep your secret, and I'll keep mine."

Alice's eyes lit up. She inched to the edge of her chair, "Your secret?"

Tess shrugged. "How about this guy?" she pushed a file across the table to Alice.

"Forget the file, Tess, do tell!"

"Nope. No Kevin, no details," she kept her nose in the files.

"Ugh!" Alice stood and paced. "There's really nothing to tell. We've been hanging out. That's it. You know me, there's never anything more."

Tess lifted her eyes, "Yeah, and why is that, exactly?"

Alice threw herself onto the chair, "God, really? I don't know. There just isn't. I'm not like you, I don't get all lovey-dovey and needy."

Tess didn't know if she should be hurt or flattered. She decided to go for the latter and lifted her eyebrows.

"He's…I don't know, fun?" Alice said.

"Fun?"

"Maybe. I don't know. There isn't anything going on or anything. We hang out, have drinks, dinner, maybe a movie. Sometimes he calls."

"Wait, you actually talk to him on the phone? More than the one-word answers you give me?"

Alice turned her back, hair resting perfectly below the line of her shoulders. "Maybe. Sometimes." Then she spun around, "Your turn!"

Flustered, Tess flipped though the papers she'd been holding.

Alice sat on the table next to the papers, flattened them with her palm. "Well? What's the secret?"

"It's not a secret, really. I've just been thinking a lot, that's all."

"About the baby?"

Tess squared her shoulders, her face serious. "No, not about the baby. I cleaned out Beau's closet."

"You did!" Alice's excitement made Tess smile. "Good girl!"

"It wasn't anything big. I just got to thinking, and, well, it's been months, and surely if he had been—" she waved her hand, pushing back the tears that welled in her eyes. "It was time, that's all."

"I'm so proud of you! That must have been very difficult."

"Not as difficult as I'd thought, actually," the truth of the statement stung. "I called Carol, too."

"Who are you and what have you done with Tess Johnson?" Alice joked.

Tess laughed. "I know. I had to. It was time." She looked at Alice, really looked at her for the first time in weeks. Her eyes had softened. *Kevin.* "Thanks, Alice."

"What're friends for?" Alice laughed. "I never would have imagined. Good for you."

"There's more," Tess admitted.

Alice opened her eyes wide and bobbed her head forward, "Should I brace myself?"

"Shut up," Tess said and pushed back from the table. She stood, turned her back to Alice, and said, "I don't even know how to tell you this."

"You're really a man?" Alice teased.

"Worse, I think."

"You're closing the office?" pain streaked across her face.

"Never." Tess sat on the table next to Alice, swinging her feet. "I kissed Louie Tole—twice."

Alice shrieked, "Oh, thank God!"

"What?"

"I mean, if you closed the office what the hell would I do?" she playfully pushed Tess. "That's your big secret?"

"No, the closet was my big secret, but this, indiscretion, has been bothering me—sort of."

"Indiscretion?" Alice kicked her feet in time with Tess's. "My dear, that is not an indiscretion. That's a much-needed taste of life, so to speak."

They both laughed.

"Speaking of taste, how was it?" Alice asked.

"Jesus, Al!" Tess got up and grabbed a file, giving Alice the sign that they needed to get back to work. "You're such a pig."

"Me? I'm not the one who kissed a could-be client."

Tess's face became serious. "Oh, God, you're right. What've I done?"

"Oh, please. Get over it. It doesn't sound like you've done nearly enough."

"You would know," Tess was only partially joking. "Who's your latest conquest?"

"Reporting my sex life was not in the job description when I took this job."

"Kevin?" Tess asked.

"No, and don't you breathe a word of it. I'm more of a one-night-stander. Not even that," she looked up toward the ceiling, as if she were contemplating just the right words. "A few-hour-banger, yeah, that's it, then, get the hell out, and I won't call you."

"Alice Workman! How have I not known this about you for all these years?"

Alice shrugged. "I guess I'm not a bag 'n' bragger."

Chapter Fourteen

Tension whipped through the afternoon like a sandstorm. The children were excessively needy and whiney, taking their cues from the adults who were short tempered as they awaited their transport across the desert.

They had remained in the small building except to use the lavatory, a wooden platform built over a hole in the ground. The stench had been overwhelming, feces and urine stained the edges of the wood where others had missed their aim. Beau had barely been able to restrain himself from retching.

He stood beside Suha and Abdul Hadi in the corner of the building. Their whispers, he'd hoped, would be indiscernible to the others. Suha wrung her hands nervously as they discussed the possible outcomes of the next leg of their journey. The reality of them all perishing was something Beau tried to push aside. He had to believe he'd make it back home. He'd promised. Hell, he needed to believe in order to get through each moment of each day.

The heavy sound of truck tires crunching sand drew their attention, inciting fear so strong, Beau wasn't sure he could manage to function around it. His heart pumped fast and hard in his chest. His muscles clenched throughout his body. He knew he had to remain strong for the sake of the children, for the sake of the women. That knowledge did nothing to calm his panicked state.

The roar of the truck frightened the children. Athra's arms shot up as she scurried up her mother's body. Edham held tight to Samira's leg. Samira rushed to Beau's side, a pleading look in her eyes. Zeid remained two steps from his mother's reach, hovering somewhere between terrified child and tough pre-adolescent.

Abdul Hadi met three armed Iraqi men in the doorway. His demeanor was calm, his words fast, aggressive. The men waved their guns in Beau's direction. Beau was unable to translate each word of the heated discussion, but the gist did not escape him. His presence was a threat, a threat they were not ready to cover. Abdul Hadi argued with the men, pulling pieces of his clothing toward the men, touching his hair, his beard. The men looked Beau over, and for once, Beau was thankful for his poor hygiene. One of the men walked out of the building, leaving the other two to argue with Abdul Hadi. The third man returned, tossing a duffle bag in Abdul Hadi's direction.

The men swiftly left the building. Abdul Hadi quickly emptied the duffle, tossing pieces of clothing to Beau. Ten minutes later, the vehicle pulled away from the camp. The group sat in the rear of the truck, Beau's head swathed in fabric, his body in the soldier's clothing. The women huddled with the children, even Zeid could not mask his fear of the armed soldier who sat amongst them. Abdul

Hadi sat across from Suha, watchful and strong. The safety of the camp fell away in the distance.

They had been traveling for hours. Athra lay curled at her mother's feet atop a blanket, the vibration of the truck had lulled her to sleep. Zeid had been silent during the long, hot trip. He moved next to Abdul Hadi, his head held high when the soldier eyed him suspiciously, as if to say that he was a man, and, therefore, could move about as one.

He nudged Abdul Hadi's arm and asked in Arabic, "To where are we going?"

Abdul Hadi did not answer. He looked warily at the soldier, whom he knew was part of the underground movement and was there to assist them, but still he did not fully trust the man.

"What will happen to us when we arrive?" Zeid pushed.

Abdul Hadi spoke without taking his eyes from the soldier's, "Hush. We are going where they take us."

"Where? To our city?" Zeid ignored the pinched look of frustration on Abdul Hadi's face.

"We will go where they take us," he repeated.

Suddenly the brakes screeched, and the group was thrown forward. Athra cried out in terror. Edham clenched his mother's arm, his nails tearing into her skin. Suha reached out to right Zeid, who'd crumpled forward. The soldier jumped from the truck, gun drawn. Outside the vehicle the men shouted angrily, unfamiliar male voices catapulted through the thin tarp that covered the rear of the vehicle.

Beau shot a worried look to Abdul Hadi.

He held up his hand, commanding silence.

They listened.

"We're at the airfield," Abdul Hadi whispered.

"That's it? We're done? Now we're safe?"

Abdul Hadi looked incredulously at Beau. He shook his head, his tone serious. "We are not safe until we are out of the country."

Samira protectively covered Athra's ears.

The rear of the truck swung open. Two Iraqi soldiers spat instructions in Arabic. Suha pushed Beau forward, guiding him toward the intended location. He kept his head bent low. Edham tugged at Beau's pants leg. He lifted the boy easily into his arms, feeling Edham's heart pounding against his thin chest. Abdul Hadi whispered to Beau to follow his lead.

Three armed men stood before a small plane. Two of them approached, staring at both Beau and Abdul Hadi. Abdul Hadi spoke rapidly, pointing to Beau, then motioning to his ear.

Suha translated in whispers, doing her best to hide her words by angling her face down toward the ground.

Abdul Hadi told the men that Beau was hard of hearing due to a recent explosion.

Suha whispered to Beau, "Not a word. Silence."

The men circled Beau, eyeing him up and down. It was not a stretch for Beau to play the part of being injured or shell-shocked. Memories of the recent months were fresh. His eyes remained low, watching the boot-clad feet of the men scuff along the sand. His nerves were live wires. He expected to be torn from the group at any moment and shot.

From a nearby vehicle came another large dark-skinned man. Beau stole a glance. The man looked more American than Iraqi. For a split second, Beau was tempted to speak to him in English, to explain how he had landed amongst the group. Before he could utter a word, the man shoved papers into each of their hands, speaking forcefully in Arabic, "Identification."

In the distance, a truck dusted up sand as it sped in their direction.

Suddenly, the men aimed their rifles in the direction of the approaching vehicle, shouting and pushing Beau and the others toward the airplane. Beau carried Edham, snagging Zeid's collar with his free hand and pulling him toward the plane. Athra clung to Samira's chest, sobbing loudly. Gunfire rang out seconds before they reached the plane. The engine roared, concealing the men's wild shouts and the pops of the gunfire. Beau threw Edham and Zeid into the open door of the airplane. Abdul Hadi hoisted Samira and Athra into the plane. They scrambled across the airplane floor. Abdul Hadi lifted himself into the airplane and grabbed Suha's arm, Beau lifted her from behind, into the belly of the plane. He jumped on the edge as the airplane lifted from the ground, falling atop Samira as the plane careened sideways. The door slammed shut. Gunfire rang out beneath the belly of the plane.

The children's frantic screams and sobs echoed in the small plane.

Abdul Hadi hushed them, grabbing Zeid by the shoulders and commanding him to get a hold of himself for the good of his mother.

Beau checked Samira for cuts, broken bones. Beyond the screams, Beau heard a moan. Suha lay across a seat, her body oozing blood from several dark holes. He rushed to her, lifting her across his lap, pushing his hands into the holes in her ravaged body.

"Suha!" His shout was drowned out by the roar of the airplane and the pilot's incessant curses. Beau frantically tried to stop the bleeding, clinging to Suha's body as his own was thrust from side to side from the turbulent ascent of the plane. Blood seeped through his fingers in thick, steady streams. He tore apart the fabric that had hidden his face and pressed the rumpled cloth into the wounds. "Don't you leave me," he pleaded through gritted teeth. "Come on, come on!"

Samira shrieked, crawling to Suha's side. She ripped the remaining fabric and pushed it against Suha's chest, desperately trying to cover the three bullet holes that spewed blood across her body, praying frantically in Arabic. Her hands shook, blood pooling beneath them.

Suha's eyes opened, then slowly closed.

"Suha!" Beau yelled. He pushed her matted hair from her eyes. "Abdul Hadi!" he yelled.

Abdul Hadi took Beau's hands from her wounds, Beau fought him. Abdul Hadi shook his head.

Tears streamed from Beau's cheeks, his body quaked. "No! No!" he shook Suha's body, shaking Suha. "Come on! Damn it, Suha! Come on!" He grabbed her hand and squeezed as hard as he was able.

Suha's eyes fluttered beneath her lids. She tried to suck in air, gurgling, emitting a painful, choking sound.

"Ja...meel," she managed.

"No!" Beau yelled and pulled her body against his heaving chest.

Samira threw herself across Suha's back, oblivious to her children's wails. Beau sobbed, holding Samira with one of his blood-soaked hands and pressing Suha's lifeless body against him with the other.

Chapter Fifteen

Tess fished through her closet looking for just the right outfit. Her bed was already covered with cast-offs— a little black v-neck dress? Too revealing. Black slacks and a blouse? The pants would never fit around her expanding waist. A blue sheath? Too matronly. The phone rang. She instantly regretted not checking her frustration before saying hello.

"Uh-oh," Louie said. "Something's got you tied in knots."

If you only knew, Tess thought. "No, I'm just...finishing some last-minute work," she lied.

"So we're still on? Eight o'clock?"

Tess nervously bit her lip, "Mm-hmm." Tess made arrangements to meet him at the movie theater in case she chickened out of what she knew was coming. The relationship was developing into something more, and she wasn't sure she had the strength to stop it.

They sat in the dark theater, their forearms pressing against one another's on the arm rest. Tess felt like a high schooler in a pair of jeans, a low-cut blouse that showed off her newfound cleavage, and heels that would even make Shrek feel sexy. Despite her best efforts to ignore her desires, the simple act of crossing her legs when wearing heels suddenly seemed to hold a sensual connotation—the way her foot arched, her leg appeared longer, sleeker. What had she been thinking? Concentrating on the movie was out of the question. She had all she could do to keep her heart from jumping out of her chest. She felt more than saw Louie glance at her—*damn him, all relaxed and confident.*

He laid his hand on hers, and heat rose to her neck. She hadn't felt that way since…Beau. Beau! What was she doing? She took a deep breath and shook her head. *Oh, my God, I'm a slut.* She slipped her hand out of his and set it in her lap.

When the movie ended, Louie stood and stretched. Trying to quell her inner turmoil, Tess fumbled with her phone, concentrating on turning it back on, having turned it off for the movie. It vibrated immediately. She answered as they made their way to the exit.

Kevin's panic-stricken voice made her heart race. "Tess? Where the hell are you? Get to Sibley Hospital as soon as you can. It's Alice."

Tess pushed through the emergency room doors and made a beeline for the receptionist. "Alice Workm—"

"Tess! This way." Tess followed Kevin through a set of electric doors. The worry in his eyes told Tess this was no minor injury. They rushed down the sterile hallway, overwhelmed by the smell of antiseptic, dodging white-clad nurses.

"What's happened?" she asked.

The look Kevin gave her sent a chill up her spine. He stopped in front of a curtain.

Tess tried to push past him. He grabbed her arm, "Tess," he swallowed hard. "It's not pretty. She's holding up okay, but—"

"What happened?" she pushed past him, opening the curtain and stopped dead in her tracks. Gauze covered Alice's left eye, her chin was deep red and swollen. The ends of her hair were matted with blood.

"Oh, my God," Tess shrank into a cold metal chair next to the bed feeling as though she'd been kicked in the gut. She reached under the sheet for Alice's hand. Thick bandages covered her wrist. Tess dropped her eyes to Alice's other wrist, also covered in a thick bandage. "What happened?"

Alice opened her mouth slowly, her voice a whisper, "He…" She swiped at the tears on her cheeks.

Tess gently wrapped her arms around Alice's trembling body. "Never mind, don't try to talk."

"You warned me," Alice said to Tess.

"Oh, honey, no. This isn't your fault," Tess said.

Alice nodded. "You asked if I worried, and I blew you off. I was scared. I was scared with every man I brought home," she sobbed.

Kevin turned away.

"It's true!" she said to Kevin. "I'm pathetic," she cried. "A fool."

Kevin turned back toward her.

"You are not pathetic, Alice," Tess said. She glared at Kevin.

Kevin's clenched jaw muscles twitched.

"Whoever did this, he's pathetic," Tess hissed. She held Alice until she calmed down.

A nurse came in and read Alice's chart. "How're you doing, honey? I see that you refused a sedative earlier. Are you ready for one now?" Her sweet tone didn't fit her bleached-white skin and pitch black hair.

Tess lifted an eyebrow at the piercing in the young nurse's eyebrow.

Alice reached for the pill with trembling fingers. She put it on her tongue and gulped it down with a quick shot of water, wincing at the pain as it slid down her throat.

"Al, I'm going to talk to the doctor, will you be okay for a minute?"

Alice clenched the sheet in her fist, nodded.

"I'll just be a sec," Tess said and grabbed Kevin as she walked through the curtain. "What the fuck happened? Who did this to her?" she seethed. Tess paced outside the curtain, her insides boiling with rage.

"I found her in her condo. I stopped by on my way to the movies, and as I got off the elevator, I saw the back of some guy running toward the stairs and caught her door before it could close." He turned away, shaking his head.

"What?" Tess demanded.

"She was tied up, Tess, naked. The fucker beat the shit out of her." Kevin slammed the side of his fist against the doorjamb.

"Easy," a nurse said as she walked by.

"Jesus, who would do this to her? Did you call the police? Did they get him?"

He nodded. "They came and took a report, but I only saw him from the back. She knows him, Tess. He's one of her..."

Tess felt nauseous. "Oh, my God. But she was just at my house this morning."

"He was waiting for her when she got home—inside."

Tess bit her lower lip. "Poor Alice."

"She's not talking. She won't tell them who he is."

"She has to! He'll do this to some other woman," she said.

"She knows that. The police have gone over everything." He gave Tess a look of apology. "She called you."

"What? When?" Tess's mind ran a mile a minute. The movies, her phone had been off. She pulled her phone out of her purse—one voice mail message. "Oh no. Oh God." She chewed her fingernail while listening to the frantic message: "Help!" Alice's voice piercing; indecipherable struggling noises; Alice screaming; an angry male voice, snarling, "My turn, bitch!" The sound of flesh pounding flesh cracked through the line, followed by Alice's shriek. The line went dead.

Tess slid down to the cold linoleum floor, her back against the wall, face buried in her hands.

For the first time ever, Tess walked tentatively into her home, wondering who, or what, might be waiting for her behind the closed doors. He was out there somewhere—Alice's attacker. A chill ran down Tess's back. Tess couldn't help but think that Alice must have known this could happen, and just as quickly hated herself for thinking it. She ran from room to room, closing curtains and opening closet doors. She checked to be sure all the doors were locked, and finally fell, exhausted, into a hot bath.

Tess lay on the bed, staring at the empty closet. She could feel Beau everywhere. Her body ached for him, for closure, and at the same time, she hoped never to receive closure because that would mean he was truly never coming back. Yet, no matter how much she tried, she couldn't dismiss her growing desire for Louie's touch. It had been so long since Tess had felt the heat of another, smelled the lingering aroma of sex. She wrapped her arms around her burgeoning waist and rolled over onto Beau's side of the bed, burying her head in his pillow. "Oh,

Beau," she whispered, "you promised to come back." Tess drifted into sleep, and finally, into a dream. *She stood in the middle of the street in the pouring rain, shivering, wearing a drenched t-shirt and maternity jeans, her belly protruding like a mountain. In one direction was Beau, battered and bloody, his hand outstretched, his sunken eyes pleading, fading. In the other direction, Louie beckoned, life emitting from his very being.*

Chapter Sixteen

Samira clung to Suha's lifeless, bloody body. How would she manage without her, without the woman who had rescued her from her abusive life and promised her a life without fear? She was riddled with trepidation—leaving the only country she'd ever known without a man to support her or Suha to guide her. Her stomach ached worse than when Safaa had beaten her. She watched her children, huddled together, their tear-streaked cheeks swollen and red. Suha's death brought a broken look to Zeid. Paralyzed by the fear that prickled her limbs, she could not let go of Suha's body. She could not go to her children, comfort them, when she herself could not accept Suha's senseless death.

Beau pried Samira's trembling fingers from Suha's body. He pressed her against him, slowly guiding her to her children's side. He laid Suha's body in the back of the airplane, going through the motions without thought, and returned to Samira's side. Samira laid her head against Beau's shoulder. Athra climbed into her lap, her thumb jammed into her mouth. Edham inched his trembling body next to Beau. Zeid remained at a distance.

"She was a strong woman," Abdul Hadi said.

Samira stared at the floor before her, feeling her heartbeat against Beau's side, gathering what little strength she could from him.

"She accomplished her goal, Samira," Abdul Hadi said. "She was a strong woman."

"Her goal was never to die," Samira whispered in Arabic.

"She saved you and the children. That was her goal," he paused. "She was not afraid of death."

Samira looked away, ashamed. She'd been the cause of Suha's death.

Zeid's high-pitched voice broke through the thick curtain of grief. "It's his fault!" He pointed to Beau with a look of disdain.

"Hush, Zeid," Samira demanded, no louder than a whisper.

"He did it! We should never have left Iraq. I hate him! I hate you!"

Abdul Hadi turned stern eyes in the boy's direction. "Your father would be ashamed, boy! Suha saved your life. She gave you what many children of the war will never have—safety. She gave her life for you, child, not for him. She gave her life for your brother and sister, for your mother. Do not disrespect your mother or Suha again in my presence."

Zeid shrunk back, jaw clenched, his eyes shooting darts.

Beau could not understand many of the words he spoke, but he understood the looks he received from the terrified boy, and he did not blame Zeid for his hatred. Instead, Beau wanted to try harder to ease the child's pain.

The flight went on for many hours. The pilot's deep voice rattled on and on as he spoke into the radio.

As Abdul Hadi translated, he methodically washed the blood from Samira's cheeks and hands, as if he'd done it a hundred times before. He used the bottles of drinking water and scrubbed the floor of the airplane where Suha's body had left its mark, then he covered her body with blankets so the children would not be forced to bear witness any longer.

Beau watched Abdul Hadi, embarrassed by his inability to help Abdul Hadi. His head dripped perspiration. The rumbling of the engine made his stomach queasy.

"He's warning the airbase that we're coming in on a private plane," Abdul Hadi explained. "He's begging them not to shoot us down."

Beau pulled Edham close, memories of the helicopter crash careening through his mind.

When the small plane had rumbled and tipped, Beau saw flashes in his mind of the men he'd traveled with in the helicopter: Gary Marks, the lanky young reporter who rued being away from his family but who was indebted to Mr. Fulan for giving him a job ten years earlier without education or experience. Gary had sat across from Beau, his head back, eyes closed.

"Hey, man," Beau had said. "It'll be okay. We're almost done." Beau could see the terror in his eyes.

Gary didn't respond.

"Is it the flying?" Beau asked.

He nodded.

"Shit, that's the easy part. Getting these people to trust us, that's the hard part."

Gary didn't say anything, his knuckles stark white against the green of the belt.

"He's been flying for years," Beau said reassuringly.

"It's not him that I'm worried about," Gary stared into the black night, listening to sand whip against the small window of the helicopter.

The forty-something pilot, Joe, turned his pitted face and scruffy mane toward them and smiled, his deep voice boomed through the cabin. "We're in the Green Zone, dude. Nothing to worry about," he assured them.

"He just said the sandstorm threw him off course ten minutes ago," Gary said under his breath. His bloodshot eyes teared up.

Beau tightened his seat belt and reached for the lump in his pants pocket, feeling mildly better. *I'll come back to you.*

The thick stench of sand heightened the tension in the close quarters. A distant whistling sound suddenly became deafening, milliseconds before impact, ripping the men from their belts and tossing them like rag dolls within the aircraft's fuselage. The helicopter had spun out of control. Screams of terror filled the fiery compartment. Beau's eyes locked on Gary's terrified stare. He'd grabbed hold of Gary's arm. The second missile had hit the center of the helicopter, ripping Gary's body backward, sending Beau, and Gary's arm, slamming against the hard metal of what was left of the helicopter. Blood spewed through the air. Beau fought to stay conscious. A rapid succession of explosions lit up the sky, tearing the helicopter to bits and ravaging Beau's body. His broken body sailed through the fiery sky. By the time he hit the Earth, a mile and a half from where they would later find the debris, he felt no pain.

It seemed a lifetime ago that he'd woken up in the makeshift shelter, Suha hovering over him. A lump formed in his throat as he thought of her nursing him back to health, teaching him Arabic as he taught her English. The thought made him long for his own mother. Beau covered his eyes, promising himself, once again, that he'd make it home. Samira sighed, and Beau looked into her vacant stare. He reached for her hand.

So strong was the urge to hold Samira, to make the children feel safe and loved, that it sent Beau's mind into a tailspin, his loyalty divided. He loved his wife, he'd never questioned that love, and he wasn't questioning it now, though at that very moment he knew that he loved Samira, Athra, Zeid, and Edham. *Edham.* The boy held a place within Beau's heart that he could not imagine being filled by anyone else. Beau forced himself to look away. He took Tess's picture from his pocket, smoothing it across his leg. What kind of man was he, he wondered, to love more than one woman? He battled the dilemma within the confines of his mind, desperately trying to convince himself that the feeling, the pull to protect, was driven by circumstance, not by desire.

The pilot's voice boomed through the airplane, shouting orders in Arabic. Abdul Hadi was on his feet in seconds, answering the man and waking the children. "We are going to land," he said, as he pushed the children and Samira toward the two tiny seats. Samira held Athra on her lap, Zeid and Edham huddled together on the other seat, their slender fingers working quickly to fasten the seatbelts.

"Will we be killed?" Zeid's voice trembled.

Samira placed her hand on his leg.

"No. Now be silent," Abdul Hadi commanded.

The plane hit the ground hard, sending Beau and Suha's body tumbling toward the front of the small cabin. Samira clutched Athra, frantically reaching for Edham's arm. Athra's wail competed with the screeching tires of the plane. Beau scrambled back toward them, crouching in front of Samira and the children, reaching his arms around the four of them and grabbing the backs of their seats, securing them against him. The plane lurched forward, then rolled swiftly to a stop.

Beau's heart pounded in his chest. His mind swam through the fear and the hope that swelled within him as he checked the children. The fear in Samira's eyes was palpable.

"It's okay," he reassured her.

Zeid frantically tried to unlatch his seatbelt. Edham squirmed out from under the tether and climbed Beau as if he were a tree. Outside the plane, the tarmac was a flurry of movement. Armed vehicles rushed the plane. The pilot spoke fervently to Abdul Hadi, who had reached for a gun. Although Beau's Arabic wasn't perfect, he knew the command, "No weapons!"

Abdul Hadi released the weapon. He spoke above the children's sobs, "Soldiers will come. Do not be scared."

Zeid's voice broke through his sobs in an accusatory, piercing scream, "American soldiers? Traitor!"

Abdul Hadi glared at him, rising to his full height, looming above the child. "Know who your enemies are, boy!"

Samira pulled Zeid against her side, silencing him.

The pilot yelled down to the tarmac, "I have clearance!" His hands were raised high above his head. "Authorization, we have authorization." He moved cautiously to lower the stairs. American soldiers were up the stairs, firearms ready, before Beau could utter a word. They grabbed the pilot and Abdul Hadi roughly by the arms, herding them down to the tarmac. A soldier grabbed Beau's arm, shoving him toward the stairs.

Beau shook himself free. "I'm an American photographer," he explained, Edham in his arms, the boy's gangly arms around his neck.

Zeid hid behind his mother's leg, his tough demeanor of only days before quickly forgotten, leaving him vulnerable, exposed.

Samira's body shook. She kept her eyes trained on the ground, holding Athra tightly against her chest. The soldier pushed them toward the exit. More American soldiers waited below, barking orders and asking questions too fast for Beau to respond. Beau tried to clarify the situation, but there was too much commotion.

Abdul Hadi and the pilot were whisked away in an armored vehicle. An officer stepped from a jeep. Beau lowered Edham to his side, pushing the boy behind his leg, his hand remaining on the boy's trembling shoulder. Beau's heart rammed against his ribcage. He took a deep breath, standing tall, thrusting his chest forward.

"What's your name, son?" the officer asked.

Beau's throat swelled, from fear or relief he couldn't decipher. He spoke his full name for the first time in months, "Beau Johnson, sir, American photographer with *War Time Magazine.*"

The officer's shoes were spit shined, the fabric of his jacket pulled against the thickness of his arms. He squinted, raising his eyebrow at Beau's Iraqi attire, the blood on his shirt. He extended his hand and gave Beau a curt nod, "Colonel Larner, United States Army."

Beau reached for his hand. A young thin soldier stood by Colonel Larner's side and spoke in a hushed and hurried tone, his words muffled.

"Where did you say you were from, Mr. Johnson?"

"I...Maryland, sir. Bethesda, Maryland. I was sent to Iraq by Mr. Hakim Fulan, president of *War Time Magazine*, to photograph the changes in family life since the inception of the war." Beau began to sweat under the stares of the soldiers. He pulled Edham into his arms and took a step back, aligning his body with Samira's. "There was a helicopter crash—"

"Do you have identification, Mr. Johnson?"

Beau shifted his weight, moving Edham to the other hip, "It was destroyed, in the helicopter crash. Everything was lost," he said, then quickly added, "I swear, I'm—"

Suddenly, Samira dashed toward the airplane screaming, "Suha!" Athra sobbed uncontrollably in her arms. In the space of a second, two large soldiers caught Samira by the arms. One of the soldiers ripped Athra from Samira's arms.

The child's arms shot out toward her mother, "*Ummi! Ummi!*"

Samira reached for Athra, fighting against the soldier's steadfast grips. She spat in Arabic, "Let me go! Suha! Suha!" She twisted her body, tears streaming down her cheeks. Zeid punched at the soldiers' legs, yelling harsh words.

Beau snatched Athra from the soldier's hands. "She's trying to get to Suha, the dead woman!" he shook off the young soldier's hand as they tried to restrain him. He stared angrily at the soldiers that held Samira like a hostage.

"She needs to see her! She's not a criminal!" he turned toward Colonel Larner, "Please, sir, she's scared, she has no one." Beau's biceps were being squeezed by two large soldiers, who'd replaced the younger one's efforts. Beau knew he had no identification, he was dressed like an Iraqi, they had no reason to believe his story any more than they had to believe that Samira wasn't some sort of terrorist.

Colonel Larner motioned for the soldiers to stand down.

Beau rushed to Samira's side, grabbing Zeid's gangly arm and pulling him away from pounding the soldier's leg.

"Sweep the plane," Colonel Larner ordered. The soldiers who had restrained Samira rushed into the plane, guns drawn.

"I swear, we're not here to harm anyone. I am who I say I am. She's just a mother, protecting her children."

Minutes later, the soldiers disembarked. "All clear, sir," the shorter of the two men said in a surprisingly high-pitched voice. "As the pilot reported, there is one deceased woman, multiple gunshot wounds, nothing else."

Colonel Larner ordered three armed men to assist Beau, Samira, and her children back onto the plane.

Samira sobbed, "Suha! I will not leave her!"

With his arm around her shoulder, Beau leaned close to her and whispered, "Suha got us here." Samira turned and looked at Beau, then collapsed into his strong embrace.

Maryland

Alice leaned across the white chaise lounge in her living room, motioning for Tess to come in close. "Want a drink?" she whispered. Before Tess could answer, Alice spoke over her shoulder. "Kev, could you bring us some ice water, please?"

Tess rose. Alice pulled her down with a conspiratorial smirk. "Watch," she said. It had been a month since Alice's attack, and when Tess wasn't with her, Kevin was.

"You're horrible," Tess laughed.

Alice shrugged.

"You're enjoying this!" Tess shook her head. "Aren't you supposed to have some remorse over using him like this? Didn't this…event…have any impact on you?"

Alice looked down. "Yes, it had an impact! Jesus, Tess, how can you even say that? I cried on your shoulder for weeks trying to understand why it happened."

"It was days," Tess said, then quickly added, "not that I'm judging you. I know you were scarred by what happened, it's just that Kevin's so sweet, and you're using him."

"Who says I'm *using* him?" Alice asked.

Tess watched Kevin filling two glasses with water. She thought of Beau and missed how they used to take care of each other. She missed his smile, the way he remembered to use one and a half Sweet 'n Lows in her tea instead of two. Sadness inched up her limbs, settling on her shoulders like a weight.

"I'm sorry. I didn't mean that," she said to Alice.

Alice waved it off, accepting the drink from Kevin, and touching his arm in a way that gave Tess pause. Kevin's eyes connected with Alice's and held them.

Tess's eyes grew wide. "Thank you," she accepted the glass of water Kevin offered, and declined the coaster he'd offered.

"I'm taking the trash down, Al," Kevin said and left the condo.

Tess leaned forward and whispered, "Okay, spill. What was *that*?"

Alice stood and walked to the window. "He thinks he's keeping me safe," she said.

"Alice, you can't do this to him. He's a nice guy. If you don't like him—"

Alice spun around, "Who says I don't like him?"

"Alice, it's Kevin. You've never given him a second look. Don't you think this is just a rebound? Someone to make you feel secure? A band aid?"

Alice flopped onto the sofa. "Give me a little credit, Tess. I'm not an idiot." She took a gulp of water and laid her head back. "I know I never gave him the time of day, but when Beau—" she swallowed. "When everything changed, and you weren't talking to anyone, we became close."

"Close?"

"Not like that," Alice said with a glare. "It's just, he's, I don't know, not like the other guys. Besides, I'm not sleeping with him, so he's got no ulterior motive or anything. I actually like being with him."

"Do you guys even talk?"

"Yeah, surprising as it might sound, we talk a lot—about everything." She looked away, then back at Tess. "I told him everything. It just came out one night when you were out with Louie. I told him about all the men. Tess, I told him everything."

Tess's jaw dropped. "No way."

"Way. And you know what? I feel so much better having told him. It's like the attack, feeling so vulnerable when I thought I was so in control, it took away the façade, all that awful anger came rushing out that night."

"Oh, Alice," Tess put her hand on Alice's hand.

"It's okay, really," Alice wiped a tear from the corner of her eye. "He got it. He understood, and you want to know the best part? He didn't judge me, he didn't pry, didn't get jealous or make me feel like a loser, or a slut," she blushed, sat up. "He just listened. That's it, listened, and you know what? It felt good." She shrugged, "He's been coming over ever since. It's nice."

Kevin came through the front door, "Hey, Tess, how's Louie? Have you told him yet?"

"Told him what?" she looked at Alice out of the corner of her eye.

Alice lifted her eyebrow, put her hands up in surrender.

"Jesus, Alice." Tess sneered.

"Really? You can't believe that I wouldn't notice." Kevin put a hand next to Alice on the back of the couch and mumbled under his breath, "There's no hiding a basketball."

"As long as we're coming clean," Alice glanced at Kevin, who looked away, "I'm really sorry for not telling you that I was going to Beau's memorial. I should have told you," Alice looked down at her hands.

Kevin sat down next to Alice, "Yeah, me, too."

The familiar smell of Kevin's Old Spice stirred Tess's memories of the four of them: Beau, Kevin, Alice, and Tess. Tess's leg bounced, her chest constricted. She thought of their last night together as a group, the week before Beau had left, when they'd been playing the stranger game. Tess remembered the playful look in Beau's eyes, the way he had spoken directly to her, as if she were the only person in the room—quintessential Beau. That night, Beau had chosen Louie as the target of their game, when his impending trip had tarnished the usual levity of the game.

"Oh, no," Tess said, interrupting a conversation between Alice and Kevin.

"What? You sort of spaced out there for a minute," Kevin said.

"It all makes sense," she said quietly, as if talking to herself. "This is a huge mistake." Tess stood, heading for the door. "It was Louie, at Olazzo's that night. Remember? The stranger game? Now I get it. I've gotta go." She grabbed her purse and keys. "I can't do this. What was I thinking?"

Alice hurried down the hall with her. "Tess, what's wrong? So what if he was the guy? What's the big deal?"

Tess pushed the elevator button, her face strained and tight, "Don't you see? It's a sign. I have no business being with him or anyone else right now." She stepped into the elevator, "Besides, I think he's married."

Tess climbed into her Prius and dialed Louie's cell phone number.

Louie's enthusiastic voice greeted her, "Hey!"

Tess clenched the phone, her voice caught in her throat. What on Earth had she been thinking? It was so obvious—the phone calls, the need to rush away at any moment.

"Tess?"

"I can't do this. I can't see you anymore," Tess said and hung up the phone. The strange realization that it was Saturday came to mind. She'd be alone on Sunday once again. Tess leaned her forehead against the steering wheel and cried, ignoring the ringing of the phone.

Germany

Edham looked on with wide eyes as the convoy of armored vehicles moved along the road on its way from the airport to the army base. He began to speak in quick, excited sentences. His mother immediately shushed him, pressing him tightly against her ribs in the rear seat of the vehicle.

Beau turned at the sound of the boy's excited voice. Edham smiled, a rare sight over the past few days.

Samira chastised Edham with a sharp whisper, her fearful tone did not go unnoticed by Beau. Edham's face became somber.

Zeid's tiny jaw muscles worked furiously in tune to his clenching teeth.

They rode the rest of the way in silence.

Beau breathed a sigh of relief when the army base came into sight. Samira's face hung heavily, her lips turned down at the ends, the soft curves of her cheeks indiscernible. She'd aged ten years in the past few days. Beau wondered if the hopeful wonder would ever return to her eyes. He reached over the back of the seat and touched her hand.

"Samira?" he quickly realized she had to use the name she was given on her new identification, Ai'ishah. Their new identities were going to be difficult to remember. The children's lives were forever changed. All that they knew was gone. They'd been thrown into a foreign world. Beau pulled back his hand, lowering his eyes.

Samira raised her eyes, full of sadness. Suha's death had left her empty.

He reached over the seat again, and this time he took her hand in his. Using what he'd hoped was correct Arabic, he whispered, "Aasef. I'm sorry."

Tears slipped down her cheek. Athra reached up and touched the tear with her tiny index finger, then rested her cheek against her mother's chest.

Maryland

Tess drove up the hill toward her home. Just as she turned into the driveway, a car flew past her.

"Slow down!"

Louie's angry voice startled Tess. She climbed out of the car and spun around, looking for him. How had she missed his car, parked directly across the street?

"Damned kids," Louie murmured, still looking in the direction of the speeding car which was now long gone.

Tess hurried past him without acknowledgment.

Louie sidled up next to her on the cement walkway. "Tess, wait!" he pleaded. "What's wrong?"

She fumbled for her house key, ignoring the question, her blood pressure rising with every second. She dropped the keys and bent to get them, Louie bent down as well, their heads colliding.

"Ouch!" she yanked the keys from his hands and quickly unlocked the door.

"Tess," he pushed his way inside, "do you mind telling me what the hell is going on? You're acting crazy."

She stopped, turned toward him, teeth clenched, "Crazy? I'm not acting crazy. This is the first sane thing I've done in what seems like forever."

"Damn it, Tess. What is it? Is it the baby?" the words were out of his mouth before he had time to think.

Tess's jaw dropped open, "How—"

Louie's voice softened, "Come on, really? Have you looked in a mirror? How could I miss it?" Louie turned away, "Just because you don't say something out loud doesn't mean it isn't real," he said.

Tess spun on her heels and raced upstairs.

Louie found her standing in front of the full-length mirror in her bedroom—the distressed look in her eyes as blatant as the belly itself.

What had she seen in the mirror every day? How did she miss what was so obvious—the arc protruding from her abdomen?

"Did you think I wouldn't notice?" Louie said from behind her.

Tears sprang to Tess's eyes. "I don't know what I thought. It doesn't matter anyway." She sat on the edge of the bed, her hands hanging at her sides, her head bowed.

"At first I thought maybe you were just gaining weight or something, but, well, when you kept getting a little bigger every week, I figured it out. It doesn't change how I feel, Tess."

"It's not yours," her voice was nearly a whisper.

He laughed. "Yeah, well, the last time I looked, it still took sex to make a baby."

"I guess that was a dumb thing to say."

"If it's not the baby, then what is it? Why do you want to stop seeing me?" Louie's voice cracked. "I want to be with you," he reached over to put his hand on her belly, "and this baby is part of you—"

Tess pushed his hand away. She was so confused. How could she describe the tingle in her stomach when they were together, the way her heart soared each time the phone rang, and the disappointment that felt like a physical blow when it wasn't him calling? How could she admit that while she carried her husband's baby, it was him she longed to feel inside her, and that the guilt that followed the desire had swallowed her whole? How could she voice the sadness over her lingering doubts—

Madonna's "Vogue" broke the uncomfortable silence.

Tess rolled her eyes and left the room, leaving Louie to answer his call in private. Two minutes later, Louie came out of the bedroom, his face pale, his eyebrows furrowed.

"I…I have to go," he said quietly.

"Of course you do," Tess said and stormed into her bedroom, slamming the door behind her.

Louie clenched his jaw in time to the ringing of the cell phone which lay on the seat beside him. He couldn't bring himself to ignore it and answered.

"What?" He wondered how long he could keep this up. He knew the answer—he was all she had.

"I think someone's trying to get out of the basement," panic flew through the airwaves.

Louie rolled his eyes. Her raspy voice grated on his nerves. *Not today.* "There's no one in the basement," his tone was firm.

"I hear them, they're turning the handle. Maybe I should call the police?"

"Karen, I promise, there's no one in the basement. Just go back to the couch and relax. I'll be over as soon as I can." He turned the car around and let out a sigh. "How much have you had to drink today?"

"Nothing."

"Karen."

"I…I was thinking of her and…and…" her voice trailed off.

You and I both. "I'm on my way."

Tess balanced her cell phone on her shoulder as she spoke to Alice and simultaneously stuffed her clothes into a small suitcase. "What do we have going on the next few days? I think I need to get away for a while." She had to figure out her life, and she knew she couldn't do it with Louie and his wife, or girlfriend, at the ready.

"Just the one position. Are you alright?" Alice asked.

Tess took a deep breath. Was she being fair to Alice? It'd only been a month since she'd been attacked. Thanksgiving was fast approaching, and the thought of facing the memories the holiday would stir made Tess's heartbeat race. Would she have to sit across the table from the long faces of her mother and father-in-law? Could she do it? Even more importantly, should she make an appearance? Would Beau want her to? *What am I doing?* "I don't know. I can stay if you need me to. Geez, I'm such a selfish bitch, aren't I?" She pulled the shirts from her suitcase and threw them onto the bed. "Here you're dealing with real life-altering issues, and I'm the one running away."

"Don't be silly. I'm fine. I told you, I'm almost thankful that asshole attacked me. I'm better now. Really."

"You're sure?" she tentatively stuffed the shirts back into the suitcase, the tension easing from her shoulders. "Think you can wrap that one up yourself?" Tess asked. "I'm going to Ocean City, I think." *Where'd that come from?* Tess wondered. She had only been to Ocean City once, with Beau, the previous summer.

"'Course. Ocean City?"

"I don't know, I guess. I have to go someplace where I can think. Someplace that's not here," she zipped the suitcase with determination. "Sure you can handle it?" Tess took a deep breath. She rested her hand on her stomach. She could do this. She would do this. "I mean really hold down the fort? No cell phones, no access to me?"

Alice's voice strained, "Sure. Are you alright?"

Tess nodded, then realized Alice couldn't hear her nod. "Fine, I just need to...put this whole thing to rest, and I can't do it here. It's too—" *hard, sad, confusing, emotionally wrenching?* She said goodbye to Alice, wondering what in the hell her going away would accomplish.

Her phone rang, the backlight illuminated Louie's name on the screen. Tess pushed the Ignore button and turned her cell phone off. She didn't want to hear his excuses. It occurred to her that she had yet to hear any type of excuse or explanation from Louie about his mysterious phone calls, and if that was how he wanted to play it, well, that was just fine with her. The last thing she needed in her life was more drama.

A streak of light filtered in through the drawn curtains. Cigarette smoke hovered in the air like mist in the rainforest. Louie found Karen slumped on the couch, an empty bottle of Scotch lying on the floor. Her eyes were closed, her gray hair matted and greasy, the thin cotton sweater she wore buttoned askew. He sighed, picked up the bottle.

"Sorry," Karen slurred.

Louie clenched his teeth. He carried the bottle into the kitchen and stopped dead in his tracks. The kitchen table was covered with photographs, framed and loose. Louie's face fell flat. He lowered himself into an oak chair and set the bottle on the tile floor. He lifted a thick silver frame, staring into the eyes of his dead fiancée, Rebecca. He ran his index finger along her two-dimensional face, the outline of her brown hair. *Bec.* It had been almost a year since he'd packed away the photographs, or rather the shrine, he'd erected in his living room, months since he'd come home in the evenings and told those photographs about his day—about how nothing mattered anymore since she'd gone. He set the frame back down on the table and gathered a stack of photos—their engagement pictures. Nausea, or maybe it was just plain pain, swelled in the pit of his stomach. Her eyes looked right into his soul, and it felt as if she knew his despair had been easing. Tess had changed him. She'd mattered. She'd needed him.

"I'm sorry, Bec," he said.

"Lou-ie?" Karen leaned against the door jamb, her body swaying.

Louie closed his eyes. If Rebecca's death had stolen Louie's reason for being, it had just about killed her mother. Karen's occasional drink had turned into a nine A.M. ritual, at first, to get her over her only daughter's senseless death, and as the days passed slowly into weeks, drinking had become the only way she could make it from one hour to the next. Louie had seen her addiction evolving, he'd even tried to convince her to stop, but he'd been trying to survive his own internal battle. Rising each day to show up at work had become a chore. He'd let phone calls and deadlines slip. If not for the determination of his partners, he'd never have been able to redeem himself. The firm suffered. Excuses came like coffee on a fatigue-filled day, often and necessary.

He lifted the engagement photo that had run in his hometown newspaper: Rebecca sat on a swing, looking over her shoulder and into his eyes. A chill ran through him. He remembered seeing the message on his desk, *Rebecca, 2:17, please call asap.* His pulse fevered. The unanswerable questions returned to plague him. Why hadn't he called her back right away? Why had he left her waiting for two hours? He'd returned the call of four clients, all while his silenced cell phone gathered message after frantic message from Rebecca. It had been a cold October afternoon, the type of day where gray engulfed not only the sky, but every breath you took, chilling you to the bone. Rebecca had gone to meet a new client in southeast D.C. He hadn't thought anything of it. As a social worker, Rebecca often visited clients in unsavory areas. She knew how to handle herself. "I'm careful," she'd told him. "I can spot the danger signs."

For weeks, he'd replayed her messages.

"I had a great meeting. The boy's parents are really trying to clean up their act." Her voice grew tense. *"Uh-oh, some guys are leaning on my car. Jesus Christ, really?"* she sighed, hung up.

Goddamn clients.

"Louie, please pick up." Silence. *"I just want you on the phone. They're not moving, and I'm almost to the car. I'm just gonna turn around and go back to the complex."*

She spoke so quickly, high whispers—she could have been playing a prank.

"They're following me. Louie, I'm scared."

It was no prank.

"Stop it. Stop! Help!"

The phone landed on the pavement with a crack. The line had gone dead.

Chapter Seventeen

The smell of saltwater drenched the air as Tess drove across the low bridge and the tips of the Ocean City hotels came into view. The last time she'd crossed that bridge, she and Beau had cheered. The memory of their anticipation of the spur-of-the-moment getaway brought a smile to her lips. She touched her belly, "Oh, Beau," she sighed.

She pulled onto the main drag, telltale signs of the beach town lined the road. Brightly-colored surf shops and the boardwalk eased the tension in Tess's shoulders. Her previous worries momentarily set aside. Even in the cold of almost-winter, people walked along the streets. The attire was different, sweatshirts instead of bathing suits, but the aura of a carefree existence remained. She reached for her cell phone to call Alice and let her know she'd arrived, then remembered she was on a communication-free vacation, the cell phone nicely hidden in the trunk of the car. She smiled. *Cool,* she thought, and her hand drifted back to the steering wheel. She inhaled the calming sea air and blew it out slowly. "I can do this," she said. "This is good."

Tess felt like a kid playing hooky in her hooded sweatshirt and sweatpants which were about all that fit her anymore. She grabbed her bags from the trunk, momentarily contemplated her cell phone, decided it was better off out of sight, then slammed the trunk shut.

The condo was just as fresh as she'd remembered. She laid her bags on the over-stuffed white couch, taking in the soothing hues of the ocean-blue recliner and sky-blue shag carpet. As seventies as it seemed, the shag carpet fit perfectly into the vacation feel of the condo. Tess swung open the balcony door and stepped into the brisk air, wondering why it was that the ocean brought such a sense of openness, while the city made her feel closed. She was glad she'd stopped for a pack of virgin strawberry daiquiris on the way. She grabbed one from her bag and put the rest in the empty refrigerator. If she couldn't drink, at least she could pretend to drown her sorrows.

Her heartbeat quickened as she opened the kitchen drawer and reached for the thickest, shiniest coaster she could find. She ran her hands over the cool ceramic. A chill ran up her spine—a ghost of times remembered. Tess closed her eyes, relishing the security the coaster brought to her.

An hour and two lame daiquiris later, Tess showered and headed out for a walk. The cold air stung her face, whipping her hair behind her. She was pleasantly surprised to find most of the stores remained open so late in the season. She walked through a small gift shop, touching the rough lines of the painted shells and smooth curves of the wave-beaten rocks. She read through gift cards, her heart sinking with longing for Beau.

She walked down the windy boardwalk. If she concentrated hard enough, Tess could feel Beau's thick palm in her own, though his smile eluded her, just out of reach of her memory. She furrowed her brow, trying to push his image free of the ties that bound it, the ties that had been so necessary in order for her to keep her sanity.

Children's laughter flitted through the air. Tess sat on the edge of the boardwalk, her legs kicking up and down. She leaned back, resting one hand on her belly. Her hand lifted, not of her volition. Her eyes grew wide, dropping to stare at her belly. She pressed her hand tighter against the mound. A moment later, the same sensation, only softer, pressed upon her palm. "Oh, my God," Tess said, her face tight. Again, she felt the flutter in her belly. "Oh, my God, oh, my—" A grin stretched across her face, then quickly faded. Had she somehow missed this sensation before? Had her thoughts been so tangled up that she'd been oblivious to the life growing within her? She pressed her hand harder, willing the baby to kick. A momentary flutter whispered across her palm. She looked around, excited to tell someone about the life within her, the life she'd been ignoring, the sensations she'd been blocking from her mind, dismissing as normal aches and pains. She bit her lower lip, breathing hard and fast. Tears slipped down her cheeks. She was actually doing it—she was going to have a baby, Beau's baby. Tess cried at the revelation, laughing through the tears.

A twenty-something guy in surfer shorts and a sweatshirt approached Tess, his hand outstretched, a flyer flapping in the wind. "Cool duds at the Surf Pro Shop," he said, then noticed her tears. "Oh, uh, sorry," he mumbled awkwardly, turning quickly away.

Tess wiped her eyes, the smile glued across her face. She walked down the boardwalk, calculating how long Beau had been gone, how many weeks it had been since her last period, and how, in total, it equated to about five months. *Five months. Can that be right?* she wondered. She thought of the images she'd seen on the computer the first day she'd found out she was pregnant and what the baby would look like at five months of gestation. Her hand moved once again to her belly.

Tess wondered if passersby noticed her elation. She was sure that she had an aura of light around her. She had changed. It seemed that everywhere she looked, she noticed mothers with their children, the way the fathers looked proud, protective. She had abruptly become someone other than Tess Johnson, Business Owner and Grieving Wife. She was going to be Tess Johnson, Mother. She'd joined the millions of other women in a silent sisterhood, one of the esteemed women giving knowing looks to each other. She would know the pain of childbirth and the love described by mothers as larger than life itself. Even Tess's gait had changed. Instead of hurrying, looking for a distraction, hunching just enough to try and hide her belly, she stood tall, thrusting her pregnant belly out a little further.

Chapter Eighteen

Curled up in front of the television, Tess half-watched, half-thought about her life. She thought of Beau and all that he'd miss, that he'd already missed. She thought vaguely about going out to find a wifi café, feeling the pull—albeit a weak one—to check Skype just one more time.

Tess sat up and leaned forward, conscious, for the first time, of the way she had to lift her torso upward in order to lean forward comfortably. *When does one more time end?* she wondered. She shook her head and spoke as if she were convincing someone other than herself, "You can't do this. He's not coming back. You're raising this baby alone. You're moving forward." She sighed and leaned back against the soft pillows. The corners of her lips twitched downward, a stream of tears followed. Tess let her body fall to the side. "It's not fair," she whispered. "It's just not fair."

Morning found Tess sitting on the couch clutching a crumpled piece of paper on which she'd written:

1.Do not think about Beau OR Louie!

2.Find myself, be alone, get strong

3.Read about babies

That was as far as she'd gotten. She lay back, rubbing her stomach. An unexpected laugh escaped her lips. How could she think Louie wouldn't notice that she was pregnant? There she went, thinking of Louie. No more, she reminded herself. She could get through this, and she'd be damned if she needed some man by her side. No, she corrected herself, she would get through this.

Tess walked along the beach, her sweats rolled up, thick sweatshirt bulging. The sun rose, warming the air to a comfortable degree. She took a picture for a young couple, and got a Henna tattoo of a pocket watch on her forearm, with the words, *until we meet again,* written above it. Lunch was Boardwalk Fries, again, and then she headed back to the beach where she sat for hours, thinking of nothing in particular and watching families pass by. The rhythmic tug and pull of the surf soothed her sorrow. She lay back, listening to the crashing waves against the shore and their soft roll as they retreated from the beach. Spray from the waves dotted her face—the smell of saltwater filled her senses. Tess closed her eyes and imagined what her life would be like with a baby on her hip. How would she work? Find daycare? Would she be a good mother? She envisioned the baby, a girl, she was sure, with a mop of dark hair, thick like Beau's, and blue eyes like her own. The warmth of the sun beat down on her face, lulling her into a light nap.

Tess awoke to her stomach growling. "Don't you worry, little one, I'll feed you." She patted her stomach, swelling with pride. It was Thursday, she realized, *Sandwich night*. She and Beau had named nights by what they'd done together, Thursday was sandwich night, Friday was book and brew night, hitting Barnes and Noble and a local brewery, Monday was fix-it-yourself night, where they ate leftovers or whatever looked enticing at the moment. Revisiting old habits brought the ever-present shadow of sadness.

She drove toward the convenience store, the slow drivers plucking at her nerves. By the time she reached the convenience store, she could feel the redness in her cheeks, knew there was a sneer on her lips. *Goddamn sandwich night.* She shouldn't have to do this alone. Who was she kidding?

She walked determinedly into the store, picked up bread and turkey, and stared accusingly at the roast beef, Beau's favorite. Tears welled in her eyes. Damn it. She turned away and strode toward the register.

"Hungry?" The kid behind the register couldn't have been more than eighteen years old, with surf-ready bangs that hid his eyes and a rail-skinny body.

Too many drugs and not enough food, Tess thought to herself. "Yes," she said, pushing her money across the counter.

"Cool," he reached for the money, moving as if he were in slow motion.

Tess's foot tapped. Her impatience at ineptitude had returned, taking her by surprise. She hadn't felt that particular frustration since she'd arrived. She stilled her foot. "Thank you," she said.

"No prob. Enjoy," the kid said.

Tess put the food away, thinking of the young cashier, and envying his relaxed attitude. She poured herself a virgin daiquiri. *At this rate I'd be drunk every day,* she chuckled. She reached for a napkin, stopping mid-reach. The coasters were still in the drawer, but she could feel them in her hand. Her nerves tingled. Oh, how she'd missed the safety and neatness of the coasters! She retrieved the stack of them from the drawer, welcoming their familiar size and shape. She set them out on the small round table in a perfect parade in order of color, darkest to lightest, then reversing the order. She stacked them, widest to narrowest, then replaced them in the original order she'd arranged. She spread her hands flat on the table before her, as if she could create an impenetrable space between her and the coasters, and stared at them. Her heartbeat quickened, pounding against her chest, her obsession returning.

The first time the coasters had soothed her, she'd been only a child. Her father and mother had been fighting—again. It had seemed to seven-year-old Tess that they fought almost every day and there was nothing she could do about it. Tess remembered the sinking feeling in the pit of her stomach, the fear as she had withdrawn to the kitchen, and the calming sensation the coasters had brought.

She closed her eyes now, as she remembered the party she'd thrown for Beau, the way she'd felt when Kevin hadn't used a coaster. The way she'd felt when Beau had. Goosebumps formed on her arms. The return of her desire to control the coasters pressed in on her. She didn't know if she was climbing out of her depression, or falling back into it.

"Goddamn it!"

Chapter Nineteen

Friday morning, Tess was up with the sun and full of determination. She pedaled down the main drag, driven by her newfound conviction. She'd take control of her life, and she'd be damned if she'd let self-pity—or men—dissuade her. At six-fifty, she pulled up in front of the convenience store. It was closed. She decided to wait the ten minutes for it to open, parked her bike, and impatiently tapped her foot on the pavement. At five after seven, she paced, her arms crossed across her chest. At seven-twenty, she threw her hands up in the air and climbed back onto her bike.

Surfer-boy walked around the corner, his shirt rumpled, hair askew, eyes barely open. "Oh, hey," he said, nonchalantly, "Sorry I'm late. Rough night," he laughed.

"Right," Tess climbed back down from her bike and stood behind him, breathing heavily.

"Wrapped a little tight?" he said in an I-have-no-idea-I'm-being-rude fashion.

Tess walked past him and grabbed a Luna Bar and a bottle of water. She slammed them on the counter and looked away.

"Luna Bar? Dude, do you even know what you're eating? This stuff isn't fit for animals."

"I'm not a dude, and yes, I know exactly what I'm eating. I've been eating them for ten years."

"Gnarly," he said and rang up her purchase. He put the items in a bag, held it close to his chest, and stared at her.

"What?" Tess snapped.

The left side of his lips lifted into a cockeyed smile. He shrugged. "Just trying to figure you out. You're here alone, right?"

Not by choice. Tess rolled her eyes.

"To de-stress? Isn't that what you call it, de-stressing?" When she didn't answer he said, "Chillin', you know."

Tess sighed loudly and reached her hand out for the bag.

"Thought so. You know, this is the perfect place for chillin'. That's why I'm here."

"Is it now?" she asked.

He nodded. "Yup, taking a year off from my master's program. Physics."

Tess smirked.

"I know, right? Me, physics? That's what everyone thinks. I'm smart. 3.8 GPA."

Tess felt her jaw slacken.

"You see me, and you think, that dude's nothin', lazy kid who does nothin' but hang at the beach." He handed her his bag and turned away to straighten the shelves.

Tess flushed. He was dead-on. She was such a mess, even her efforts at relaxing had failed. She could be there to help Alice heal, but she couldn't even keep a band aid on her own wounds. She walked out the door, her head hung a little lower than it was when she'd first arrived.

Tess stood on the balcony watching the sunrise, contemplating her latest craving—bacon and eggs. She showered, dressed, and drove back to the convenience store.

"Forget something?" surfer boy asked with a touch of sarcasm.

Tess ignored his remark. She was feeling more in control by the moment, and she wasn't going to let some college dropout ruin her morning. She grabbed the groceries and set them on the counter.

"You are hungry," he said, slowly picking up each item, inspecting it for a price, and then punching the numbers into the cash register. "Cool, bacon."

"Can you please just hurry?" *Shit, that was rude.* "Sorry, I'm just hungry."

He stopped ringing up the items and looked at her. "Got a date or just hungry?" he ran his hand through his hair, revealing eyes an even brighter blue than Tess's.

"Uh...hungry," Tess fiddled with her wallet.

"Y'oughtta try English's breakfast buffet. It's the bomb."

"Thanks, I'll do that," she said, wishing he'd hurry.

He totaled the register and looked toward the door, making no effort to take Tess's money. "Ya know," he said, "I used to be like you, all tied up in knots all the time, rushing from one thing to the next. Then I realized that life is going to happen whether I rush through it or not." He shrugged and accepted her money. "Might as well enjoy it a little."

Tess wondered why getting back into her old routine made her feel like she was relaxing, when all it was really doing was creating a mandate for things she had to get done in a specific fashion.

As she drove toward the condo, she thought of surfer boy. What right did he have to make her feel bad about her life? She had finally been feeling more in control. Damn it! Heat rushed up her chest. By the time she arrived she was livid. She walked in the door, picked up the socks she'd left on the floor, threw away the bottle from her daiquiri, lined up the coasters, and vacuumed and dusted the entire condo. She flopped on to the couch. She was back. She was in control. *Damn you surfer and your wayward ideas.* We'll see where you end up in two years. "Physics," she laughed.

Still, she couldn't shake the feeling that her life was spiraling in a whirlpool and she was just trying to stay afloat. *Maybe I am tied in knots. Stuck.* Tess thought about Beau. "He's not coming back," she said aloud. She knew she had to let him go, but she had, hadn't she? She'd boxed up his belongings. She'd even kissed Louie. *What am I doing? How can I create a future for my baby if I can't move beyond the past?*

Tess packed and unpacked her bag—twice. She stormed into the kitchen and put the coasters ceremoniously into the drawer. "I don't need you," she scoffed, and slapped her hands together as if wiping off dirt.

Tess parked in front of the convenience store, which was closed, of course, and handwrote a note. *Thank you. If you ever need help finding a professional job, call me.* She crumpled it up, and began again. *Thank you,* she wrote, and signed it, *the pregnant woman who was tied in knots. Pregnant.* Just writing the word made her happy. She headed toward English's for their breakfast buffet, and then drove toward home, determined to set her life on the right path.

Tess watched the beach town fall away in the rearview mirror. "Okay, gnarly boy, here goes. Time to let go, enjoy life."

Tess breezed through the front door of her house, pausing momentarily as thoughts of Beau billowed around her. She pushed the thoughts of him away, determined not to spend any more time pining for someone who would never return. She threw her bags on the couch, each step toward the front door filled with resolve. *Enjoy life a little,* she thought. *That's just what I intend to do.*

The house phone rang as she pulled the door closed behind her. She stood on the porch contemplating the phone call. Her heartbeat sped up as she listened to the incessant ringing. She put her keys into the lock and turned, feeling the deadbolt slide open. There was a tightening around Tess's eyes. She bit her lower lip and shook her head, *No. I'm not doing this. No more pining.* She spun on her heels, pulled the door closed behind her, and headed for her car.

Tess started the Prius and gripped the leather steering wheel, her muscles taut. She took a deep breath, exhaling slowly as she turned off the car and climbed back out, heading for the house.

Tess opened the drawer next to the refrigerator and stared at the coasters. "Shut up," she commanded. She gathered them, fumbling with the awkward mass in her arms. Tess stared at them for a long time, her parents' arguments echoed in her mind. She understood the reasons she felt the need to control her environment, but even with that control, that modicum of making things right in her life, Beau still was taken away. *Let go of your crutches, Tess,* she told herself. She tried forcing a laugh, emitting a half-grunt instead.

Tess thought of Alice and all she'd been through, her need to control the intimacy in her life. She thought of

Kevin's visits, how they abruptly ended when she wouldn't let Beau go, and how much she missed his positive energy. *Control.* She tried to attach some element of control to Beau's need for international exposure. "Come on," she urged herself. Her shoulders slumped. It was no use. Beau hadn't been seeking control at all. She leaned against the counter, talking as if she were speaking to a friend. "He's gone. All the coasters in the world won't bring him back." She closed her eyes, willing herself to be strong. She held the coasters above the trash, hesitated and turned back to the drawer. "You're a crutch!" she seethed. "You didn't do a damn thing but distract me." Tess's face reddened. "I'm tired of waiting, tired of wondering." She quickly threw the pile of coasters into the trash, breathing heavily and staring blankly at the colors and shapes which seemed to be pointing at her. Before she could change her mind, she rushed out the front door.

Germany

The dirt on Beau's hands and face felt as if it were ground into his skin. He reached up to run his hand through his hair, his fingers caught in the tangled mess. He craved a real shower.

Samira and her children sat on metal chairs just outside the small room where Beau sat in front of a large army-issue desk, the black telephone before him. He would finally hear her voice. His heart leapt against his chest as he dialed her cell phone number. The ringing phone was like music to his ears. *Pick up, Tess. Please, pick up.*

"Hi, this is Tess Johnson. You've reached my voice mail."

"Damn," Beau disconnected the call and dialed their home phone number so fast that he almost misdialed. He breathed hard, anticipating her voice—six rings, seven, eight. Beau closed his eyes, wondering why the answering machine wasn't picking up. He wanted so badly to speak to Tess that his chest ached with disappointment.

Beau took a deep breath and dialed Kevin's number. He answered on the second ring.

"Kevin? It's Beau," Beau listened to the stunned silence. "Kevin?"

"Who is this?" Kevin sounded as if he might climb through the phone line and pummel him.

"Kevin! It's me. It's Beau, man. I'm in Germany."

"What the—"

"Kevin, listen. Do you know where Tess is?" he asked. Before Kevin could answer he said, "Listen, Kev, there was an accident, but I survived it. It's a long story, but listen, please. I'm coming home."

"Beau?"

Beau pushed past the shock in Kevin's voice, unable to slow his words. "I want to surprise Tess. I couldn't reach her, but, please, don't tell her I'm coming home. I've got a day of processing here, but then I'm coming home," the words tasted sweet on Beau's tongue. "I'm coming home, man. Can you get me at the airport?"

"What? Yeah," Kevin took a deep breath. "Beau, we thought you were dead," his voice cracked with emotion. A moment of silence stretched between them. "Man, it's good to hear your voice. Are you okay? What are you doing in Germany?"

"I'll tell you everything when I get back, it's complicated. Please, Kevin, don't tell Tess. I want to be the one to tell her. I want to see her face. God, I want to see her face." Beau reached for Tess's picture. "Don't tell anyone, okay?" Beau pleaded, excited about his plan.

"What about your parents? They had a memorial for you. God, Beau, you're alive, man, alive!"

Sadness settled as a lump in Beau's throat. He was unable to hold back the tears that filled his eyes. "Don't say a word—to anyone. I want to tell them," his voice cracked. *My parents.* He wiped his eyes on his sleeve. "I wanna be the one to tell them, please."

Two American soldiers entered the barren, narrow hallway, their boots clomping loudly as they neared Samira. She stared at the floor, twisting her hands nervously in her lap. A rush of cool air startled Samira as the men passed by. She wished Beau would come out of the room. She looked at her children, each on a cold metal chair, dark moons under their little eyes, the boys' feet swaying beneath them, Athra's curled under her little body. Fear prickled Samira's limbs. Where would she go? What would she do without Suha? She couldn't speak the language, save for a few broken sentences. What had she been thinking? She'd had no business leaving Iraq. Who was she to think she could give her children something more than a life of fear? They'd still live in fear, she thought, just a different type of fear.

Beau sat in the empty chair next to Samira and let out a long sigh.

"All is good?" she asked in a tiny, tentative voice.

Fear shadowed Samira's eyes. Lines had formed around her lips, and her body sagged, fatigued. She watched Beau as he looked down at his own clothing, then back at the children's—stained, wrinkled, their eyes haunted, untrusting. Embarrassment reddened her cheeks.

Edham slipped off his chair and walked sleepily to Beau who lifted him off of the linoleum floor and into his lap without so much as a thought. Edham had become like a fifth limb.

Samira watched her son settle against Beau's chest. Her lower lip began to quiver. Beau reached for her hand, entwining his fingers with hers, and squeezed, ever so lightly. The ends of her lips lifted, and she closed her eyes.

It was Zeid who spoke the truth, rattling Beau to his core. "No one wants special marbles."

Chapter Twenty

Beau looked out the window of the airplane as it descended onto the runway. *I never thought Dulles Airport would look so good,* he thought.

Edham's nails dug into his arm.

"It's okay, buddy," Beau said, and he glanced at Samira across the aisle. Beau looked into her beautiful, dark eyes and thought he saw a twinkle of hope. He smiled.

The plane jolted forward as it touched down, then slowed with the high-pitched sound of speed against brakes.

Athra screamed.

Samira wrapped her thin arms around Athra's tiny, shaking body, and looked over her shoulder at Beau, a pleading look in her eyes.

"She's scared. She remembers Suha," Beau said, then reached across the aisle and touched Samira's back, as if to say, *It's okay, I'm right here.*

Athra calmed, and Edham clenched Beau's arm in a death grip. Zeid stared straight ahead, his muscles taut. Beau knew it must have taken all of Zeid's will not to let his fear become apparent.

"Samira?" The gray-haired woman extended her hand, accompanied by a broad, welcoming smile. "This must be Zeid, Edham, and Athra. I'm Sandra Wallace, Colonel Larner had asked that we get you settled at the army base for a few days, just until you're situated with where you'll be staying."

Kevin thought his heart might explode. Emotions bubbled up within him. Beau was alive, there, standing right in front of him. He walked past the little gray-haired woman with his arms open wide. "Beau!" he gushed.

Tears welled in Beau's eyes as he pushed into Kevin's arms.

"Man, I can't believe you're here. Hell, I can't believe you're alive," Kevin said.

"I'm very much alive," Beau laughed, then hugged Kevin again.

"Come on, let's get you home."

Beau turned back toward Samira, who stood silently behind him, holding Athra, Edham, and Zeid at her side. His smile faded, the reality of what being home meant coalesced with the joy of his long-awaited arrival. He put a protective arm on Samira's lower back.

"Samira, this is Kevin. Kevin, this is Samira, and Zeid, Edham, and Athra."

"Nice to meet you," he smiled. "You met on the plane?" Kevin was anxious to leave. He'd had a hard enough time keeping Beau's secret from Tess, the last thing he wanted was a delay.

"I have so much to tell you," Kevin said, oblivious to Beau's quandary. He felt as if he might burst with happiness and wanted nothing more than to give that excitement to the woman who deserved it the most, Tess. She hadn't been the same since the news of Beau's death, and this was sure to make her world right again. "Wait until you see Tess, she's show—"

Kevin caught a worried look that passed between Samira and Beau.

Beau's hand rested on Edham's shoulder, his other arm still around Samira, a tender look on his face. The smile faded from Kevin's lips.

They'd spent forty-five minutes settling the children in the van with Samira and Sandra, whom Athra had immediately taken a liking to. Zeid hadn't spoken a word, glaring at Kevin with a scowl on his face. It had taken fifteen minutes for Beau to pry Edham's arms from around his neck. Kevin watched with interest as his friend lovingly maneuvered around what appeared to Kevin to be a newfound family.

Route 495 was bumper-to-bumper. Beau explained what had happened after the helicopter crash. He told Kevin about how Suha had found him and nursed him back to health, about their travels through the desert, and the danger his presence had brought to the group. He told Kevin about the camps, and eventually, about their escape and Suha's death.

It was almost too much for Kevin to digest. It explained Beau's loss of weight, the crisp, leathery tone of his skin, his limp, and even the weariness in his eyes— like a POW that'd finally been rescued. What Kevin didn't understand was the part of Beau's journey that had brought him and Samira together like a couple. What exactly had happened in the desert between the two of them that Beau was not telling him? He'd watched Beau's smile fade when they'd left the airport, and he'd hoped Beau wasn't thinking about the woman and her children.

Tess sat in her Prius with the engine running, windows rolled down. The cool afternoon breeze tickled her cheeks. She turned the radio up loud, mapping the quickest route to Louie's office in her mind. Her resolve strengthened. She was ready to apologize to Louie and tell him she wanted to move forward, to date him. *Date.* The word sent a tingle of excitement up Tess's arms. She lowered her hands to her belly. "We're gonna be just fine," she whispered.

Tess put the car in reverse, reaching across the passenger seat, feeling for her cell phone. She reached behind the seat, feeling with her fingers along the floor. The Prius rolled into the street as she thought, *Trunk.* She placed her foot on the brake pedal, glancing over to her right as she righted herself on the seat, then she glanced over her left shoulder. Kevin's truck moved slowly up the hill toward the house. As the truck neared, and the passenger came into focus, the hair on the back of her neck prickled. Her eyebrows pressed together as she leaned forward, straining to see more clearly, her heart galloping against her chest. Tears filled her eyes. "Beau?" escaped her lips like the wind. An engine roared somewhere in the distance. A red car flew over the hill, catching air beneath its tires.

Tess heard them scream and turned to look the other way just as the car careened into the rear of the Prius, spinning it into the air, throwing Tess against the door. Her head smacked against the window, shattering the glass like spears into her face. The world grew blurry. Tess's eyes rolled back in her head. The airbag hit her jaw and neck, slamming them back milliseconds before the car smashed into the trunk of the large weeping willow.

Just before the end, just before the car came to rest, just as the weeping willow grasped the Prius in a twisted embrace, there was a moment. There was a moment in which a wisp of consciousness flowed like vivid electricity through fluttering synapses, a moment that whistled into eternity—*Beau*—then flittered into a nothing that ever was.

Chapter Twenty-One

Beau pushed through the large double doors and into the bitter air of the intensive care unit, his facial muscles twitching. Kevin steered Beau toward the waiting room. Beau took two steps into the waiting room, then turned and walked back out.

"This is where we wait," Kevin said.

Beau shook his head, walking toward the double doors that separated the patient care area from the waiting room.

Kevin grabbed him by the arm. "Beau, this is the waiting room," he said, reading disorientation in Beau's eyes. "C'mon, buddy," he urged and guided him back.

Beau stared straight ahead, his body numb.

A gray-haired woman sat knitting, stopping every few seconds to wipe her eyes. In the seats next to Kevin, a young woman sat with her head on the shoulder of an older woman, her face drawn, her eyes rimmed in red.

Lives held on by strings, family members hoped for miracles.

Where was his goddamned miracle, Beau wondered? Had he already used it up? Was returning to the United States his one chance at good fortune? Did he somehow steal Tess's chance at survival? Was this his penance for his loyalty to Samira? Each unanswered question tightened Beau's chest. Minutes passed like hours.

"Do you want me to call your parents?" Kevin asked.

Beau shook his head. "I can't...don't."

"Want me to get you a drink?" Kevin nervously played with his keys.

Beau heard the words Kevin spoke but couldn't comprehend or focus on them. If only he'd called Tess, she wouldn't have been driving. She'd have been in the house waiting for him, or she'd have met him at the airport. *Goddamn it*. The accident was his fault. He'd been selfish to want to surprise her. Beau paced, crossing his arms over his chest. He leaned his head against the door jamb, then turned and lifted a fist above his head, poised to strike the wall.

The old woman stopped knitting and shrank back in her chair.

"C'mon," Kevin tried to bring him back to his chair.

Beau twisted out of his grip. "This is my fault," his spat. "Me and my goddamn five-year plan," he seethed. "What the fuck makes me so special?" He turned and walked to the nurses' station.

Kevin followed.

The nurse looked up from the desk, "Yes?"

"My wife is in there. How is she? What's happening?" Beau demanded.

The nurse's eyes softened, "What's your wife's name, sir?"

"Tess, Tess Johnson," he said with hope.

She looked down at the schedules before her. "The doctor is still with her. If you'll just have a seat, they'll be with you as soon as they're done evaluating her." Her voice left no room for negotiation.

Beau was not going to be dissuaded. "I want to see her," he said. "Where are they?" He took two steps to the right.

The nurse rose quickly and stood between Beau and the doors.

"Sir, you can't go into the operating room. I know you're upset, but please wait in the waiting room. I assure you, the doctor will see you as soon as they are finished." She gestured toward Kevin and escorted them back to the waiting room.

Two hours later, a tall woman wearing blue scrubs and a surgical cap came into the waiting room, "Mr. Johnson?"

Beau sprang to his feet, his heart pounding, "Yes?"

"I'm Dr. Kelly," she extended her hand.

"How is she?" Beau couldn't slow his mind or his mouth, "What's happening? Is she alive? Is she o—"

Dr. Kelly spoke calmly, "She's undergone a great deal of trauma. She's in a coma."

A pain, greater than any pain he'd endured while in Iraq, ran through Beau's heart. *Coma?*

Practiced at speaking with grieving families, Dr. Kelly urged Beau to sit and continued with her explanation. "Head trauma can cause the brain to swell. When the brain swells, the fluid pushes up against the skull. The swelling can cause the brain to push on the brain stem. We're controlling the swelling and hoping to reduce it with a drug called Mannitol."

"What if the swelling doesn't go down?" Beau's voice quivered.

"Let's hope it does," she said matter-of-factly. "This medication takes fluid from the brain and passes it through the kidneys. We'll monitor her closely." She paused, letting Beau digest the information. "The baby is fine, so far, but we'll have—"

Beau grabbed her forearm. "Baby? My wife isn't pregnant." A rush of relief swept through him. "That's the wrong person." Beau turned to Kevin with a glimmer of hope in his eyes.

Dr. Kelly flipped through her chart.

Kevin took a deep breath and opened his mouth to speak. The doctor beat him to it. "Tess Abigail Johnson?" She looked to Kevin for confirmation.

He nodded.

Beau's legs weakened, he backed into a chair and sank into it.

Kevin went to him, "I didn't say anything at first because I thought Tess would want to tell you," Kevin's face reddened, "and then, I just didn't think of it."

Beau ran his hand down his face, then lowered his face into his hands, his elbows propped on his knees.

"I'm sorry," Dr. Kelly drew her eyebrows together in confusion. "You didn't know?"

Chapter Twenty-Two

Monitors beeped in irregular rhythms. Tess lay unconscious, a ventilator mask strapped to her face, its ominous pump and suck echoed in the stark room. Sickeningly-dark purple and red bruises covered the left side of her jaw, disappearing beneath the bandages that covered all but her eyes and ran beneath the brace wrapped around her neck. Tubes ran from her arm to an intravenous fluid bag which hung beside her bed on a metal pole. Across her chest were small plastic circles with metal nubs on the top, like faux robotic nipples, each one connected to a wire that ran to another monitor, beeping in a constant tempo.

Nausea rose in Beau's throat. He stood above Tess, his hand resting upon hers, his eyes drawn toward her swollen belly and the fetal heart monitor strapped across it. Beau tensed with each approaching footstep.

"She's a very lucky woman, Mr. Johnson." Dr. Kelly's voice was soft and thoughtful as she checked the monitors. She reviewed the chart as she spoke, "The next twenty-four hours are critical."

Beau's body revolted against the words, standing stiff, refusing to turn and face her. His throat grew dry. He tried to find his voice and failed. Beau didn't want to hear about the next few hours and what could happen. He wished he could cover his ears like a child and create a silent cocoon. He wanted Dr. Kelly to tell him that everything would be fine. He needed her to assure him that his wife would be okay. He wanted assurances that he knew the doctor could not give.

Beau covered his face with his hand, trying to block the antiseptic smell that settled around him and failing to discern the stream of information that Dr. Kelly spewed. Everything felt wrong. Beau's face reddened, his breathing came in fast bursts. The sun shouldn't be shining. People in the hall shouldn't be walking around as if his life were not falling apart. The damn doctor should be hovering over Tess, making her better, not watching and waiting and speaking in terms of statistics.

"Mr. Johnson?" she touched his shoulder.

Beau bristled.

"Perhaps you should sit down. This is a lot to digest." She guided him to a chair. "Take a few deep breaths."

He did, the redness slowly drained from his face.

"That's better," she said. "The good news is that the Mannitol seems to be working, and her kidneys are draining appropriately."

Beau sat in the chair next to Tess's bed and laid his head on her hand and wept.

Darkness seeped through the blinds. A nurse came in to check on Tess, smiling at Beau in a way that said, *You're the poor husband.*

"Mr. Johnson?"

Beau lifted his head in response to the high-pitched voice. There was that pitying smile again.

"Your parents are waiting outside the ICU," she spoke matter-of-factly, unaware that they'd believed Beau to be dead. "Your wife can only have one visitor at a time."

Beau trudged wearily toward the double doors, avoiding the sorrowful glances of the nurses. The earlier surge of adrenaline had left him hollow, unable to corral his thoughts. He stopped just short of the doors. The oversized doors swung open, a grief-stricken woman who looked as if her whole life held on by a string walked in. He watched the doors shut solidly behind her. Each time the doors opened, he tried to walk through them. He was unable, his feet heavy as lead. He knew his parents needed to see him as much as he needed to see them. He craved his father's strength, the sound of his deep voice, *You're lookin' good, son. We're proud of you.* He envisioned his mother, her sandy bob bouncing as she'd run up and hug him like she'd never let go. Just the thought of the surge of emotion made Beau dizzy. He backed against the wall, sliding down, resting on his heels. Beau rubbed the back of his neck, wincing at the crick that was on its way to full-blown pain.

His legs grew cold. He used the wall for support as he rose to his feet.

"Are you okay, sir?" It was the petite nurse who had told him his parents were there to see him.

He stared at her, unseeing.

She touched his arm. "Sir? Do you need a doctor?"

Red lights blinked on the walls, and a calm, electronic voice boomed from a loudspeaker above Beau. "Code blue, room 242. Code blue, room 242."

Two men in scrubs rushed past Beau and the nurse.

"That's Tess's room!" Beau yelled and pushed past the nurse. "Tess!"

A nurse stopped him from entering the room. He peered around her, "What's going on?" Through the window behind the nurse he saw the two men in scrubs, their voices silenced by the closed door. Their actions were swift. One of them grabbed something from the wall. "What's that? What's he doing?" Beau's voice cracked.

The taller of the men looked down at Tess's stomach, then up at the other man. His eyebrows pulled together. He shook his head.

"Defibrillator," the nurse said. "They'll take good care of her. They're the best code team around."

Dr. Kelly pushed past them and entered the room. A second later, the blinds were closed.

"She's stable," Dr. Kelly said, watching for the telltale sign of relief, for Beau's shoulders to drop a quarter inch. They didn't. "She stopped breathing, from an arrhythmia, we think."

The questions in his mind formed faster than he could speak. "Arrhythmia? What's that? Why? How?"

"Your wife has undergone an incredible amount of stress, and the baby takes everything it needs from her, leaving her…not quite as strong as she might be otherwise. We believe she had a ventricular arrhythmia, possibly caused by stress, or perhaps by an underlying conduction problem to the heart."

Beau's lips pushed tightly together as he listened, trying to follow her explanation. "Conduction problem?"

"We can't be sure. We're monitoring her—and the baby. Hopefully, this was an anomaly. If she stops breathing again, we may need to take the baby."

The blood drained from Beau's face.

"We would do an emergency cesarean section," she explained. "If this is a conduction problem, then there are a few ways to proceed, none of which we'd want to chance while she's carrying a baby." Dr. Kelly handed Tess's chart to a heavyset nurse. "Your wife is very strong, Mr. Johnson, but comas are very tenuous, and the baby is very premature. We'll have to monitor her and see what we're dealing with. Let's hope this was a one-time event caused by the stress of the accident."

Chapter Twenty-Three

The next morning, Beau awoke to the portly nurse bustling around Tess. Jet lag settled upon him like a night of hard drinking. He pried his eyelids apart, gathering his thoughts. *Tess. Hospital.*

"Good morning, Mr. Johnson," she said with a warm southern drawl and a sincere smile. "I'm sorry I woke you."

Beau sat up in the chair, his back ached from slouching all night. "It's okay," he said with a yawn. "How is she?"

"Why, she's just lovely, isn't she?" she tucked Tess's blanket around her still body. "Can I get you something? A pillow? Blanket?"

"No, thank you," Beau said. "How long do you think she'll be in a coma?"

"Sweetie, I think she'll be in there just as long as she needs to be." She bent close to Beau. He could feel her breath on his cheek, "I've seen them stay in a coma for weeks, I've seen them stay in a coma for hours. It just depends on how tired they are, that's all."

Beau smiled. *Yes*, he thought, *maybe that's it.*

"And look at her!" she exclaimed. "Look at that belly. You're going to be a father!"

Beau gazed over at Tess's rising abdomen. *My baby.*

"See this monitor?" She pointed to the monitor that was strapped to Tess's stomach. "That there's a fetal heart monitor. If anything goes wrong with your baby, we'll know like that." She snapped her fingers and walked toward the door. "But don't you worry yourself over her, she's safe and warm inside her mama."

Beau watched her waddle out into the hall, desperately wanting to believe her. He brushed Tess's bangs away from the bandages and kissed her forehead.

"Why didn't you tell me?" he whispered.

Her stillness seemed to magnify his question.

Her skin was warm and soft. The faint scent of vanilla lay under the bitterness of the antiseptic. He picked up her limp hand and drew the letter "I" with his index finger, then he drew a heart. His eyes drifted to her swollen middle. He released her hand and turned away, perplexed, his brows furrowing in confusion.

Outside the intensive care unit, Alice, Kevin, and Beau's parents waited for news. Alice had convinced an ICU nurse that she'd gone to school with into giving them enough information to know that Tess was still in a coma and that the baby was doing fine.

"Why hasn't he come out to see us?" Carol Johnson's eyes were red. She gripped a tissue as if it were a security blanket.

Her husband, Robert, sat forward, elbows leaning on his knees. He turned toward her and shook his head. "He'll never leave her side."

"Two minutes, that's all I want with him." Carol stood, her arms crossed, her shoulders rounded forward. "I just need to see him," she said in a thin voice.

Robert reached up and pulled her gently back toward her seat. His enormous hand encircled her tiny forearm. "We'll wait, Carol. He'll be out when he's able."

"I'm going to get coffee. Carol?" Alice asked.

Carol sank down beside her husband.

Kevin stood. "I'll go."

"Shouldn't we call Louie?" Alice asked in an urgent, hushed tone.

"No," Kevin answered.

"But he's got no idea she's here," Alice pleaded.

"Beau's here. What are you gonna do, have another guy come in and be like, 'Um, here I am. I was sleeping with your wife.'?" He glared at her.

"We don't even know they were sleeping together." Alice picked up her pace. "I'm going to the ladies' room. I'll meet you at the cafeteria."

Safely secluded in the ladies' room, Alice withdrew her cell phone and called Directory Assistance. "Bethesda, Maryland. Tole, Louis Tole, please."

The pleasantly-plump nurse changed Tess's IV bag. "There, that should do." The nurse moved gracefully despite her large size. "How're you holding up, hon?" she asked Beau with a smile in her eyes. She took a washcloth and dabbed the exposed parts of Tess's face. "Let's see what we have here," she bent down to check the bag of urine that hung from the side of the bed.

Three nights without sleep had left Beau shaky, his eyes swollen and tired.

"What a good girl," the nurse said. She emptied the urine and replaced the collection bag, then turned back toward Beau. "Oh, hon, you're looking a little tired. Why don't you go get yourself some breakfast? Your family's still waiting out there for you."

Beau rose to his feet. He'd forgotten about his parents. Suddenly it dawned on him that he'd forgotten about Samira all together. "Shit," he mumbled.

"Something wrong?" the nurse startled.

"Nothing. I...forgot something," Beau paced. He'd left Samira at the army base with her children and an interpreter. She was safe. It was her fear that worried him. He was all she had, all she knew. He withdrew his cell phone.

"Uh-uh, hon. No cell phones in the ICU," she shook her head. "Why don't you just use this bedside phone?" She tapped the green receiver next to the bed.

"Right," Beau said. He waited until the nurse left, closing the door behind her. Beau picked up the phone and dialed. "Mr. Fulan?"

"Yes?" he said.

"It's Beau Johnson." Beau squeezed his eyes shut, ready for the disbelief, then the joy, both of which came quickly.

"Yes, I'm thrilled to be home," he proceeded to explain Tess's situation to Mr. Fulan, then asked for the biggest favor he'd ever had to ask of the man, and hoped Mr. Fulan would agree. "I traveled with a young Iraqi woman and her children. She speaks little English, and she doesn't know anybody." Beau ran his hand through his hair, his eyes washing over Tess. "I was hoping you might be willing to go sit with her, just for a few hours. I don't know who else to—"

Before he could finish, Mr. Fulan interrupted, "It's the least I can do."

Beau took a deep breath and pushed through the doors that separated the ICU from the waiting room. His mother glanced up, tears instantly filled her eyes. She brought her hand up to her mouth, tissue pressing against her teeth. Beau's eyes welled with tears.

Carol stood, trembling. The wrinkles on her face were new, the gray in her hair seemed out of place.

Robert rose to his feet, his strong demeanor melted before Beau's eyes. Tears streamed down his cheeks.

Beau bit his upper lip, unable to keep his tears at bay. His father's embrace sent his heart racing. His mother's frailty brought sobs from Beau.

"Son," his father's voice cracked.

Beau squeezed them to him. Until that moment, he hadn't realized how much he'd needed them. He'd been running on adrenaline, using all of his energy to get from one painful second to the next. His defenses down, he reverted back to a scared ten-year-old. "I'm sorry," he cried. "I'm so sorry. I shouldn't have gone. It's all my fault."

Robert kissed the top of Beau's head, then rested his cheek there, fitting perfectly. "No, son, no. Thank God you're home."

Carol cried softly. She pulled back from Beau, looked him up and down, then pulled him to her again.

"Mom," he whispered.

Kevin and Alice stood to the side, holding hands. Alice turned away from the private scene, wiping her own sadness away.

"I'm sorry I didn't come out yesterday," Beau said. They sat in the chairs, Carol's knuckles white around Beau's hand.

Carol shook her head. She reached across the seat and stroked Beau's cheek.

"How's she doing?" Robert asked.

"She's still in a coma," he wiped his eyes. "She stopped breathing—" sobs stole his words.

"Oh, son," Robert put his arm around Beau.

"They said it might've been caused by the stress of the accident." He stared straight ahead, hoping they were right. "She's pregnant," his eyebrows lifted.

"We know. Alice told us," Robert said. "And how's the baby?" his tone was gentle.

"So far, so good."

One by one, they had gone in to see Tess, Alice first, then Carol, Robert, and, finally, Kevin.

"She's gonna be okay." Carol sat next to Alice and squeezed her hand.

Alice cried openly.

Carol drew strength from comforting Alice. She'd needed a purpose. She gathered Alice in her arms and consoled her.

Beau and Robert sat silently staring at the double doors. Every passing second was one less he had with Tess. Beau's leg bumped up and down. He twisted his wedding band.

Kevin burst through the doors, his face sheet white. "Beau, she stopped breathing. Get in there."

Beau was through the doors and down the hall in seconds. Tess's door was closed, the curtains drawn. "What's going on?" he yelled to a nurse sitting at the desk down the hall.

"She stopped breathing, hon. They're taking care of her." The southern nurse from earlier came to stand beside him.

"Why? I thought it was a fluke!"

"We don't know yet, sir."

Tess's door flew open. The doctor led the way, followed by nurses pushing Tess on a gurney. Beau ran beside them, "What happened? Where are you taking her?" he yelled.

"It wasn't an anomaly, Mr. Johnson. She must have a conduction issue," she motioned for the nurses to take

Tess into the operating room. "We have to take the baby. If we don't, they both might die."

Beau couldn't even acknowledge that he'd heard her. His tongue felt as if it had doubled in size. His throat was closing. *Tess might die.*

"Mr. Johnson, every second counts. I need your consent."

A nurse rushed over with a clipboard and put a pen in Beau's hand.

He looked at her with tears in his eyes. "Will she be okay?" his voice was barely a whisper.

"We're trying to save her. There are no guarantees about the baby. She's very premature, but many—"

"Tess!" *Why don't they understand?* "Is Tess going to live?" Beau grabbed the clipboard from the nurse and scribbled his name.

"We're doing everything we can."

Chapter Twenty-Four

"She's stable. She had a conduction problem to the heart. We did an ablation of the pathway to the heart," Dr. Kelly spoke to the Johnsons, Kevin, and Alice in the waiting room.

Stable. As reassuring as that word should have been, Beau found it unnerving. He clenched his jaw. She had been *stable* before. "What does that mean, an ablation?"

"There are nerves, pathways, that stimulate the heart. Sometimes there's an aberrant pathway that doesn't conduct properly, causing abnormal electrical activity to the heart. We're lucky we caught it. We burned the aberrant pathway that was causing the arrhythmia. She should be fine now."

Beau ran his hand through his hair. He crossed his arms and asked, "And the baby?"

Dr. Kelly took a deep breath, lowering her eyes for a nanosecond—enough time for Beau to notice, and for the world around him to stand still. "She's in the neonatal intensive care unit."

"She?" If a heart could swell to twice its normal size, Beau's heart did it. His heart beat against his chest so hard he could feel it behind his eyes. Tears sprang to his eyes. "A girl," he whispered.

"She?" Carol repeated.

Robert touched her shoulder, and nodded, as if to say, *Not now, Carol.*

"Yes. She's very premature, Mr. Johnson. A baby's ability to survive outside the womb increases dramatically between twenty-four and twenty-eight weeks, increasing from about forty percent at the beginning of the twenty-fourth week to more than eighty percent just four weeks later." She paused, letting the information sink in.

Beau squeezed his arms tighter around his chest. "And she's?"

"Roughly twenty-six weeks."

Beau quickly calculated how many weeks he'd been gone. His gaze narrowed.

Dr. Kelly interrupted his thoughts. "Before the twenty-eighth week of pregnancy, almost all babies will have short-term complications, like difficulty breathing, as your baby is having."

My baby?

"Some preemies will also have some long-term problems, and others—"

Carol gasped, turned her back.

Robert took a step closer to Beau.

"There are no guarantees, and unfortunately, we can't predict the outcome at this time." Dr. Kelly looked over her shoulder, following Beau's glare.

His eyes fixed on Alice. Alice crossed and uncrossed her arms. Her eyes danced around the waiting room. Beau took three heavy steps in her direction.

"Beau? What is it?" Robert asked.

Beau put a hand out behind him, palm up. Robert took the hint.

Alice feigned a smile. "A girl," her voice shook.

"Alice? Twenty-six weeks? What the hell is—"

Alice took two steps backwards. She looked up and saw Louie hurrying down the corridor. "Beau, I—"

"Alice, I came as quickly as I could. Is she alright?" Louie burst into the waiting room.

Alice spun around, "Louie, she's—"

Beau breathed heavily through his nose. "Louie?" He stood eye-to-eye with Louie, sizing him up. The angular nose, thick eyebrows, and curly hair might look decidedly nerdy on some, but on Louie, it had a handsome appeal.

Louie reached out his hand and in a serious tone said, "Louie Tole."

Beau's face reddened. Louie's friendly demeanor and the concern in his eyes brought his good looks to the forefront. Beau's gut twisted, pushing an acidic taste to his mouth. He couldn't look away from the man's thin pink lips. "Beau Johnson," his words were heated.

Louie lowered his hand, he looked to Alice, back at Beau, then took in the rest of the waiting room, the grieving parents, the doctor, worried and rushed, Kevin, standing behind Beau, arms crossed, eyes trained on Louie. "I'm a…a…friend of Tess."

"He's our client," Alice piped in. "We're helping him fill a position. We've been working very closely the last few weeks, and Louie—"

"I've become good friends with Tess. I was worried about her."

"You called him?" Kevin accused Alice with a disapproving look.

Alice looked down. "Yes, I…I thought I should."

"Mr. Johnson, I'll come back," Dr. Kelly said and hurried down the hall. Beau had forgotten she was in the room.

Beau paced, his limp more pronounced. "The baby...she's twenty-six weeks?" He looked from Louie to Alice.

Robert put his hand on Beau's shoulder. "Son, let's all calm down and talk about this. We all thought you were gone, even Tess."

Beau shrugged him off. He looked at Kevin. "You knew," he pointed in the general direction of Louie, "about them?"

Kevin looked from Beau to Louie and back again, then gave a small nod and lowered his eyes.

"Beau," Louie said, "I'm not sure what you think's going on, but I can assure you—"

A nurse rushed into the waiting room, abruptly stopping the deteriorating scene. "Mr. Johnson?" she said hurriedly.

Beau turned, his eyes on fire.

"There's a problem in the NICU."

Chapter Twenty-Five

"Jesus, Alice. I can't believe you called him. What were you thinking?" Kevin fumed as he and Alice walked down the hall to the cafeteria.

"I thought he should know," she said.

Kevin glared at her.

"I screwed up, okay? I didn't think it through." Alice stopped and leaned against the wall. "She's my best friend. All I was thinking about was her. She'd been spending all this time with him. I didn't even think about Beau. I know he's here, but, I mean, I thought...I don't know what I thought." Tears streamed down her face. "I'm scared, Kevin. She could die." She turned away.

Kevin put his arm around her, hovering between angry and in love. "She's not gonna die," he said.

Alice sniffled, leaning into him. "She could. Beau will never forgive her—or me. What've I done?" Her eyes darted about the hall.

"Geez, Al. Why'd you do it?"

"I don't know." She pulled back and looked up at him. "I thought he needed to be here." She looked away. "Maybe I'm one of those people."

"What people?"

"One of those people who has to ruin other people's lives, I don't know," she buried her face in her hands.

"You're not that person. You care, that's all. You knew he'd be worried. It'll be okay." Kevin looked up at the ceiling and closed his eyes. *Okay* was one thing he was not sure things would ever be again.

Louie leafed through an old copy of *People Magazine* in the waiting room of the neonatal intensive care unit. His eyes moved from the pages of the magazine to Robert and Carol. He set the magazine down and leaned forward, clasping his hands between his legs, "I'm really sorry about what's happened to Tess and the baby. I didn't mean to upset Beau."

Robert lifted his gaze, his face unreadable. "We're all in a state of shock."

Carol clenched Robert's hand. Her thin, arched eyebrows lifted, but her eyes remained dark. "So, are you and Tess," she waved her hand in the air, clutching a tissue, "dating?"

Louie looked down at the floor. He shrugged. "To be honest, I'm not sure what you'd call it, but yes, we were spending time together."

Carol leaned into Robert's side, as if the words had pushed her against him.

Robert put his arm around Carol. "This is going to be a difficult situation for everyone involved."

Each time someone walked by the waiting room, the three of them looked up, expecting to see Beau, who'd excused himself to the men's room fifteen minutes earlier.

"We weren't, um, we hadn't..." Louie blushed. "What I'm trying to say is that we were close, but it's not what Beau thinks. We weren't...intimate."

Carol closed her eyes, her words came out in a rush of breath, "Oh, thank God."

Alice came in with Kevin trailing behind her. Her eyes were swollen, her face drawn.

"I'm sorry," she said to them all. "I didn't mean to cause trouble for anyone. I just thought Louie should know what'd happened."

"That's alright, Alice. We know you didn't mean any harm, dear," Carol said.

Louie stood. "I can leave." He put his hands in his jeans pockets. "I mean, I don't want to. I want to know how Tess is doing, but I don't want to cause anymore pain for Beau, or for you two."

Robert and Carol spoke in unison.

"You don't have to leave," Robert said.

"Maybe that would be best," Carol said.

Louie took a deep breath and let it out slowly. He shrugged and extended his hand to Robert. "I'm truly sorry if I caused you any grief. It wasn't my intent."

Robert tucked his chin into his chest, his eyes serious. He shook Louie's hand.

"I'll call you," Alice said as Louie passed by, catching, out of the corner of her eye, Kevin glaring at her.

Beau stood beside Tess's bed, his nerves afire. He stared at her bandaged face. "Damn it, Tess," he said through gritted teeth. He paced, his injured leg throbbed. "How could you do this to us?" The monitors lulled him into a daze. His eyes glazed over.

"Hey, sugar, how're you holding up?"

Her southern drawl pulled him back to the moment. "Hi," he said, lowering himself into his seat.

"I hear you're a proud papa now. Congratulations." She checked Tess's vital signs, humming. "What're you going to name that sweet little treasure of yours?"

Beau shrugged.

"You're gonna wait and see what Mama says, are you?" She tucked Tess's blanket around her body. "Well, I think that's mighty nice. Give her something to wake up for."

"Do you think she can hear me?" Beau asked.

"I'd like to think so. I've seen some miraculous things happen in my day." She walked toward the door then turned back around. "Talk to her, sweetie. She needs you as much as you need her."

Beau sat in the chair for a long time, staring at Tess, the sunshine streamed across Tess's chest. He'd worked so hard to come back home to her, and now, he wasn't sure he could ever look at her the same way. How could she have thrown away their relationship so quickly? How could she have slept with another guy so soon after he'd left the country? The veins in Beau's neck bulged. He clenched and unclenched his fists.

Beau's thoughts turned to Iraq, the day he'd awakened in the tent with Suha caring for him. He hadn't known where he was or who she was. There had been only one thought on his mind: Getting back to Tess. He remembered Samira watching him from across the tent and Edham clinging to his hand as they took their daily therapeutic walks. He heard Athra's piercing scream when she was ripped from Samira's arms. Beads of sweat formed on his forehead.

He looked at Tess's broken, bandaged body with fresh tears in his eyes.

"What have I done?" he asked. "I've ruined our lives. I can't live without you." He clenched his teeth, "But I can't," he pushed back from her, wiping his eyes with his sleeve, "I can't even look at you without seeing him."

Chapter Twenty-Six

Samira leaned against the cool cinderblock wall of the army barrack where she and the children had stayed the night before. Her stomach growled. She wished she'd eaten more of the hearty meal they'd fed them the evening before, but she'd been too nervous. The children had been famished. She'd thought Zeid and Edham would be up for hours with bellyaches, but they'd slept right through the night. Only Athra had awakened several times, crying and reaching out for Samira.

Samira lifted the shade, bringing sun across the children's cots. She knelt in the center of the small room, her knees pressed against the concrete floor. She bent forward and prayed. She prayed for Suha, who had not been washed and wrapped in a clean, white cloth by a loving family member. She hadn't been buried after a special prayer had been said in her honor. She hadn't been buried the same day. Samira prayed that the absence of those acts would not disgrace her in her afterlife.

Edham knelt next to Samira, his hands clasped together. He rocked in time with his mother. When her body slowed, he spoke. "I miss Mr. Beau, Mother." His long dark lashes blinked rapidly, awaiting an assurance that was not to come.

Zeid stared at him from the edge of the cot where he sat.

Samira leaned back on her heels and ran her fingers through the bush of hair just above Edham's right ear. She kissed his cheek.

"I am glad to be without him," Zeid's cutting words pierced Edham like a spear.

Edham jumped to his feet and ran shoulder first into his brother's chest, propelling him backward with a howl of anger. He punched his brother's ribs over and over again.

Samira grabbed him from behind, "Edham! Release him!"

Tears streamed from Edham's eyes, his heart pounded, his arms hammered Zeid's chest with such speed and force that he feared he would not be able to stop.

Zeid pushed at Edham's chest. "Get off!"

"You are just like Father! I hate you! I hate you!" Edham yelled. "I love Mr. Beau!"

Samira yanked Edham's right arm so hard it startled Edham out of his hate-driven reverie. He spun and stared at her, his lower lip quivering. He collapsed into her arms, sobbing and panting until his sobs became hiccups.

"He's crazy, Mother," Zeid wrapped his reddened arms around his knees and pushed back toward the wall.

Samira stroked Edham's back, holding him against her chest, "Calm, Edham. We're all scared." She shushed Zeid before any more words could escape his mouth, staring at him with remorse in her eyes.

Athra crawled up onto the cot, her thumb jammed into her mouth, and sat next to Zeid, her wide eyes flitted from Zeid to her mother, then back again.

A knock at the door shot three sets of worried eyes in Samira's direction. She gently led Edham to the other cot. "They heard us," she scolded. She wished Suha were there. Fear swelled in her chest. She held up a trembling hand, palm facing the children, signaling them to stay put. She covered her head with her *hijab* and reached her other hand toward the door handle. Her slim fingers wrapped around the cold metal. The lock sprang open. Samira pulled the door open an inch and peered into the hall. A man in uniform stood with a tall, dark-haired man. Samira dropped her eyes. The man's pressed trousers lay perfectly above his shiny black designer shoes. His dark skin and thick dark hair were comfortably familiar.

The man lowered his eyes and gave a slight bow. "Ms. Samira?" His voice was calm and low.

Samira's eyes filled with fear. She peered out from behind the door.

"I am Mr. Fulan. Beau Johnson asked me to come." Hearing her native language in conjunction with Beau's name sent a chill of relief through her body. She took a loud deep breath and glanced back into the room, where Athra huddled between Edham and Zeid, and for the first time in many years, she knew they were going to be okay.

Chapter Twenty-Seven

Beau paced outside the entrance to the hospital emergency room, favoring his left leg and sweating, despite the cool air. His hands reflexively clenched and unclenched. He'd never allowed himself to think about what Tess might do if she'd believed he was dead. He'd never gotten past the thought of coming home. *Tess has a boyfriend.* He reached up and rubbed the ache in his arm. He'd calculated and recalculated at least one hundred times—he'd been gone for almost twenty-eight weeks. There was no way the baby was his. He sank down onto a bench, grasping the sides of his head.

"There you are," Alice said, exasperated.

Beau flinched at the sound of Alice's voice.

"We've been looking all over for you."

Beau stood and backed away.

"Beau? She's okay, they stabilized her," Alice misread his distress.

Beau turned his back and mumbled, "Get away from me."

Alice, unable to hear him clearly, approached.

Beau spun around and seethed, "Get the hell away from me."

She stiffened, her jaw slack.

Beau brushed past her and stormed into the hospital, taking the elevator up to the NICU.

Beau's anger renewed with each *Ding!* of the elevator announcing the floors between the lobby and the NICU. By the time the doors opened into the NICU, his jaw was clenched so tight his temples throbbed. He stepped out of the elevator and into the bright hallway, squinting to the left where the babies were kept behind an enormous window. Louie stood with his back to the elevators, his forehead resting against the window. Next to him, Carol was enveloped by Robert's embrace. She looked up at Robert, said something, then raised a tissue to her face. Beau's throat thickened, the veins in his forehead ached. He stepped backward into the elevator and watched the doors close, remaining unseen by the others.

The cabbie pulled up in front of the small yellow house. Tess's mangled car had been removed, traces of glass and splinters of metal lay beneath the injured willow. Beau stared at the traumatized tree as if in a trance. He felt his anger—and perhaps his life—being sucked from him, one image at a time.

"This it, buddy?"

Beau nodded, paid the cab driver, then pushed himself out of the vehicle. He stood on the front walk until he was sure his legs would not fail him, then dragged himself to the shed in the backyard where he retrieved the spare key to the house.

Beau stood in the foyer, disturbed by the unfamiliar smell of his home. He set the keys on the table next to the door and closed the door behind him. Silence permeated the house like an unwanted visitor.

The coziness of the home he'd left had been obliterated. He opened the foyer closet to grab the zip-up sweatshirt he'd kept there and was startled to see only Tess's blue windbreaker and winter coat. He walked past the coffee table in the living room, once littered with photography magazines and snapshots, now bare. The den looked like one in a model home, stripped of all personal effects. He sat in the leather chair, inhaling deeply. His lips curled up at the ends. At least his chair still smelled familiar. He ran his thick fingers along the edge of the desk, exhaling in a way that said, *This is more like it. This is home.* He opened the top desk drawer—then quickly shut it. He pulled the other drawers open, one by one—all empty.

Beau bounded up the stairs two at a time. He threw the bedroom closet open. "What the—"

He ripped open his empty bureau drawers, sending them crashing to the floor. Beau sank down onto the bed, burying his face in his hands. He'd been erased from Tess's life, and it cut him like an ice pick to the heart. He ignored the ringing of the house phone. He clenched his eyes shut and rocked back and forth, unable to cry and wishing he could.

"What the fuck," he mumbled.

The phone rang incessantly.

The muscles in Beau's arms flexed. He crossed the bedroom in two steps, yanked the phone cord from the wall and threw the phone, sending shards of plastic across the bedroom floor. He pushed Tess's books and perfume off the bedside table with one swipe of his arm, then ripped her closet doors open and tore out every piece of clothing, hurling them across the room. Panting like a wrestler after a brawl, he stomped downstairs, grabbed his car keys, and burned rubber out of the driveway, hoping someone would hit his car and wrap him around a tree.

Chapter Twenty-Eight

The purple bruises had deepened and begun yellowing across Tess's jaw, tugging at Beau's heart. He stood in the shadows of the room, every fiber of his being pulling him toward her. The rage in his chest stopped him. She'd abandoned him. Beau wrung his hands together. His head throbbed, and his shoulders ached. The pain in his leg had become an angry reminder of all that was bad in his life. He punched his thigh, wincing at the pain. His eyes darted around the cold room bouncing from the sterile flooring, to the white walls, and settling on the medical equipment standing sentry at her bedside. His heart raced. He didn't know whether to ravage her room or climb into the bed like a needy child. He was stuck in a middle ground that was neither safe nor sane.

Tess's chest rose with each aided breath. *Wake up,* he silently urged her. *Tell me I have it all wrong,* he pleaded. He hoped for a flutter of her eyelids, for her finger to twitch, some mystical sign that she'd heard him, that she knew he needed her. Even the air in her room remained still.

Beau crossed the room out of the shadows and into the streak of light from the monitors. He hovered above her. The longing to touch Tess's skin was so strong, he could almost feel her softness on his fingertips. He reached for her, then pulled his hand back slowly, holding it under the bicep of his other arm, as if his hand had a mind of its own and might betray his anger. The hand won. He ran a trembling finger along her skin, shivering with the soft familiarity of it.

He took the photo of Tess that he'd carried with him in Iraq out of his pocket and laid it on her stomach, watching it rise and fall. Tears filled his eyes. He closed his eyes and breathed in the antiseptic smell of the room, his teeth grinding against each other. His hand squeezed Tess's arm until he felt the sharpness of her bone press against his palm. He released her, leaving an indented white streak where each finger had laid and a twinge in his wrist. The lump in his pocket silently beckoned, pressing against his thigh. Beau shoved his hand deep into his pocket, making a fist around the circular memory.

"How could you do it?" he fumed. He withdrew the watch, raising it to his forehead and imprinting the cold engraving into his mind, his eyes clenched shut. Thoughts of Tess and Louie assaulted him. His stomach burned, bile rose in his throat. Beau bit the acrid taste of hatred that grew within him, a guttural sound pushed from his lips. He lowered his fists and stared at Tess's battered body, steeling himself against the guilt that drew his shoulders down. He wiped his hand up and down his face, forcing the tears to stop. He shoved the pocket watch under the edge of the blanket.

"Hey there, sugar," the cheerfulness of the southern nurse's greeting was in sharp contrast to the storm brewing within Beau.

He pushed past her, muttering under his breath, "I should've never come back."

The hall was suspiciously quiet. Beau's gait was stiff, threatening, every footstep determined. The nurse looked up as he neared the desk. He lifted his eyes above her gaze, set his jaw. The nurse answered the telephone as Beau passed the desk.

"Yes, sir, I'll check."

Beau slowed, peering over his shoulder as the nurse left her station for the supply room. His eyes bounced wildly down the empty hallway, settling on three pill bottles left next to the nurse's computer. Beau's nostrils flared, his heart raced. Those pills, any pills, would do the trick. He pushed forward, reached a sweaty hand over the counter, pocketing the pills, and spinning toward the exit. A nurse exited a patient room, smiled at Beau. Beau looked down at the floor, chewing on the inside of his cheek as he pushed through the doors and into the corridor. He took the stairs two at a time to the ground floor.

Chapter Twenty-Nine

The lights in Tess's room had been turned down, barely lighter than the darkness of night outside the shaded window. Alice sat rigid, her eyes downcast, Tess's hand in her own. "Do you think she can hear us?" She turned to face Kevin. "I'm glad they let us both come in this time, but I'm not sure if that's a good sign or a bad one."

Kevin shrugged, the bags under his eyes pronounced, his lips set in a hard line.

The grooves between Tess's eyes had faded, leaving her skin smooth, an attribute that had been missing since Beau had left for Iraq. Her almost translucent skin sent a shiver down Alice's back. She cleared her throat in an effort to stifle the sobs that had lodged in her throat.

"I couldn't take another second with Beau's mom," Alice whispered. "She's a doll, but it's just so sad. What the hell is Beau thinking? Where is he?"

Kevin shrugged again. He knew she wasn't looking for an answer, and he was in no shape to make one up. His best friend had returned from the dead only to abandon his wife and child. Kevin sighed, slumped into a chair.

"Do you think they'll stay all night with the baby?" She didn't wait for an answer, "I do. God, I hope she makes it. The baby, I mean."

Kevin lifted his eyes.

"Tess, too, of course," she rubbed her neck, wishing the day had never begun. "What do we do now?" she stared at the darkened blinds. "Maybe you should try to find Beau."

Kevin stood, headed for the door.

"Are you not talking to me now?"Alice snapped.

Kevin closed his eyes, turned around slowly. He shook his head, his voice calm, low, "There's just nothing to say."

Tears slipped down Alice's cheek. "Why?" she hissed. "Because I called Louie? Because Tess is dying? Because her baby's dying?" She threw her hands up, sending the chair toppling behind her.

A nurse appeared in the doorway.

"All of it, I guess." He walked past the nurse and out of the room.

The nurse walked gently into the room and righted the chair. Alice leaned against the wall, her hands covering her face.

"Are you okay, sugar?" the "ar" sounded like "ah".

Alice sniffled, shrugged.

"I'm Mary, hon, Ms. Johnson's nurse, and if you need anything at all, I'm right here." Mary hummed, giving Alice her space and checking each of the lines that led from the machines to Tess's body and arms. "Poor thing. She's been through an awful lot," she said.

An uncomfortable silence stretched between them. Alice shifted against the wall. "Do you think she'll make it?"

Mary waited one beat too long before answering. Alice's hands trembled.

"We'd like to hope so," Mary said. She replaced the IV bag and headed for the door.

Chapter Thirty

Beau sped along Route 15 North, dodging cars like bullets. Suburbia fell away behind him, replaced with placid pastures. The storm brewing within him did not ease with the scenery. His muscles remained tense, his jaw clenched, knuckles white-gripping the steering wheel.

The tires screeched as he careened onto an unmarked dirt road just outside of Thurmont. He eased off the gas, and the car rolled toward the darkened forest before him.

He parked in front of a small wooden shack, just a mile from the main road, though the thick woods felt like another world altogether. He climbed from the car, wound so tight he breathed in short, clipped bursts—a tiger ready to pounce. He slammed the door and placed his hands flat upon the hood of the car. Images of Tess exploded in his mind: Tess's eyes holding his gaze for a split second before her car was rammed, Tess's battered body pulled from the wreckage, her face torn and bloody. He hadn't seen her swollen belly, he'd been so focused on her breathing. *Her belly. The baby. Goddamned baby.* Why couldn't she have waited? Was she in that much of a hurry to have a family? He'd have reconsidered his goddamned five-year plan if he'd known she wanted a baby so goddamned bad. Or would he, he wondered? It didn't fucking matter if he would or wouldn't have changed his plans. What kind of wife gets pregnant weeks after her husband leaves the country? Had she been cheating all along, just waiting for him to go away so she could be alone with another man? With Louie? *Fucking Louie!* Who the fuck was he, anyway? Some goddamned prick who has to sleep with another man's wife, that's who.

The sour, woody smell of the cabin hung in the stale air. He threw his aching body on the matted and worn plaid couch, his eyes drawn to the gun mounted above the ancient wood-burning stove, a gun Kevin had used several times. Kevin's grandfather's hunting cabin had served as a place of contemplation for Beau many times in the past—when he had been thinking of proposing to Tess, and more recently, before he'd accepted the assignment in Iraq. In both of those cases, he'd been in control of the decisions. He knew what he'd wanted when he'd arrived, and he'd used the cabin as a sort of driving-home of his decisions, a place to rationalize his thoughts. Now, his world was spiraling out of control, and he couldn't stop it. Fatigue clouded his mind, his nerves burned. He had no idea what he wanted, and to make matters worse, the woman he loved most in the world may not live long enough for him to decide. The realization startled him. He leaned forward and ran his hand through his hair. How would he live without her? It was one thing to get a divorce. She'd go her way and he'd go his, leaving town if he had to, to escape the pain of seeing her with *him.* She'd still be around, safe, even if hate bore a hole in his gut. She'd be *alive.* If she died, he'd no longer be able to reach out if he wanted to. There'd be no chance. No chance for what? Reconciliation? For him to steal her back from *him? Fuck that!* His head swam in circles.

The warped wooden planks creaked beneath Beau's weight as he paced the floor, each heavy step an echo of his pain. His nostrils flared. Veins rose across his forehead and down his neck. He lifted his eyes to the gun. He crossed the room.

His fingers fit perfectly around the smooth wooden stock of the gun. He ran his other hand along the barrel. Beau backed onto the couch, the weight of the gun comforting across his lap. He worked his jaw muscles until a stabbing pain shot up past his ear, snapping him out of his stupor. A deep breath later he retrieved a shotgun shell from the bureau in the corner and loaded the gun. Beau hoisted the gun over his shoulder, holding the butt of the gun in his right hand, and walked out back.

Moments later, a single shot rang out and echoed within the umbrella of the forest.

Chapter Thirty-One

The door closed behind Samira, reverberating in the cold, industrial room. She stood, frozen in despair, staring at the white sheet before her under which Suha's body lay atop a stainless steel table. A putrid smell hung in the air—rotting eggs and something sharp, like ammonia. Samira tried to breathe through her mouth, the aroma drenching even the taste buds on her tongue. She looked over her shoulder toward the door, desperately wanting to turn and run, to escape the reality of Suha's death. She knew she could not. Goosebumps climbed up her arms in rapid succession. She turned back toward the table, feeling the emptiness of the room closing in around her. She had to do this. Suha had already missed the proper burial she should have had, and knowing that had crushed Samira's heart. She'd thought that Beau had deserted her, and though she'd been wrong, she still hadn't been able to shake the loneliness that had engulfed her. She summoned every bit of her courage. It was up to her to properly wash and pray for Suha, and she prayed for the strength to carry out the task.

Her feet moved forward in short, tentative shuffles. Suha was the strong one, not Samira. How would she do this? She thought of Suha's ability to push past the gruesome or difficult, and tried to glean strength from her memory. Images of Beau sailed through her mind: the night Suha had found him, his body bloodied and broken; the way she and Suha had struggled to carry him into the tent; and the unfamiliar tension that had clenched her stomach the first time she'd seen him. She thought of the camera she'd found in the desert and hidden from him like a child, guilty of thievery. She pushed past that guilt. This was not Beau. There would be no healing—for Suha or Samira. She closed her eyes and willed herself to be strong, turning again toward the door, debating retreat. No, she thought. She would not desert Suha, the woman who had saved her and her children from sure demise. Suha would have done this for her. Samira pressed on.

Samira repeatedly drenched the washcloth and squeezed it out. Anything to give her a little more time, a bit of space between her and Suha's dead body. Her hands shook so badly that she wasn't sure she'd be able to actually manage the task. She knew she was stalling, a flush warmed her cheeks. Samira lowered her head in shame and prayed, then set her shoulders back, gritted her teeth, and gathered her courage like a protective shield around her.

The sheet covered Suha's body and face, drawn up to her scalp. Her thin, greasy hair was exposed, a sticky dark mass. Samira lifted a trembling hand and touched the sheet, then quickly pulled her hand back, tears slipping down her cheeks. A quick, sharp whimper shot from her throat. She closed her eyes again and prayed—this time for her own strength. She squeezed her eyes closed as hard as she could until she saw red and yellow dots. When she opened them, there was a gray film cast before her. She waited for it to clear. Samira swallowed hard, then lowered the sheet from Suha's face.

Her hand flew to her gaping mouth. Unable to stifle the declaration of her pain and sorrow, she cried out. Bile rose in her throat, causing her to turn away. She rocked back onto her heels. The thumbs of her fisted hands pressed hard against her chin. Closing her eyes, she willed away the harsh image of the green/blue tint of Suha's face, the waxy sheen of her skin. She prayed for many minutes, her heart galloping within her small chest. Blood rushed to her ears, muffling the world around her. Several moments passed before the rushing blood calmed and she could once again hear the silence in the room.

Samira's stomach churned, pushing the tea she'd had for breakfast into her throat. She swallowed against the acidic intruder, her muscles tense, and went to work washing Suha with careful, tentative movements. Strokes of the washcloth left indentations in Suha's skin, unnerving Samira anew each time one appeared. She moved her way down to Suha's chest, three dry wounds stared back at her, accusing, haunting. The shock of the vicious holes knocked her off balance. Samira stepped back from the table. Her knees weakened, sending her down to the cold floor in an awkward hunched over mound, her pigeon-toed feet crossed beneath her. The washcloth lay in a wet heap on the floor, water bleeding into a puddle.

Forty minutes later Samira had finished the macabre job of washing Suha's front and sides. She'd pushed past the disgust, shifting into automaton mode. Her thin fingers pushed Suha's body, rolling her from her back onto her stomach. The sheet fell away, landing on the water-specked floor. Purple bruises covered Suha's back, sending a shock through Samira. She dropped Suha's body like a hot coal, stepping backward, as it connected with the cold stainless steel with a loud *Thud!* The backs of Suha's thick thighs were deep purple and black, the backs of her knees a morbid gray. Bruises, thick like mortar, hid the waxy sheen of the aged flesh of Suha's buttocks, the backs of her arms, and her heels. Samira tried to regain a steady breath. Prayers tumbled from her mouth. The slight blistering of Suha's skin repulsed her. She moved forward to finish the job, her face pinched, the final images of Suha's battered body seared into her mind like a nightmare.

Chapter Thirty-Two

"I've called his house several times, his cell phone, checked with his parents—I can't find him anywhere." Kevin hadn't been worried when he'd first set out to find Beau. Beau was a sensible man, after all. He might have been angry about Louie, but he'd walk it off. *Unless.* A disturbing sensation began to nag at the back of his mind.

"Maybe he's around the hospital somewhere," Alice lifted the blinds. Moonlight streaked across Tess's bed. Halos of light illuminated areas of the parking lot. She turned back toward Kevin, thinking of Tess and the baby. "Have you checked the cafeteria? How about the bathrooms? He's got to be somewhere. He wouldn't leave Tess," Tess's name fell timidly from her lips. "Oh no, Kevin, what if he thinks—"

"I'm two steps ahead of you," Kevin rushed out the door as realization struck them both.

The NICU was a flourish of activity, nurses rushed from one room to the next. The pink and blue scrubs somehow lightened the severity of the environment. Alice found Robert leaning on his elbows, his face in his hands, and Carol, staring at nothing in particular. They were the only people in the waiting room.

The distraught look in Carol's eyes was almost too much for Alice to take. Her son was, in essence, missing *again*, and her premature granddaughter was gravely ill. Alice reached out to touch her arm, then pulled back, uncomfortable with the gesture. She sat, back straight, hands in her lap. Even Carol's hair had lost its sheen over the past several hours. Alice's face softened. She reached again for Carol's arm, touching it lightly.

Carol turned toward her, her eyelids heavy.

"How're you doing?" The caring tone of her own voice surprised her.

Carol lifted the ends of her lips, reaching for a smile, but falling short.

"How's the baby?" Alice asked.

Robert sat up, inhaling deeply through his nose, exhaling slowly through his mouth, the sadness in his eyes unmistakable.

"Oh, I'm so sorry," Alice said.

Robert shook his head. "They're doing all they can," he said quietly.

Carol turned her blank stare to the entrance again.

"I'm sure she'll be okay. The doctors here are very good. Sibley is one of the best hospitals in the area." Alice knew her words sounded as hollow to them as they did to her.

Robert nodded, looked down at his lap.

"Have you seen Beau?" Alice's confidence had disappeared, replaced with a tentative, unfamiliar nature.

Robert shook his head.

"Kevin's looking for him." Alice closed her eyes and willed herself to be strong. This was her fault, the pain, Beau's disappearance. "I'm sorry," she offered.

Robert looked up, met her eyes, and held them.

"About inviting Louie—I'm sorry. I just thought—"

"That man didn't cause this," he said in a calm, even voice.

"No, but I think Beau left because of him, and that's my fault." She held his gaze.

"Alice, life isn't full of easy choices. For whatever reason, you thought he should be here. I respect that. All that matters at this moment is that the baby and Tess pull through. Beau's back, and that, in and of itself, is a gift. Now we need to hold the rest of his family together." The weight of the situation bound them together in the small room.

Kevin raced from floor to floor of the hospital, checking bathrooms, waiting rooms, and hallways. He pushed through the front doors and checked the perimeter of the building. Where the hell was he?

Driving in D.C. after seven in the evening has its advantages. Kevin made it to Bethesda in twenty minutes. He parked along the curb in front of Beau's house and raced to the garage—Beau's car was gone. He looked away from the mangled tree, struck by its gnarled beauty in the moonlight. He focused on finding Beau. His mind ran through a list of Beau's hangouts, which included only his house, the ESPN Sports Bar during football season (and only if Kevin agreed to watch the game with him), and the hunting camp. He climbed into his truck and headed north.

The hood of Beau's car was cool, he'd been there a while. Kevin opened the front door, sure he'd find Beau on the couch. The emptiness of the pitch black room worried him.

"Beau?" he called.

He was met with silence.

Kevin turned on the overhead light and looked around the small cabin. Nothing was out of place. He stepped back outside and onto the back porch. "Beau?" he hollered.

He turned back, eying the kitchen. The bureau drawer was open. He walked slowly toward it, wondering what Beau could have taken from the junk-filled drawer. The open box of shells answered his thoughts. Kevin's eyes shot to the empty wall above the stove. "Shit." He rushed back outside. "Beau?" he yelled. He hurried to the edge of the woods and called out again.

There was no answer.

The silent forest reached for him. Kevin took a step toward the woods, then heard a *Thud!* behind him.

"Beau?" He ran toward the sound. "Beau!" he yelled into the night.

Kevin had become accustomed to the darkness, able to make out the shapes of the small shed and wooden table his father had built when he was just a boy.

"Beau?" He yanked the shed door open, feeling his way through the camping equipment, tools, and hunting paraphernalia. Adrenaline drove him toward the forest. His heart pounded like a hammer against his chest.

"Go away."

Kevin spun around at the sound of Beau's weary, broken voice.

"Beau?" he scanned the forest.

"Get outta here," Beau spat.

Kevin followed his voice and found Beau sitting on the forest floor, his back against a tree. The coppery, sour stench of blood stopped Kevin in his tracks. He reached for Beau, then he saw the gun lying on the ground, the butt against Beau's leg, his shirt saturated with blood. Kevin grabbed him by the collar and shook him, "What did you do?" he yelled.

Beau's head lolled back against the tree. A mocking laugh escaped his lips.

Kevin tried to pull him to his feet. Beau pushed away from him, staggering backward.

"I got the mother fucker," he laughed.

Kevin's pulse raced, he kicked the gun away with his foot. "Jesus, Beau," his voice cracked. Kevin walked slowly toward Beau, his hands up, fingers spread. "Beau, come on. Let's get you to the—"

Beau's face lit into an eerie, unstable smile. Just as Kevin touched his shirt, Beau sidestepped him and dove for the gun, turning it on Kevin.

Kevin put his hands up and backed away, "Beau, man, come on. What're you doin'?"

"What the fuck'm I doin', he asks." Beau staggered backwards, deeper into the woods. "I'll tell you what I'm doin'." Beau took two steps and collapsed on the forest floor.

"Jesus!" Kevin ran to his side, grabbed the gun, and snapped open the now-empty chamber. He threw the gun behind him.

Beau lifted his head. "I got 'im, Kev. I got that mother fucker." The laugh that followed was a wicked little laugh, the likes of which Kevin could never imagine coming from his best friend.

"We've got to get you to the hospital." Kevin looped his arms under Beau's armpits and dragged him toward the truck.

Beau's feet dragged on his heels, his legs dangled limply. His arm sprang out to the side, index finger extended. "There he is!"

Kevin looked in the direction he pointed. There, on the ground, lay a raccoon the size of a small dog, its fur matted with blood, its legs reaching for the sky.

Beau pried himself from Kevin's arms, wobbling toward the raccoon. "Mother fucker," he kicked the dead raccoon.

"Whoa, man. What're you doing?" Kevin tried to pull Beau away from the dead animal.

Beau pushed out of his grip like a crazed animal, grunting and fighting. He kicked the carcass again and again. "Mother fucker ruined my life." His rage exploded through his toes, sending the raccoon's limp body hurtling into a tree. "Goddamn son of a bitch."

Kevin watched his friend destroy the body of the animal. He moved swift and hard. Sweat covered his face. *Thank God,* Kevin thought, *at least Beau didn't shoot himself.*

Beau panted, grunting against his own body's fatigue. He picked up the raccoon and heaved it into the woods with a primitive, indecipherable yell, then sank down onto his heels, his head in his hands, and sobbed.

The fight had left Beau's body. It had taken Kevin thirty minutes to get Beau into the truck. Beau stared straight ahead, his head resting against the window, bobbing against it with each dip in the road. Beau's chest, stomach, and arms were a map of scratches and punctures. It was two o'clock in the morning, and Beau hadn't slept in days—more accurately, it had probably been months. As he neared Beau's street, Kevin watched Beau in his peripheral vision, worried about what seeing what had just been an accident scene would do to Beau in his tenuous state.

"Hey, buddy, why don't we get cleaned up at my place?" he suggested.

Beau didn't respond.

Kevin took that as agreement and passed Beau's street.

"Go back," Beau's words were robotic, cold.

"Are you sure? I'm not sure it's a good—"

"Go back." This time he meant it.

Kevin turned the truck around and headed up the steep hill toward Beau's house. The street was dark, punctuated by patches of streetlight illumination. Kevin was thankful for the camouflage of night. He parked the truck in the driveway.

Beau didn't stir.

Worried for his friend, Kevin let out a loud breath. When Beau didn't move, he said, "Ready?"

Beau spoke quietly, "How could she do it?" He stared at the house.

Kevin fidgeted with his keys. He'd always been straightforward with Beau, and now he wasn't sure if he should be honest or whether he should sugarcoat the whole Louie situation.

Beau didn't wait for an answer.

"Did Alice know?"

Kevin looked down at his keys and nodded, "Mm-hmm."

"How long?"

"I don't—"

"How long, Kevin?" Beau's voice escalated. "How long was she seeing that asshole before I left town?"

At first Kevin didn't understand what he meant, "Before?"

Beau turned toward him, his eyes piercing Kevin's confidence. "How fucking long was my wife having an affair?"

Kevin leaned back against the door, his hands warding off Beau's encroachment of his space.

"Beau, she wasn't seeing him before," his voice wavered.

Beau grit his teeth. "How long?"

"She thought you were dead," Kevin said. Then louder, "Dead, man. She thought you were dead. We all did." His chest heaved with anger, "And what about you? What's going on with that...that woman?"

Beau turned his fierceness on the truck, slamming his fist first into the dashboard, then the door. He yelled, "How long was she fucking that guy before I left?"

Kevin's confidence returned. "She wasn't," he yelled. "Beau, man, she wasn't doing anything. I...I don't think she even started seeing him until long after you were...well...after we thought you were dead." Kevin pleaded, "C'mon, you know Tess wouldn't do that. Beau, listen, I won't mention that woman—Samira—but Jesus, what's going on between you two?"

"Keep her out of this!" Beau's eyes were cold as stone. "Tess had a fucking baby, Kevin," Beau punched the door with the side of his hand.

Kevin bit back his growing fury over Samira. *One thing at a time.* "Beau, listen to me. That's your baby, man, your baby!"

Beau shook his head. "She's twenty-six weeks, Kevin. I was gone longer than that."

"Then they're wrong." Kevin stared him down.

"She's less than two and a half pounds!"

"They're wrong." Kevin's anger mirrored Beau's, though on the opposite end of the spectrum.

It was nearly five o'clock in the morning when Beau and Kevin arrived in the NICU. Beau's parents and Alice had gone home. The hospital was in nighttime mode, dim lights and quiet corridors.

"Mr. Johnson, nice to see you." The neonatal nurse stood beside Beau and Kevin. She looked through the glass at the tiny baby in the incubator. "She's a strong little girl," she said.

Beau mustered a smile, though his insides were tangled like a rebellious child's confusion.

"How's she doing," Kevin read her nametag and added, "Susan?"

"She's a tough little cookie. She's not giving up." She smiled and walked away.

"Well that's good news," Kevin said to Beau.

Beau turned his back to the window, "I wanna see Tess."

The monitors loomed like ominous monsters. Tess's swollen belly looked like a deflated balloon, still puffy but not bulbous. Beau was relieved to see that she no longer needed the ventilator. He dropped his eyes to her hand. He lifted the blanket, gently touched the pocket watch, then moved it to rest under Tess's hand. A tear slid down his cheek. His legs had become dead weight. He leaned against Tess's bed. *Why did you give up on me?* Love and hate battled in his mind. He was too tired to combat his own thoughts.

He walked around to the foot of the bed, where the web of wires and IV lines were nonexistent, and looked up at his wife. She was beautiful. Even with her face covered in grape bruises and gauze covering her apple-plump cheeks. Beau's heart stirred. He moved to the far side of the bed and reached for her hand, heavy and warm. He wrote the letter "I", drew a heart with his index finger, and wrote the letter "U", then clasped her small hand within both of his scratched and battered palms and brought it to his forehead.

"What am I going to do?" he whispered. He climbed into the bed and lay on his side, his right arm under his head, his left arm stretched across Tess's chest. He inched closer, until he could feel her body move with each shallow breath. The rhythmic beeps lulled him to sleep.

The beeping had stopped, replaced by one dull and steady high-pitched hum. In Beau's dream, the television screen had gone to one of those tests of the local area broadcasting system. Someone was tugging on his side, pulling him off the couch.

"Get him out of here, stat!" the male doctor ordered.

Beau awoke to being pulled off of Tess's bed and shoved out of the room. "What's wrong? What happened?" Blinking rapidly, he tried to pull his mind out of its slumbering state.

Tess's door slammed, the blinds closed. Beau was left floundering in the hall, listening to a frantic "Clear!" every few seconds from behind the door. He paced.

Mary came to his side, having just come on her shift. "They're doing all they can, darlin'," she said.

He panicked. "What happened? What's going on?"

"She coded again," Mary reached out, touched Beau's forearm.

"Coded?"

"Stopped breathing," she explained.

Beau's features crumbled. He covered his face with his hands, then moved toward Tess's door. Mary put herself between him and the door.

"I'm sorry, hon, but I can't let you go in there," her voice was sweet, yet firm.

"She's my wife!" He tried to push past her.

A tall, thick orderly moved beside Mary in quick fashion. "I'm sorry, sir, but you have to wait in the hall. Let the code team do their work. There's nothing you can do in there."

Minutes passed as if stretched into hours—too many minutes. Beau leaned against the wall, his chest constricted. His stomach turned and twisted. *Let her live*, played over and over in his mind like a broken record. If only he could be in the room. *She has to make it.* In that moment, he knew that no matter what she'd done while he was away, he did not want to be without her.

Nurses filed out of Tess's room, unable to meet Beau's eyes. An unfamiliar male doctor followed, his face a mask of apprehension.

Beau rushed up to him, "Is she okay?"

The doctor looked at him without saying a word, lowered his eyes.

Beau grabbed his arm, "She's okay, right?" Tears sprang from his eyes. His voice rose. "Tell me she's alright!" he pleaded.

"She's stabilized."

Beau let out a breath. "Thank you," he grabbed the doctor's hand and shook it. "Thank you," he said, wiping his eyes.

The doctor separated his hand gently from Beau's. "She's stabilized, for now, Mr. Johnson, but she wasn't breathing for several minutes."

"But she's okay?" Beau's eyes lit up, his hands fisted.

The doctor looked at Mary, who lowered her eyes.

A hunk of lead formed in Beau's gut.

"We've got her on life support."

Life support?

He let the words sink in before continuing, "Your wife's been through a lot, Mr. Johnson. She was in a complete state of anoxia for nine full minutes. She was legally dead."

A cold pain shot through Beau's chest and arms. "But...but she's on life support. She just has to get strong enough to breathe again, right?" Beau's voice rose and cracked.

The doctor shook his head. "It means we're breathing *for* her. Without oxygen, brain cells are destroyed after four to six minutes. Tess was without oxygen for nine minutes." He sighed, softened his voice. "Recovery is not an outcome I would hope for. She'll likely be in a vegetative state for the rest of her life. I'm sorry."

Chapter Thirty-Three

Kevin left Beau alone with Tess. He'd wanted to stay, but Beau had refused to let him remain in the room. Against Kevin's better judgment, he'd left the hospital. He wasn't going to fight with a man whose wife was on the verge of death. Rage mounted within him. His best friend was going to lose his wife *and* he thought she'd had an affair. Beau's coming home should have been a time of celebration, instead, it was a nightmare. He should have called Tess, let her know Beau was coming home, then she'd have been in the house, not in her car. The unraveling of his best friend's life was his fault. He pushed hard on the gas pedal, needing an outlet for his mounting anger. He headed toward Alice's condo.

The lights in Alice's window were out. Kevin's heart thumped against his chest as he took the stairs two by two to Alice's floor, then pounded on the door. When she didn't answer, he banged, two, three, four more times— each rap echoed in the empty corridor.

Alice peered out of the peephole, pulling her bathrobe tight around her small waist and opening the door, "Kevin?" Her voice carried the weight of sleep. She opened the door. "Did you find Beau?"

Kevin pushed into the condo, his arms tense, "Why'd you do it, Al?"

"What?" she said innocently, taken aback by his anger.

"Why'd you call Louie?"

Alice tucked her hair behind her ear and sat on the couch. "I don't know," she said softly. "I guess I felt like he should be there."

"Why?" his voice rose.

"What do you mean, why? They were *dating*, you know that," her voice twisted with irritation.

"But you knew Beau was back!" He paced the floor, stopping in front of Alice, arms crossed, red-faced. "You knew it would cause trouble!"

"Kevin—"

"Was she having an affair before Beau left?" he spat.

"No!"

"Is the baby *Louie's*?"

"No, Kevin. Jesus," she stood and walked into the kitchen.

Kevin followed.

"Then why, Alice?" his voice rocketed between the ceramic tile and the ceiling.

"Please lower your voice. It's hardly morning yet," she put a pot of water on the stove, her hands trembling. "The baby's Beau's. You know that. Why are you yelling at me?"

"She's dying, Alice. Tess is dying, and Beau thinks she had an affair and that the baby's Louie's."

The spoon Alice had been holding clanked to the floor. Her legs weakened. She grabbed the counter. "She's...she's—"

"Shit." Kevin lowered his voice, "I'm sorry, Al. I shouldn't have blurted it out like that."

"Dying?" she asked in a frightened voice.

Kevin nodded and reached out to her.

She pushed him away and turned her back. "You come in here accusing Tess of having someone else's baby, yelling at me, and *now* you tell me she's dying?" She spun around, her cheeks drenched in tears, her eyes venomous. "How dare you!"

"Ali—"

Alice's body shook, her legs would not carry her to the door. She clung to the countertop, her fingertips white with force. "Get out," she demanded. "Get out, get out, get out!" Her shrieks followed Kevin down the hall and into the elevator.

"She's…she's—" Alice's sobs stole her voice.

"What is it, Alice? Slow down, honey," Carol placed her left hand atop of the right, in an effort to stop the receiver from shaking. She wished Robert were there. She turned and looked toward the empty living room, then turned back toward the kitchen counter.

"She's not good. Kevin said she might not make it."

The receiver dropped from Carol's hand, slamming into the cabinets, swinging from its cord like a hanging victim. Her ability to think, to move, to comprehend, slipped away. Her hands hung limply at her sides. Carol didn't hear Robert's footsteps as he stepped from the carpet onto the ceramic tile of the kitchen floor. She didn't hear his high, panicked voice as he called her name. Carol's body collapsed into a heap on the cold kitchen floor.

"Carol!" Robert gasped, crouching beside her. His wife stared straight ahead, tears streaming down her cheeks. He touched her forehead, leaned her back against the cabinet. "Carol, what's happened? Can you hear me?"

Carol heard his voice, but couldn't find her own.

Robert grabbed a dishtowel and soaked it in cold water. He wiped her brow, her cheeks. "Carol?"

She blinked, turned toward his voice, as if just noticing he was there.

"What is it? What's happened? Should I call a doctor?"

Carol leaned forward, reaching for his shirt. She grasped his open cardigan in two tight fists, and pulled him toward her. Her forehead rested against his chest. She stayed there, silently crying, unable to tell her husband that their son's life was about to change forever. It wasn't fair. He'd just relieved their grief, only to be given his own.

Chapter Thirty-Four

This wasn't supposed to happen—none of it. Beau was supposed to return and Tess was supposed to jump into his arms, ecstatic to hold him. It wasn't fair, and Beau was dead set on making someone pay. His body taut with anger, he clutched the bedrails of Tess's bed so tightly they shook. *Louie. Fucking Louie.* Beau blazed with hatred. Breath shot from his nostrils fast and hard. He turned to leave, took two purposeful steps, then turned back. *Later,* he resolved.

The doctors were wrong. This wasn't the end. Beau leaned over Tess's body until his face was within inches of hers, the breathing tube a small viper, barely separating them.

"Wake up," he said sternly.

Tess's body remained still, her eyelids did not move.

"Wake up," his voice rose, his hands moved up the rail to the stainless steel curve near Tess's head.

"Wake up." His hands hovered above Tess.

"Wake the fuck up," he yelled. He clenched her shoulders and shook her. Her head bobbed up and down, her arms hung limp, like a rag doll's. He shook her harder, his voice gaining strength with each shake. "Wake up! Wake up! Wake up!"

Mary rushed into the room. "Mr. Johnson!" She grabbed his arms, pulling with all her might against his adrenaline-infused body. "Release her!"

Beau swiped his right arm backward, casting Mary off like a flea.

Mary pushed the emergency call button repeatedly. She grabbed at his arms again, pulling hard. "Let go! You'll hurt her!"

"Wake up! Wake up, Tess!" he raged, pushing her body into the mattress. Mary's voice, the monitors, faded into white noise. It was just he and Tess in the room, tunnel vision. *Wake her,* he heard in his mind. *Wake her now.*

Two orderlies rushed into the room, each grabbing one of his arms and dragging him away as he flailed and twisted, screaming, "Get up, Tess! Wake up!"

"Get him into room 210," Mary ordered.

Beau saw Tess slipping away before his eyes as he was dragged out of the room.

The orderlies stood, arms crossed in front of the door of room 210, an interior room with a couch, a table, two chairs, and despair. Beau paced, crossing and uncrossing his arms, pondering how he might get out of the damn room. He had to get to Tess. She had to wake up. This was a mistake, a goddamn mistake! It wasn't she who got hit by the car, it couldn't have been. This was a nightmare. It had to be. When would he wake up? He dug his nails into his forearms, trying to wake himself, sure the events weren't real. Blood filled the crescent-shaped punctures.

Beau looked up at the squeak of the door.

"Mr. Johnson." Dr. Kelly's eyes were serious, her lips set firmly in a line. "Let's sit down, shall we?" She motioned to the couch.

Beau sat on one of the upholstered chairs. He leaned forward, elbows on knees, his legs bouncing, eyes trained on his clasped fists.

"I understand—" Dr. Kelly began.

"It's a mistake." His gruff voice caused Dr. Kelly to lean back, distancing herself from him. "She's not brain dead."

"Mr. Johnson, it's very common—"

Beau pushed to his feet, paced. "Don't tell me what's common. Tess isn't common." He turned to face Dr. Kelly.

"I can assure you—"

"Don't assure me." He moved closer to her. "Don't fucking assure me. You don't know Tess. You don't know me."

"Yes," she said in a confirmatory tone. "I don't know Tess, or you, but I know medicine. I can assure you, all tests indicate—"

"Tests? I don't care about fucking tests! I know my wife, and she's not brain dead." He turned away, took two steps, then spun back toward her. "She's sharp as a tack, able to do a hundred things at once without thinking about it. You're wrong, Dr. Kelly, wrong."

"Mr. Johnson, if it will make you feel more assured, I will order a retake of the tests. This is a difficult process." Dr. Kelly stood, her voice softened. "I can assure you, we have no reason to indicate anything other than what the tests show."

Beau stared her down, arms crossed, muscles twitching. He felt the orderlies approach from behind, and turned, giving them a don't-even-think-about-it look.

"We can't have you assaulting your wife, Mr. Johnson. You will only injure her further."

"Assault? I didn't assault my wife."

"Shake, I'm sorry. You cannot shake your wife. If you're deemed a threat to her, Mr. Johnson, we'll have to ask you to refrain from seeing her."

Beau's arms fell to his sides. He let out a long breath, rubbed his hand down his face. His voice eased, "She's my wife." It sounded more like a question. Fresh tears sprang to his eyes. His anger changed to pain, vulnerability.

Dr. Kelly nodded. "Yes, she is."

"My wife," Beau said and collapsed onto the couch, his head in his hands. Beau couldn't wrap his mind around Tess's diagnosis. How could Tess be brain dead? The beautiful, bright woman he'd fallen in love with…brain dead? He cried like a child who'd lost his parent. His nose ran, his breath hitched. Salty tears dripped into his mouth.

Dr. Kelly gave a knowing glance to the orderlies. She sat next to Beau, her hand on his back.

"I'm sorry," he said, unable to stop the tears. "I'm sorry."

Chapter Thirty-Five

Alice walked down the corridor towards the office. When had the hallway become so narrow? The path that used to invigorate her now gave her a hollow feeling in the pit of her stomach. The gold Top Staffing Consultants sign appeared at the end of the hall. Each step carried the weight of Alice's grief, a grief so consuming she'd been unable to eat or sleep in more than fits and starts in the weeks since Tess's accident. She stood before the door, mentally preparing herself for the empty office. Her cell phone rang. Kevin. She pushed Ignore and sighed, lifting her right leg to support her purse as she dug for her keys. Something crinkled beneath her booted foot. Alice let out a loud breath. Missing an envelope on a hall floor came as no surprise. She was becoming all too familiar with things slipping by her lately. She retrieved the white, letter-sized envelope, and inserted the key into the lock.

The door pushed open, smooth and easy, its threshold a moat between her and the office—Tess's domain. Stacks of folders sat upon her desk, the blinking red message light on the phone flashed as loudly as a needy infant's wail in the silent room. A light jangling noise broke the silence—her keys, clanking against each other from her trembling hand. She clasped them in her palm. *You can do this.*

Stepping across the threshold was like entering a sacred place where she'd never before tread. It felt different with Tess lying in a hospital bed. Her eyes trailed the path to Tess's door, which stood open. Alice set her purse, keys, and the envelope down on her desk and walked toward the empty office. She stopped just shy of the door, her legs refusing to move forward. She returned to her desk. A lump formed in her throat, tears in her eyes. She sat on the chair behind her desk, staring at the envelope. She reached for it, expecting a note from the landlord, as it was the fifth of the month and she'd yet to pay their rent (or contact clients).

She withdrew a neatly-folded piece of white copy paper, flipped it over, and revealed a handwritten note. Her eyes drifted to the signature line. *Louie.*

Café Deluxe wasn't crowded, which was exactly what Alice had hoped for when she'd accepted Louie's invitation to meet him. She walked past the three thirty-something males at the bar, her head slightly bent, eyes trained on the ground. She shook off the shiver that ran up her spine and headed for a secluded leather booth in the back. How had she ever found that game of cat and mouse acceptable? She played with the seam of the booth in which she sat, looking up every few seconds for Louie, her insides a whirling tornado of nerves. What if Kevin saw her? What was she doing? Was she being disloyal to Beau? To Tess? *To Kevin?*

"Ma'am?"

Alice startled.

"Would you like a drink?" The waiter looked eleven years old with his side-parted hair and spirited eyes.

"Um, yes, please, piña colada." She remembered that she'd ordered that with Kevin and quickly changed her order. "Actually, I think I'll have a sour-apple martini. *" I need the big guns for this one.*

Louie arrived ten minutes later, his gait cautious, his eyes guarded. He slid into the booth across from Alice. She took note that he, too, looked as if he'd been lost on a desert island for the past two weeks without any food—or a hairbrush.

"Alice," he said.

"Hi, Louie." If discomfort had a taste, it would taste like this very moment in time.

"Listen, I didn't mean to cause—"

"You didn't," she interrupted. "It was my fault." *Damn. Tears.*

Louie handed her a napkin. "How is she?"

Alice shook her head, rolling her lips into her mouth, trying to keep from sobbing uncontrollably, as she'd been doing for what seemed like forever.

"Wha—"

Alice covered her eyes.

Louie reached across the table and took her other hand. "Alice, what happened? Is she...did she..."

Alice shook her head. "No," she sniffled. "No, she didn't."

Louie let out a loud breath.

Unable to bring herself to speak of Tess's condition, she offered, "I shouldn't have called you to come to the hospital, not with Beau there. I wasn't thinking. I'm sorry."

The waiter brought Alice's drink and took Louie's order.

"It's okay. You didn't do anything wrong. Hell, we didn't do anything wrong—or at least it didn't feel wrong." He looked away. "We thought he was dead," he whispered. The waiter returned. Louie grabbed the frosty mug and took a long swig of beer, thankful for the distraction.

"I know," she said.

"Jesus, Alice, I didn't mean to come between them."

The tenderness in Louie's voice couldn't be denied. Alice hated herself for what she knew she had to ask. "Louie?" She adjusted herself in the booth. "Did you...know Tess before he left?"

The inflection of the word "know" noted, Louie sat up straighter and looked Alice directly in the eye. "No, I didn't *know* her before he left. Jesus, Alice, what kind of guy do you think I am?"

Alice wiped her eyes, finally able to stop the river of tears. "I didn't think so. Beau thought—" there she went again, crossing loyalty lines. She shook her head, waved her hand in dismissal.

"Shit, no wonder he looked like he wanted to rip my head off."

"He thinks the baby is yours," she quickly added.

"Come on. I'm not like that." He sighed, "That's Beau's baby. The Tess I know isn't that type of person." Disgust oozed from his words. "Hell, she wanted to call it off with me anyway."

Alice let that drop. She didn't have the strength to go down that path. It didn't matter what Tess was thinking. It'll never matter again what Tess was thinking.

"I'm going crazy, Alice. I don't want to come between Tess and her husband, but...I gotta see her. I *miss* her."

Alice played with the seam in the bench again, her eyes trailing down to her lap, toward the bar, anywhere but at Louie. They were two people connected by some strange plane—two people who had once been untouchable, unbreakable, now broken by the loss of the same woman.

"Can you let her know?" he pleaded. "Don't make a big thing of it, just tell her I'm thinking of her?"

A lump swelled in Alice's throat. Perspiration formed on her brow.

"Please? I respect their relationship. Her husband's been through hell. I wouldn't come between them. I just want her to know that I didn't desert her."

Alice set her jaw. She looked at Louie with brimming tears and a trembling lower lip.

"I didn't mean to upset you, it's just—"

Alice shook her head, whispered, "She's..." She turned away, wiping the endless stream of tears. "Oh, God." Sobs tore from her chest. How could she do this? Not like Kevin. No, she couldn't be so cruel. With much pain and through hiccupping breaths, she took Louie's soft, strong hand into her own. "She's brain dead." The words felt like gravel in her throat, and, she could only imagine, like knives in Louie's heart.

Chapter Thirty-Six

The burly, pock-faced tree surgeon Robert had hired shook Beau's hand and handed him the receipt for cutting down and removing the tree that had ultimately stolen Tess's mental capacities. *Tree surgeon. Right. Murderer is more like it.* The tree was gone, a grave mound of wood chips and sawdust in its place. Is that what you do with things that don't work well anymore? Kill them? He couldn't help but wonder what would be left of Tess.

Beau watched the truck pull out of the driveway, a trailer full of wood, limbs trailing behind, bits of sawdust disappearing into the air. The house phone rang. Beau's heart fluttered. *Tess.* Then reality showed its ugly face again, and his heart deflated as quickly as it had swelled with hope. *Mom.* She was the last person he wanted to talk to. She hadn't stopped hounding him about the baby. *The baby* wasn't even his. He lumbered inside, hoping the ringing would stop before he reached the phone.

"Hi, Mom."

"Hi, honey. How are you? Did the tree surgeon show up?"

Shitty. Yes. "Fine. Yeah, they were here, took down the tree. Tell Dad thanks, will ya?"

"Of course, honey."

The silence between them thickened. Beau's face pinched. *Please don't start.*

"Honey, I was thinking…about the baby?"

"Mom*, please."*

"Just hear me out, please. I know you think Tess…strayed."

She's not a cat. She's my fucking wife.

"But I think you should forgive her, if she did…*stray*…I mean."

Beau pictured his mother standing in the kitchen, twisting the cord of her ancient wall phone around her finger, pain inking itself across her forehead.

"Mom, I gotta go," he said.

"Wait, honey, please. She's just a baby, Beau, a tiny, little piece of Tess, of you. She didn't ask for this. She's—"

"Mom!" Beau didn't mean to yell. He closed his eyes and breathed through his nose, wishing she'd shut up. *She's not a piece of me.*

"She's all you have left of her, Beau," Carol pleaded.

"Bye, Mom."

Chapter Thirty-Seven

Kevin had been sitting on the floor in front of Alice's door for twenty minutes, his arms leaning on his knees, head bowed. He'd wait for twenty hours if that's what it took for Alice to speak to him. *Alice.* She'd sure thrown him for a loop. He hadn't seen the strange attraction coming. Who knew she was so soft and vulnerable underneath the iron exterior? He hadn't handled her well that night he'd told her about Tess. He didn't blame her for being upset—okay, beyond upset. He could understand her hating him—for a while—but come on, look at what he'd been dealing with. His best friend is alive, his best friend's wife is brain dead, his friend has a baby he refuses to acknowledge, and now, this?

He and Alice had become so close. He'd learned to make the bed, give her space. Hell, he didn't even mind when she played up the sultry vixen when they were out together, even though the lecherous looks she received cut him to his core. He'd have adjusted to that, too, in time. *In time.* God, how he wanted that time.

"Ahem."

He hadn't heard Alice approach. He lifted his eyes. God, she was beautiful, even with anger etched into her face. "Hey." *Lame.* He rose to his feet.

Alice lifted her chin and put the key in her lock.

The silence crushed Kevin. He waited, hoping she'd say something, anything.

She didn't.

Kevin dug his hands deep into his pocket. The scent of her only made him miss her more. He followed her into the condo and stood by the door, waiting for her to tell him to leave. The condo looked like a freshman dorm room. Magazines littered the table, spilling onto the floor, dirty dishes lined the counter, and…was that a stain on the white chair? Kevin took two steps closer to inspect the discoloration.

Alice hung up her keys and waved to the chair, making no apologies for the new ransacked look her condo was sporting. "Sit," she said.

"It's okay," he said. "Alice?"

She set her purse on the counter and turned to face Kevin with a look that said, *What the hell do you want now?*

Kevin lifted his hands in surrender. "I'm sorry, Alice. I'm truly, desperately, unendingly sorry."

Alice dropped her gaze.

"I was out of my mind. I thought Beau had shot himself, he had blood all over." The anxiety that he'd been holding onto came tumbling forward. "He…God, Alice, he's my best friend." He sank into the chair, letting his face fall into his hands. "I'm so sorry."

Soft footsteps moved in his direction. Her hand on his back sent a shiver through his body and released his tears.

"I'm sorry," he said.

MELISSA FOSTER

Alice sat on the edge of the chair, emotional pain still tearing through her. "You shouldn't have accused me." Her heart was going to explode. "You shouldn't have told me like you did." Flush burned her face. "Goddamn it, Kevin. I hated you! Why'd you have to come back?" She folded her arms across her chest and turned toward the windows.

Kevin lifted his head. "Because I love you."

Tears filled Alice's eyes. For the umpteenth time that week, her body felt like a beehive, full of holes and whirling with turmoil. "Well, guess what? It doesn't work that way." She stood, spun around to face him. "You can't walk all over the people you love!" Her voice rose, her eyes bulged. "You can't do it. I'm losing my best friend, too, you know." She took two steps toward the kitchen, then buried her face in her hands. "This whole thing is fucked up," she cried.

Kevin was instantly by her side, "I'm sorry. I'm so sorry. I know I was wrong. I get it. I promise, Al, I'll never do it again."

Alice pulled away. She'd heard that one too many times—from her father, years ago. No, she wouldn't be the weak woman who allowed herself to be stepped on. She took a look around her condo, noticing the chaos for the first time. *What have I done?* She'd lost control. *Goddamn it!* She swallowed her pain and turned an icy stare toward Kevin.

"It's not okay."

Her cold tone startled Kevin.

"While I appreciate your apology, I'd like you to leave now."

"But—"

"I let you in, Kevin. You knew everything that I'd gone through. You're the only goddamn man I've ever let get close to me, and you've proven to me exactly what I already knew. You can let yourself out." She spun on her

264

heels and retreated to the bedroom, slamming the door behind her.

Louie's cell phone rang on the passenger seat as he sped toward the hospital. He knew who was calling and pushed the pedal down toward the floor. He had to see Tess. This couldn't be happening.

She's not yours to lose.

He gripped the steering wheel more tightly, fighting his own thoughts.

She's his.

He shifted in his seat. The phone began ringing again.

"Not now, Karen," he said through clenched teeth. The light up ahead was yellow. He floored it.

Carol's words taunted Beau, *All you have left of her.* He slowed to a stop as the light turned yellow. He was in no hurry to get to the hospital. He felt sick to his stomach every time he saw Tess and knew he had to muster the courage, or the desire, to see that baby. He wondered what Tess had been thinking as she held Louie in her arms. Did she speak to him in cute little quips like he remembered? Did they have inside jokes, secrets?

Beau focused on a spot on the dashboard as each thought stacked on the one before, building momentum. His body tensed. A prickling of frustration crawled along his skin. Honking behind him infiltrated his distress, and he lifted a hand in apology, pushing on the gas without looking away from the tiny fleck on the dashboard. Horns blared. Beau reflexively slammed on the brakes, looking up just in time to see the car speeding across the lane in front of him. *Jesus fucking Christ.*

Louie flew into a parking place, slammed the car into Park. He sat in the car and stared at the imposing brick façade of the hospital, each window watching him, accusing him. He knew he would be crossing a line the minute he walked into the hospital. He had no business seeing Tess. Her husband was back in town, her *husband.* He'd never be her husband. He'd never be Rebecca's husband. He let out a frustrated moan.

Tess had cast him away. Why hadn't he just told her about Karen? He'd seen her face each time he took one of Karen's calls. He knew he should've told Tess about her, but Karen was separate from Tess—his private burden to bear. Tess hadn't needed to be part of that craziness. She'd lost her husband, had a baby to care for. He thought he could protect her from the ugly remains that death leaves behind, and instead, he'd lost her forever. He'd known it when she'd gone away, and he was sure of it now, as he sat in the hospital parking lot ignoring Karen's call.

Beau slogged across the parking lot, still recovering from the near-miss at the stop light. Part of him wished the car had knocked him to hell. At least then he'd be out of his misery. His thoughts turned to his parents, and instantly guilt made each step more difficult.

A car door slammed behind him.

Beau reached for his cell phone. He needed to apologize to his mother. Tess had the affair, not her. He dialed her number. The hair on the back of his neck stood up when a man walked past his car. He glanced up. *Shit.* He clicked End Call, shoved the phone in his pocket, and set his shoulders back.

"Hey, asshole." His nerves were on fire.

Louie turned around. His eyes locked with Beau's. His face fell flat.

"Where do you think you're going?" Beau's gruff voice matched his imposing gait.

Louie put his palms up. "I don't mean any trouble, Beau. I just wanted to see her."

Beau's fists clenched and unclenched at his sides. "You've got some nerve."

Tension rose thickly between them. Beau was a lion, ready to attack, Louie, a pleading antelope.

Louie took two steps backward. "I don't want to—"

The punch connected with his jaw with a distinct crack, sending him reeling backward.

A woman passing by grabbed her daughter and hurried inside the hospital.

Beau stood above Louie, pushing Louie back in fast, hard thumps.

Louie stumbled backward.

"You've got no right." *Thump!* "Get the fuck outta here." *Thump!*

Louie swiped at the blood dripping from his lip. "I love her." He knew it was a mistake.

Thump!

"We thought you were dead."

Thump! "So you moved right in? Just like that?" *Thump!*

Louie's back was up against a car. "It wasn't like that," he tried to explain.

"You knocked up another man's wife!" *Thump!* Beau pulled his arm back, fist tight. "You fucking prick. She's MY wife!"

Two enormous security guards grabbed Beau from behind, dragging him backward on his heels.

"Don't you dare go in there, motherfucker," Beau screamed. "Stay away from her!"

Chapter Thirty-Eight

"What were you thinking?" Kevin asked as he and Beau left the police station. "You're lucky he didn't press charges."

"He's lucky I didn't kill him," Beau fumed, marching toward Kevin's truck.

"Jesus, Beau. Don't you want to see Tess? At this rate you'll...I don't know. Something bad's gonna happen."

Beau gave him a sideways look.

Kevin rolled his eyes. "Sorry." He waited for Beau to say something.

Beau didn't respond.

"What's going on, Beau? Tess is lying in the hospital, man." He prepared for a punch, knowing he had gone too far, but he was sick of the crap Beau was pulling. His wife was lying in a hospital, brain dead, their baby was struggling for her life, and Beau was acting like a psycho teenager. Kevin was no better prepared to handle this than he was to handle the mess he was in with Alice.

"What the fuck? You think I don't know that? You think I don't think about her every second of the goddamn day? She can't fucking do anything, Kevin, and she's not coming back. I have to fucking deal with that."

Kevin turned away, his heart aching.

"You expect me to just say, *Oh, whatever. She slept with some other guy, great, no problem. I'll just play daddy to that prick's kid.*" He shot Kevin a cold look. "I got news for you, Kev," he paused, "it ain't happenin'."

Kevin wondered how long a hospital could care for a baby if a father refused to.

Beau was becoming used to the way the house felt—like returning to his childhood home after his parents had sold it—alive with memories, but lacking animation. He went upstairs and lay back on the unmade bed. He'd found the boxes of his clothes in the basement the week after Tess's accident, and he'd begun the slow process of restocking his drawers. As his eyes sailed over the half-empty box, he wished he could restock his life as easily. It had been weeks since Tess had been pronounced brain dead, and he was still too angry to make any decisions. He loathed the hospital, sitting by Tess's bed, the nurses passing him with pitying looks, treating him with kid gloves, Dr. Kelly pressing him to make a decision. How the hell do you decide to end someone's life? What if they're wrong? What if she's not brain dead, but just—he didn't know what—lost in the recesses of her own mind? He rolled onto his side. Maybe he was just being stupid.

His mother had told him to let her go, but he didn't know how. How could he? He was too mad to let her go. Selfishly, he wanted her to wake up so he could yell at her, make her feel the pain he was feeling at that very moment. He rolled over onto his back, his leg and arm aching, reminding him of the desert. Suha. He wondered what had happened to her body. *Samira. Jesus Christ.* He propped himself up on his elbow and dialed Mr. Fulan's number.

"Beau, how are you?" Mrs. Fulan's voice was laden with concern.

"I'm doing okay, thank you. I'm sorry to bother you. Is Mr. Fulan available?"

"Yes, he is."

Beau could hear her hard shoes moving across the marble floor. She covered the phone, said something in Arabic. Beau could hear the smile in her voice.

"Samira is here," she said into the receiver.

Beau hadn't expected that.

"Would you like to speak with her?" she asked.

His heartbeat quickened. "Yeah, sure."

The phone passed hands.

A tentative hello whispered through the receiver.

"Samira?"

Her small familiar voice, "Yes."

"I'm sorry about leaving. I...there's been an accident."

"Yes, I know."

Beau was thankful she understood the words he spoke. "Are you okay? The kids?"

Edham's voice piped up in the background, "Mr. Beau?"

Samira hushed him. "Yes," she said to Beau. Edham rattled on in the background. Samira hushed him again.

Beau smiled at Edham's excitement. "Can I talk to him?"

Samira handed the phone to Edham, speaking quickly in Arabic to her excited son.

"Mr. Beau!"

"Hey!" Beau felt his spirit lift for the first time in weeks. "Are you being good?"

"Good. I'm good," Edham said. "You see me?"

Beau smiled. "Yes. Soon."

Samira took the phone from Edham.

"How's Zeid? Athra?" he asked.

"Zeid? He is Zeid. Athra close to Mrs. Fulan," she said with warmth.

A brief silence passed between them.

"Sorry. Your wife," Samira offered.

"Thank you." Beau lowered his voice, "Suha?"

A strained sound came through the receiver.

"Don't. The children. I'm sorry." Beau shook his head. He should have known better. "Are you okay?"

"Yes. Mr. Fulan is very kind."

Beau let out a relieved sigh. He told Samira that he'd see her soon and spoke briefly to Mr. Fulan, who thanked him for bringing Samira and the children into their lives.

"Layla has taken the children in as siblings, and Mrs. Fulan and Samira are like sisters," Mr. Fulan had said.

Knowing that Samira and the children were safe and happy eased a weight from Beau's shoulders. He was pleased that Samira had been using her given name, rather than the fake name she'd been given. What Mr. Fulan said next, sent Beau into bittersweet hell.

"Samira gave me your camera. The photographs will be published next month. You'll gain international credit."

Beau lay back on the bed and closed his eyes.

Chapter Thirty-Nine

Alice sat in a padded wooden chair next to Tess's bed, wondering how she'd carry on without Tess in her life. She was the closest thing Alice had to a best friend. They'd had an odd relationship, that was true. Alice knew she'd been off-putting at times, perhaps exuding an aura of snootiness, but she had to believe that Tess had seen through that, of course she had.

Alice had been in the hospital room since six A.M., having woken up at five A.M. with thoughts of Tess careening through her mind. The nurses didn't seem to mind. Alice supposed that traditional visiting hours didn't come into play when a person wasn't conscious.

She'd finally notified Top Staffing Consultants' clients of Tess's condition, which explained the multitude of bouquets that lined the counters and windowsill in Tess's room. Alice had even begun to get back on track with running the business. She was driven by the belief that she was making Tess proud. Tess had worked too hard to build the business. Alice owed it to her to carry on. Today, though, something within her had guided her to Tess's bedside.

The room brightened with the rising sun. The bandages had been removed from Tess's face, exposing angry red stitches and fading multi-colored bruises. *Why her and not me?* Alice wondered. *Why did I live through my attack, and she didn't even see hers coming?* She tucked stray strands of hair behind her ear and leaned forward, her fingers lightly touching Tess's arm.

"Tess?" she whispered. "I'm sorry for everything." *Everything?* What did that really mean? She leaned forward and tried again. "I'm sorry that I was such a bitch. I'm sorry that I acted like I was better than everyone else, when really..." She looked behind her. She was alone.

Alice turned back to Tess and whispered, "When I was really scared." She closed her eyes and thought about what she really wanted to tell Tess. Tess had pulled Alice through the most difficult times in her life. She'd accepted Alice as she was without question or judgment. Tess's support had helped Alice to maintain her confidence. She needed her, plain and simple. Alice leaned back in the chair, disappointed in herself—again. She didn't know how to climb out of her internal pain and tell Tess what she felt. It would expose her own vulnerability. *To whom?* she wondered. *A woman who would never wake up? Selfish bitch.*

Alice knew her own limitations. Sure, she had been able to push past them for a short period, with Kevin, but he'd only proven to her that it was dangerous to let anyone see who she really was. She looked down at her perfectly-pressed linen suit, the three-inch taupe heels that she knew made her look elegant. She smoothed the expensive fabric that covered her thin thighs. Her eyes moved to Tess, a lonely thread weaved its way through her heart. The clothes, the stature, it wasn't what made her feel strong. It was merely a costume. She was the female version of Batman, and she needed her Robin. She needed Tess. With Tess by her side, building her up, believing in her in a way that no one ever had, looking at her in that way that said, *Sure, you're beautiful, but you're even more beautiful inside.* In her disguise, she was untouchable. Alice covered her eyes. *Without you, I'm right back at square one—that little girl that Daddy hurt.*

"Alice?" Kevin's voice interrupted her thoughts.

Alice tensed.

"I'm sorry," Kevin approached her from behind. "I didn't know you'd be here."

Alice looked away, "It's okay. I was just leaving." She rose to her feet.

Kevin reached out and touched her arm, "Al, can't we talk? I miss you."

She looked from him to Tess, the lonely tug in her gut hard to ignore.

Beau kicked the pavement outside the hospital. He was stalling. He took a few steps closer to the automatic doors. *Just go in,* he told himself.

"Mr. Johnson?"

Beau turned to face Susan, the nurse he'd seen weeks before. The one he'd almost forgotten.

"It's nice to see you." She fell in step with him, walking toward the elevator. "Here to see Baby A?"

He looked at her sideways.

She blushed. "That's what we call your baby girl."

Beau nodded, slipping his hands into his jeans pockets. "A?"

"Oh, don't worry, we're not allowed to name her. We call her A because it's first in line, you know, like the first letter in the alphabet? She turns toward you when you walk in the room now, like she's saying, 'Hey, here I am!'" Susan waved her hand in the air with a smile. "Like she wants to be seen first."

An unfamiliar sensation swelled in his chest. They arrived at the NICU and went directly to the viewing window. Beau didn't recognize Baby A. He looked over the four babies in their incubators.

Susan pointed to the largest of the babies, the only one not in an incubator. "There she is. Isn't she fantastic?"

He touched the glass between them. She'd grown so much, he couldn't believe it was the same baby.

"She's had a few bowel issues, but I guess you know that."

Beau startled. "Bowel issues? Is she alright?"

"Oh, yes," she waved the comment away. "She's shaping right up, breathing on her own pretty well. This is all pretty standard for a preemie. She was on a vent for a week or so, but she's doing well now. They're monitoring her for sleep apnea, but the doctor said she'd probably be out of the hospital very soon."

A vent? Bowel issues? His mind was tangled in knots, and Susan was pulling the ends of his strings even tighter. He feared he'd never unravel the mess he was in.

"Your mom's been here every day."

"Yeah, I know."

Susan turned to face him, crossing her arms over her chest. "It's okay, you know. You're not the only parent who hasn't been able to face your child's weakness."

Her voice was kind, her eyes gentle. So why did Beau feel as though he'd just been slapped in the face?

Chapter Forty

Carol had scrubbed the bathroom and kitchen until her fingers were raw. She'd dusted, vacuumed, and prepared and frozen enough dinners to last for weeks. It was no use. She couldn't ignore the pull to see her son. He was drowning and every lifeline she threw fell short. It had been almost two months since Tess's accident, and Beau still wasn't answering most of her phone calls, and when he did, he was short and distant. She'd lost him once, and she couldn't bear to lose him again.

She couldn't listen to Robert's passive advice for one more second. "He'll come around. Let him be, when he's ready, he'll see the baby." Carol pushed herself out of the kitchen chair. She'd minded her business for forty-something years. She'd had enough. Robert could take his children-move-naturally theory and put it where the sun doesn't shine. Carol was Beau's mother. It was time she acted like it.

"I'm going to the library," she called to Robert and headed out the front door. She'd never before lied to Robert, and it didn't sit well now. *It's for a good reason,* she rationalized.

Carol parked in the empty driveway, remembering the day Beau and Tess had purchased their little bungalow. *The perfect house for the perfect couple,* she'd said. Sadness gripped her by the shoulders. She slumped against the door of her car and waited for Beau to arrive.

Beau pulled up ten minutes later.

Their eyes met through the car window. Carol met him on the sidewalk.

"Mom, what are you doing here?"

"I missed you, honey. I figured you could use—"

"I'm fine, Mom." He brushed past her, heading for the front door.

Carol hurried behind him, the pull of a mother guiding her.

Beau pushed the door open, tossed his keys on the table next to the front door, and walked into the kitchen, his mother stopped in the living room.

Stark. That was the only word Carol could come up with to describe the feel of Beau's house. The house that had once exuded warmth, solicited smiles, was now cold and barren.

Beau grabbed a beer from the fridge and leaned against the door jamb between the kitchen and the living room. He took a long swig.

"You okay, Mom?"

His voice brought her out of her dumbstruck state, "Uh, yeah, sure, honey." She moved around the room, picking up Beau's dirty socks, unable to stop her eyes from hovering over the empty sections of the wooden shelves, where pictures of Beau and Tess used to stare happily back at her. Beau's books sat stacked in a half-open box on the floor.

"Are you moving?" she tried to quell the alarm in her voice.

"Nope," he said and trudged upstairs, taking another long pull on his beer.

Carol stood with a bundle of dirty laundry in her hands, unsure if she should follow. She bit her lower lip, wishing the world would have been kinder to her only son. She took a deep breath and marched up the stairs, tossing the socks into a hamper in Beau's cluttered bedroom. The closet doors were shut, half-full boxes of Beau's clothes leaned against the dresser, Tess's clothes strewn across the floor.

"How do you live like this?" she asked.

Beau flopped on the bed, leaned back against the headboard, and watched his mother with disinterest. He lifted his beer—and his eyebrows—in response.

Carol set her hands on her hips, suddenly thrown back to being the mother of a rebellious teenager. "I didn't raise a pig," she said and began to straighten up the room.

Beau didn't move.

"Beau Mitchell Johnson, you put that bottle down and clean up your room. What would Tess think of this?" She turned her back, knowing the mention of Tess's name might cause a stir.

Beau pushed himself to his feet. "You know what, Ma? She wouldn't think anything of it. She can't think, remember?" His anger stung Carol.

She closed her mouth, swallowing her body's desire to coddle his sadness and anger away. *You can do this. You have to.* She crossed her arms, more of a stabling of her body than a meaningful gesture.

Beau set the beer bottle on the dresser with a loud *clunk.*

Coaster? sailed through Carol's mind.

"That's right, Mom. She's gone. Oh, her body is here, and her goddamn baby, but she's nothing but a vegetable." He threw open the closet doors. "She'd already moved me out. All my shit," he spread his arms like Vanna White presenting a prize, "gone. She was all ready for that other guy to move right in and take over." He pulled open his sparse dresser drawers. "Whaddaya say to that?" He set his jaw in a smirk. His eyes glazed over.

Carol moved around the room, closing the drawers, and folding his clothes, "I think she was a grieving woman, a woman who had just lost her husband." She stared at her son's disheveled hair, tension emanating from his every muscle. Her heart ached for him. She knew her words hurt, but she pressed on—she had to. "I think she was a woman doing all she could to remain sane. Losing someone you love is not easy." She realized what she'd said, and softened her tone, "You, of all people, should know this."

"She had another man's baby."

Carol did not mistake the hurt in his voice for anger. "Maybe." She lowered herself to sit on the bed. Carol ached to tell him what Louie had said, but worry stopped her. It might seem a betrayal to her son that she'd held this knowledge that Louie had confided in her and had somehow done so behind Beau's back. Beau's love for Tess, his faith in her, had to prevail.

"No maybe, Mom. The doc said the baby was twenty-six weeks."

"The doctors told me that I'd never have a baby. Then they told me that I'd never carry you to full term." She recalled the memory as if it were yesterday. She smiled, remembering the joy of holding Beau for the first time. "Doctors can be wrong, Beau."

Beau turned away.

"That baby did not ask for this. She didn't ask to be unwanted."

Beau flushed.

"You're a smart man, Beau. If you're so inclined to believe the baby isn't yours, then do a paternity test. They do it all the time."

"And say what?" his eyes filled with tears. "Excuse me, but I think my dying wife screwed around behind my back, and before I claim this baby, I wanna know for sure?"

Carol pushed to her feet. "Yes! If that's what it takes, then yes, sure, why not?" She paused, waiting for Beau to respond. No words left his lips. "There's nothing to be ashamed of."

"What would Dad have done?"

Carol stopped and thought about the question, finally answering in a meek voice, "I have no idea what your father would have done, but it doesn't matter. This is your life, Beau. That may be your baby, and in any case, she's Tess's baby. Doesn't that mean *anything* to you?"

Beau made a grumbling noise and stomped downstairs.

Carol followed.

Beau stood in the living room, staring out the window into the side yard, his back to his mother. He turned and said to his mother, curtly, "I'll order the test."

Chapter Forty-One

"Mr. Johnson, may I speak with you?" Dr. Kelly held a folder in her hands, and led Beau to her office. "Have a seat," she motioned toward a blue tweed chair.

Beau eyes were drawn to the photos of twin girls on the desk.

Dr. Kelly smiled. "Those are my girls, Dot and Lorna."

"Cute," Beau said, feeling stupid.

"Mr. Johnson, I know you've been going through a very difficult time." She withdrew a bundle of papers from the folder. "I took the liberty of copying these articles for you." She handed him the stack.

He leafed through them: "Loved Ones and Brain Injuries", "Dealing with Death", "Living with Life Support", "The Grieving Process". Beau handed the stack back to her. "I appreciate your time, but I don't need these."

"Don't need them or don't want them?" she asked.

Beau hesitated.

"Mr. Johnson, we can keep your wife on life support for as long as you wish, but that's not going to bring her out of the vegetative state."

Beau pushed to his feet. If he sat there one more minute his head would explode.

"Mr. Johnson," she pleaded, "I would like to talk to you about a few things that perhaps you haven't considered."

Reluctantly, he lowered himself into the chair, clenching and unclenching his jaw, sure his teeth would crack.

"When a person is in the state that Tess is in, oftentimes family members will hold out hope that the injured person will somehow bounce back or wake up. I can assure you, in Tess's case, that isn't a possibility." Her eyes did not waver, her words remained confident. "The longer you wait, the more difficult it will be."

The light from the window dimmed as a cloud passed overhead, mirroring the dark thoughts running through Beau's mind. He couldn't find his voice. Every breath took tremendous effort to push from his lungs.

"There's more to consider," she continued.

Shut up. Shut up!

"I know this seems like a lot. I'm sorry for what you're going through. It's difficult for loved ones to move on when a relative is in this state. I've seen it a thousand times. People become trapped, stilled. They take three steps forward, only to visit the patient and be sent four steps back."

Tears formed in Beau's eyes. He didn't want to listen. He wanted to bolt from the room, but his feet were glued to the floor.

"Think about it, Mr. Johnson."

That's all Beau had been able to do since the car had flown over the crest of the hill and shattered his life.

Chapter Forty-Two

Beau lay on his back on Tess's side of the mattress in their bedroom that now felt too big, too empty. He looked around for some sign that he'd made the right decision. What that sign might be, he had no idea. He wished there were a magical guide, something that gave a virtual nod to people who had to make these decisions. He thought back to the pamphlets, the way they felt as though they were filled with betrayal. *Was it the right decision?* he wondered. His mother seemed to think so. The doctors definitely agreed, having pushed him in the direction of letting go. Why, then, did he feel like such a traitor? His gut burned, and his chest ached. The leg he'd broken sent searing pains through his knee. He wondered if the pains were real or imagined—his own silent form of self-punishment. He turned onto his side, closed his eyes, and inhaled through his nose. Tears rose to his eyes. He grabbed the pillow and buried his face in it, taking a deep whiff. *Nothing.* He shoved his face into the mattress, inhaled. *Nothing.* He needed her.

His pulse raced. He climbed to his knees and ripped the drawer from her bedside table, fumbling through the contents looking for her tube of CK One lotion. Where the fuck was it? He slipped to the floor and rifled through the drawer, tossing out pencils, a notepad, bottles of Motrin and Tylenol, lotion. *Lotion!* He pulled open the cap and brought it to his nose. His pulse calmed. He gripped the tube in both hands like a lifeline, squeezed a dab into his palm and rubbed his hands together, then wiped the lotion on his neck and cheeks. He lifted a stack of magazines from the deep drawer, exposing Tess's journal.

Beau stared at the journal for a long time. He'd never once considered reading her journal. He reached a shaking hand into the drawer and lifted the keeper of Tess's private thoughts into his lap.

The ringing phone broke the silence.

"Hello?"

"Honey? I just wanted to make sure you were okay," Carol's voice embraced him.

"I'm okay, Mom."

"You sure? Want me and Dad to come get you? We can drive you to the hospital."

There it was. *Reality.* Today was the day they were saying goodbye to Tess—forever.

"Beau?"

"I'm here. It's okay. I can drive myself." His hand rested on the journal, the tips of his fingers curling around the edge of the fabric-covered notebook.

"Are you sure, honey?"

"Mom."

"Okay, well, we'll see you in an hour?"

"'Kay."

Forty minutes later, Beau picked himself up from the floor, lotion safely tucked away in his pocket, and tossed Tess's journal onto the bed. He went to the bathroom, brushed his hair, and came back into the bedroom, the guilt of what was yet to come shadowed his every move. He grabbed Tess's journal and headed to the car.

Chapter Forty-Three

Tess's journal lay on the passenger seat calling to Beau as the apple had called out to Eve. Beau eyed it as he gathered his strength for what lay ahead. He shouldn't have brought it. He wasn't sure why he did. He picked it up and held it to his chest.

"Tessie," he whispered. An envelope fell from the journal, landing in his lap, his name scrawled in Tess's handwriting across the front. He set the journal on the seat, and pondered the envelope. Was it his Dear John letter, the explanation that she was leaving him? He didn't want to know.

Beau pressed his body into the warmth of his parents. His mother's tears landed on the crook of his neck. His father held him tight against his chest, his broad hand spread across Beau's back. Beau would have stayed within their embrace forever if he could, safe from the nightmare that loomed. Cognitively, Beau knew that the right thing to do, the humane thing to do, was to turn off Tess's life support, to provide closure to everyone who loved her, an end to their agony. He just wasn't sure he was capable of actually doing it.

Carol stepped back from Beau and Robert. She blew her nose, patted her eyes with a tissue. Robert lifted his hand from Beau's back, releasing him. Beau remained against his father—a child's safety revisited. Eventually he pushed back, a glazed look in his eyes. A lump inhabited his airway. He couldn't shake the feeling that he'd let everyone down, especially Tess.

Tess's face looked like a rag doll that had been stitched a few too many times. Beau saw past her marred skin. He saw milky-white smoothness, soft and inviting, the tiny dimple that formed just above the outside right corner of her mouth when she smiled, and the cute way she'd crinkled her nose when he'd mentioned the word "anchovy". Beau looked past her still body, feeling her index finger lightly pushing on his palm, the way she'd push her shoulder into his armpit and snuggled close as they walked down the street. He heard her whispering to him in the stillness of the night, *Hold me.* His heart swelled with each memory. The antiseptic smell of the room suddenly changed, as if a new scent, Tess's scent, had come in with a breeze. The unique minty, flowery aroma of her breath came back to him. Behind her closed eyelids he saw the shine of her morning glory blue eyes, dancing when she laughed at an inside joke between the two of them.

His parents, Kevin, and Alice faded away. It was just he and Tess in their last bubble of time. He felt the drag of her finger across his shoulders and spun his head around. She wasn't there. Of course she wasn't, and he wasn't hulking over photographs on the living room couch—he might never be able to pick up another camera—he was mourning the upcoming death of his wife in a stale hospital room, with people waiting for the turning off of her life support. The person lying in the bed before him, unmoving, unthinking, that was not Tess. That was an imposter, a manikin of the woman Beau loved.

Robert put an arm across Carol's shoulder, his eyes on Beau. He spoke with concern, not rushing or pushing Beau. "Son?"

Beau's eyes were red and swollen, shadowed with gray. He lifted his chin. Kevin and Alice stood apart from the family, an uncomfortable distance between the two of them.

"Sorry, man," Beau whispered through his tears.

Kevin squinted, shook his head, sending a silent message, *Don't even think about it. I'm here.*

"For all the shit I put you through, I'm so sorry," Beau said.

"No worries, man, no worries."

Beau lifted his gaze to Alice, emaciating before his eyes. Creases had formed across her forehead, her normally tight cheeks, now sunken and hollow. Her eyes had become dull, frightened. Beau's chest tightened, still believing that Alice knew about Tess's affair before he'd left for Iraq. He tried to feign a pleasant look. He failed.

Alice stiffened.

Robert put his hand on Beau's shoulder. "Son? Would it be okay if we said a few words to Tess before we leave you alone?"

"Alone?"

"We just thought...you might want a few minutes alone to say goodbye to Tess," Carol said gently.

Beau nodded.

Carol brought her husband's hand up to her lips, pressed them there, and closed her eyes. Robert pulled her into his side, kissing the top of her head. She lowered his hand. Carol brushed Tess's hair from her forehead, tears streaming down her cheeks.

Alice reached for Kevin's hand.

Beau leaned against the wall, his back to the others. He slipped the letter out of his pocket, turning it over in his hands, contemplating the weight of it. He opened the envelope and withdrew the light pink stationery. His pulse climbed with each passing second. He filled his lungs and read.

Beau, my love. You didn't come back to me. You promised. How can I not be angry? I don't want to be angry, but it's happening anyway. I trusted you. I know it's not your fault, but I have no one to blame, and my every thought carries anger.

The "me" in blame was smudged, as if a tear had fallen and washed it away.

I feel like I'm floating through each day without knowing where I'm going. I can't see anything but you. I look for you everywhere. I feel you with me, even now, when everyone says I'm crazy. I pick up the phone to call you, but you're not there. I can't see you, but I can feel you. I know you're here with me. Everyone is telling me to move on. I don't think I know how. It feels like I'm betraying you if I try to get back to normal, whatever that is. Normal won't ever be normal again.

We promised till death do we part, but I never expected it to happen so soon. I wonder what you were thinking when the helicopter went down. I wonder if you'd wished you'd never gone. I wish you'd never gone.

Nothing feels right, Beau. Food tastes bad, the sun is too bright. Your side of the bed is too empty. Do you feel me at night, when I inch over to where you should be? Do you hear me when I call out to you in the middle of the night? Damn it, Beau, I'm not cut out to handle this. I know you think I'm strong, but it's not real. Maybe one day I was, but I don't know how to be strong anymore. I'm trying to carry on because that's what everyone says that you'd want for me, but in my heart, I don't believe it. I think you'd want me to stay connected to you. I think you'd want what I want, to feel you here with me, every second of every day. I love you, Beau, and forevermore you will be with me, and I with you. I will never say goodbye. Tess

Beau was alone with Tess for what he knew would be the last time. Tears streamed down his cheeks. He held her hand in his own, his words stuck in his throat. He still hoped for a miracle that he knew would never come. *Why,* he silently asked *God, why Tess?* He swallowed past the lump that stopped his words, and found a whisper of his voice. "I can't say goodbye, Tess," he said. "I'm not strong enough for this. I don't think I can do it."

He looked down at the note in his hand, his tears coming faster. He brought his fist, and the note, to his forehead, and clenched his eyes shut. "I need you," he cried. "I am so sorry, Tess. Can you ever forgive me?"

Beau rose on shaky legs and climbed onto Tess's bed, ignoring the wires and monitors, ignoring the pain in his throbbing leg. He had to hold her one more time, to smell her, to feel her next to him. She had to know she was loved. She had to feel his love, his heart beating next to hers. He wrapped her in his arms, his left leg crossed over hers, his chest against her side. His face nuzzled into her chest for the last time; he sobbed. He cried for the loss of the only woman he'd ever loved. He cried for the time he'd already lost and for the looks he'd never see from her. He cried for the voice he'd never hear again and for the dimple he'd never wait to see appear. He cried for the baby who would never know her mother, the one they'd never raise together. Beau cried until his eyes ached and his throat threatened to stop letting air pass. He pulled the pills from his pocket, counting each one in his hand. Thirty. Tears blurred his vision as he reached for a small cup of water on the nightstand. A silly thing to be next to the bed, but Beau knew it was there for him, not for Tess. He bent his head back and tossed the pills into the back of his throat, then gulped them down with the water.

The room blackened. His pain dissipated. He couldn't feel. He couldn't think. His vision faded in and out of darkness. Beau closed his eyes against the sight of Tess. Images of her eyes, the second before the airborne car struck her, stared back at him in the dark recesses of his mind. A wail broke through his sorrow, ripping from his throat like broken glass, only he hadn't uttered a sound. He couldn't catch his breath. No, that wasn't it at all. His breath was leaving him. Sadness was a monster that clawed at every inch of him, stealing noises from his throat that no one ever heard, stealing his heart from within his chest. He hated the doctors. He hated that this day had come. Where the fuck was rewind? How could he go back? Warmth spread through his limbs. He tried to dodge the truth, huddling in his mind against the pressure of it. He knew he made the right decision. He could not live without Tess. A tear slid down his cheek, as he surrendered to the darkness.

Chapter Forty-Four

Tess's lips parted, a soft puff of air released. No one was there to witness the flutter of her eyes beneath their lids. No one was there to witness her breath as she sucked it back in.

There was a weight against her side as she tried to pull herself out of what felt like a deep, drug induced sleep. *Beau,* she thought.

Her eyes would not open. She tried to speak, but her lips would not move. With the scent of her husband comforting her, she drifted back into the darkness.

Carol couldn't wait any longer. It had been thirty minutes since they'd left Beau alone with Tess to say his goodbyes. Something told her she had to be in there. Beau was not strong enough to do this alone. She took Robert's hand, nodded to Alice and Kevin, and together they pushed through the door to Tess's room.

"Beau, honey. Are you ready for us?" she asked, walking slowly to the side of the bed where he lay. "Oh, Robert, look at him," she whispered. "He loves her so."

Robert touched Beau's leg.

Beau didn't move.

Robert shook his son's arm. "Ready son?" An empty pill bottle rolled out from underneath Beau's arm. "Jesus Christ. Get the doctor."

Kevin ran out the door and into the hallway. "Help! Doctor!"

Carol took in the pill bottle, and Beau's still body. She reached for her husband's arm, unable to speak past the lump in her throat. Her body trembled and shook.

"Oh my God," Alice sobbed, pointing to Tess's fluttering eyelids.

Two nurses burst into the room. The older one moved swiftly to the bedside and took Beau's pulse, then checked to see if he was breathing, while the other spoke to Robert.

"He was saying goodbye to Tess. We were only out there twenty or thirty minutes," Robert said.

"Call a code!" the older nurse ordered.

The younger nurse rushed from the room. Seconds later, Dr. Kelly burst into the room shouting orders, followed by the younger nurse and the code team. The code cart and a stretcher were pushed into place next to the bed.

"Get them out of here," Dr. Kelly said, as she took Beau's pulse.

"What's going on?" Carol grabbed the nurse's arm, pleading with her. "He was just saying goodbye."

The nurse hurried them out the door.

Carol watched Beau being put onto a stretcher and, as they pushed her out the door, she looked over her shoulder and saw electrodes stuck to his chest.

"She's breathing!" Dr. Kelly yelled as the door closed behind them.

Chapter Forty-Five

The beeping wouldn't stop. Beau slowly drew himself out of the darkness. The scent hit him first. He was in the hospital. *Damn it.* The pills didn't work. Tears spilled from his eyes. How would he live without Tess?

He turned to face the curtain that separated him from the other patient, his hands curled into fists. What would he do now? His eyes ran frantically from counter to counter, looking for something, anything that might help him leave this world.

A door opened. He listened to soft footsteps move behind the curtain.

"How are you, darlin'?"

Beau recognized the nurse's voice. Embarrassment warmed his chest and cheeks.

"Slowly getting there."

Beau's chest clenched. His eyes grew wide. He knew that voice. Was he crazy? It couldn't be her.

"That's good, hon. You just rest up now, and you'll be out of here in no time." The nurse moved through the curtain and smiled at Beau.

Beau's eyes were riveted to the curtain, which was slowly falling closed behind her. He caught a quick glimpse of a woman lying prone on the bed. He couldn't speak. He pushed himself upright, his legs hanging off the edge of the bed.

"Whoa, settle down there, hon. You'll rip your IV out, and trust me, you need that Narcan. You sure pulled a fast one on us." She took his arm and gently moved him back to a laying position, then leaned down and whispered in his ear, "Scared me half to death. You sure did. And that pretty wife of yours, too. What were you thinkin'?"

"My...my wife?" The words were barely audible. *Tess?* Tears instantly welled in his eyes. His head felt heavy, too big.

"Oh yes, hon. She's right here with you." She nodded toward the curtain, and then drew it slowly open.

Every muscle in his body tensed. His nerves were afire, the hairs on his arms and the back of his neck stood on end. Tess lay on the bed, her eyes closed.

Sobs bubbled up from Beau's chest. He blinked several times, hoping he wasn't dreaming. "Tess," he cried.

Tess turned her head toward Beau. As a smile spread across her cheeks, Beau's heart ached.

"Tess?"

She nodded.

"It's really you." He looked up at the nurse. "How? Is she okay? I don't understand." He swiped at his tears. Every muscle in his body pulled in her direction. "Please, take this out. I have to go to her." He held the IV tube between his fingers.

Tess turned her head and Beau saw a smile in her eyes.

"Now didn't I tell you to believe in miracles?" she asked, patting his arm. "I can't take that out, but I can walk you over with the bag on the pole if you're careful."

Beau stood, leaning on the nurse. The room swirled around him for a moment, then stilled.

"You okay?" the nurse asked.

He grinned, ear to ear. "Never better."

The five steps from his bed to Tess's were like crossing an ocean. He took her hand in his, kissed the back of it, closing his eyes and trying to hold back his tears. He sat on her bed and leaned over her, kissing her cheeks, then her forehead, and then her lips. Beau carefully slipped his arms around Tess and pressed his body to hers in a warm embrace. He felt her heart beat against him, and felt her tears through his shirt. Beau held on tight. One of his palms rested on her back, the other cupped the back of her head. He rocked her like a baby. His fingers slid under her hair, pulling her closer, soaking her in.

"I love you," he said.

"I...love...you," she managed.

Beau lowered her carefully back down to the bed and kissed her lips again.

The door opened and Carol and Robert stepped quietly into the room. It took all of Beau's strength to pull his lips from Tess's and turn his face away from her. His mother's eyes were puffy and red, wet with fresh tears, her hair uncombed. Robert's cheeks were drawn, and thick lines were etched into his forehead.

"Mom," Beau said. "I'm sorry. I'm so sorry. I couldn't imagine life without her."

Carol shook her head, then came to Tess's bedside and embraced them both.

The nurse moved to Robert's side and handed him a box of tissues for his tears. "It's a miracle of miracles," she said.

Robert nodded, holding onto the bar on the foot of the bed for support.

"I'm not sure if you're a man of faith or not," the nurse said, "but I believe it took him crossin' over to bring her back."

Chapter Forty-Six

Beau was cleared to be released from the hospital later that evening, while Tess was being kept for observation. They had yet to determine if she'd need any form of rehabilitation, but so far she was progressing nicely. Aside from being tired and having a killer headache, the doctors had high hopes of Tess experiencing a full recovery. Beau relived the nightmare of almost losing her every time he saw her face.

Tess remembered everything that had happened before the accident, but not the accident itself. For that, Beau was thankful, though it broke his heart to know that the last thing she remembered was looking at him through Kevin's windshield. If only he hadn't tried to surprise her. Maybe none of this would have happened.

Beau couldn't imagine leaving Tess's side, and he refused to leave the hospital—even for one night. The nurses agreed to let him stay with her now that she'd been moved out of the ICU. Beau had one thing left to do.

Carol and Robert were in the cafeteria. He kissed Tess, assured her he'd be right back, and then he headed in the direction of the cafeteria.

"Mr. Johnson?" Dr. Kelly called after him.

Beau turned to face her, feeling a mixture of embarrassment, determination, and elation.

She held an envelope in Beau's direction. "I have your paternity results." Her voice held no indication of the results.

Beau reached his hand out and took the sealed envelope. He stared down at it, then gripped it in both hands and tore it up, handing the shreds back to Dr. Kelly, leaving her bewildered, shaking her head.

He turned and walked down the hall. His parents, on their way back up from the cafeteria, stepped out of the elevator and walked toward him. Beau stopped walking.

"Mom? Are you coming?" he asked.

She looked at Robert, bewildered.

"Abbey's waiting, and I'm pretty sure she needs her grandmother as much as her father."

Epilogue

Beau watched Abbey toddle across the living room and tumble into Samira's arms. It had been fifteen months since Tess had recovered from the accident, and Beau still couldn't look into Abbey's luminous blue eyes without the reminder of those fateful weeks looking back at him. It no longer pained him, as it once had; now it embraced him like a hug. Abigail Tess Johnson had her mother's spirit. Headstrong and dead set on proving the entire medical community wrong, she met each of her milestones, with the exception of rolling at three months. Abigail decided to scare everyone and roll at four months instead, quickly turning that roll into a scrunch-and-push crawl at five months and twenty-nine days. That's when Beau and Tess knew they were in trouble.

"I want to hold her!" Zeid had warmed to his new life in the States. It had taken months, but he no longer regarded Beau as the enemy. The misplaced anger he'd felt had slowly dissipated. He pulled Abbey from his mother's arms and into his lap. Abbey squirmed; their giggles filled the room.

Samira smiled at Beau. She no longer looked at him as though he were an unattainable glass statue on the tallest shelf. "Suha would roll her eyes at this behavior," she laughed.

"Yes, but she'd secretly welcome it," Beau said.

"Would not!" They'd become as close as siblings and teased each other as such. Samira had quickly become fairly proficient with the English language. She seemed a reborn person to Beau. He attributed her newfound confidence to the fresh, unrepressed environment of living with the Fulans, who encouraged her to take English as a Second Language classes, and provided a supportive family life for her and her children. The filing clerk job Mr. Fulan had provided for her also gave her purpose and a chance to practice her new language skills. Ten hours per week were just enough for her to feel as though she contributed to the wellbeing of her family.

When Mr. Fulan had told Beau that Samira had found his camera and he'd been able to salvage his photographs, Beau had refused to have them published. They were a hurtful reminder of his near loss of Tess. It had taken his mother four months of pushing and begging for him to look at the touching photographs. When he had finally relented, the images jumped off the page: Iraqi families standing with the American soldiers who remained in their country protecting them, becoming one community rather than a world of "we" and "them." Beau would never forgive himself for following his dream. He'd never accept the dismissal of blame from the others, but with Tess's encouragement, he finally gave in, agreeing to publish the photos in memoriam of all of the lives lost during the war. The photographs were to be released the next day, all monetary proceeds to be given to the underground organization that helped women escape honor killings and other abuses and threats to their lives.

Edham and Athra decorated cookies at the kitchen table with Tess and Carol. Alice glowed as she showed Robert the new sparkling diamond ring on her left finger—classic cut, of course. Kevin hung back and watched, relishing the thought that he was soon to be part of the Sacred Club of Married Men.

Beau walked to where Tess sat and took her hand in his. He stood back from them all, watching, and traced the letter "I", the shape of a heart, and the letter "U" in his wife's palm.

Acknowledgments

The idea for the story within these pages came to me while I was running down State Highway in Wellfleet, Massachusetts, just months before my husband was scheduled to leave for a tour in Iraq. The story evolved as I wrote, and the Iraqi women became very important characters. I hope that I did them justice. I verified the Arabic terms used and the clothing and mannerisms portrayed with soldiers who spent time in Iraq and with the Iraqi civilians who worked with them. Many provided answers through others, sometimes in passing, during conversations in the medical facility on base. Unfortunately, those who passed on the information hadn't realized that names were important for acknowledgments. For all of those who reached out and took the time to research and guide me from afar, thank you. This book could not have come to light without your efforts. I'd be remiss if I did not also thank Hadear Kandil, a woman I've never met and with whom I've only tweeted. She was kind enough to answer my terminology questions when she had no idea who I was.

There are so many people who have stood by my side during these past few years as I've grown as a writer, and I hope I do not miss mentioning anyone. In case I do, I hope you know me well enough to realize that you are in my heart, and I deeply appreciate you all.

My mind often works faster than my fingers, and my good friend and editors, Dominique Agnew and Dale Cassidy, who are always there to make me look good. Thank you, Dominique. Many thanks to Clare Ayala, a formatting genius, and to Natasha Brown, my amazing cover designer. A special thank you to my beta readers and the women on The Women's Nest, who never fail to amaze me with their unending support and willingness to help me work through scenes, listen to me gripe, and not get turned off when my days are filled with word counts and discovering new adjectives. Thank you, Pat, Deb, Paula, Gina, Clare, Jessie, Jackie, Kian, Nel, MaryAnn, DJo, Syl, Jan, and all the other Nest sisters. Thank you, Clare Karsteadt and Kian Vencill, for always having my back. Virtual hugs to M.J. Rose and Carrie Green, who have selflessly helped me with my career without asking for anything in return. I would also like to thank trusted readers who caught errors and provided guidance, and authors who were kind enough to read my work: Joan Diamond, Sue Harrison, Kathie Shoop, and Kaira Rouda. A special thank you to my mother, Hilde Alter, who provides feedback so straightforward and honest that it takes me by surprise, and who is always right (truly, she is).

To the multitude of friends that I have made on Twitter and Facebook who encourage me, support my efforts, play my silly games, and retweet my tweets, you inspire me each and every day, and for that, I will be forever grateful. To my World Literary Café volunteers and friends, bless each one of you. I wish I could name you all, but there just isn't space.

I have an enormous family and want to thank them all for believing in me just because they love me: my brothers, Adam, Jon, Dale, Joel, Seth, and Elliott, my stepfather, Colin, my aunts and uncles, and cousins, and, of course, my grandparents who are no longer with us but are in my heart. Thank you. Steve and Sandy Foster, I am so lucky to have you in my life. Jane DeVito, thank you for being excited about my work and for taking the time to read my books.

Gratitude doesn't begin to touch on the feelings I have for my immediate family members who talk me through the moments when I'm not sure I have what it takes, who kiss me goodnight when my fingers are glued to the keyboard, and who would love me even if I didn't write. Les, Jess, and Jake, you are my biggest fans (rivaling my mother, of course) and I appreciate your support. Thank you to my big kids who are busy with their own lives but make time to congratulate me on my efforts and pretend to be interested: Noah, Zach, Brady, and Devyn. I love you all.

Lastly, I'd like to thank my readers. Your emails make me smile, your book clubs make for fun gatherings, and I will always write for you.

Melissa Foster is the award-winning author of five International bestselling novels. Her books have been recommended by USA Today's book blog, Hagerstown Magazine, The Patriot, and several other print venues. She is the founder of the Women's Nest, the World Literary Café, and Fostering Success.

Melissa hosts an annual Aspiring Authors contest for children, and she has painted and donated several murals to The Hospital for Sick Children in Washington, DC.

Melissa welcomes emails from her readers, and invitations to book-related events.

www.MelissaFoster.com